I0831967

WHEN LEAVES LISTEN

A Nature of Noise Novel

Editing & Copy by: Julie Tibbott & Krystal Elghanayan

Paperback edition published 2018

Please visit our website at www.katiefeavel.com

ISBN: 9781973558620

PROLOGUE

3-1-1-4

The four digits, seared sloppily into the flesh of Haddi's left calf, stared up at him as he sat cross-legged in the mud. He pressed his shoulders back against the bark of a fallen *hoch* tree and looked into the fire as it popped and crackled with a spirit he no longer felt.

Shia was dead.

Old scars on his knuckles throbbed in time with the stinging realization of his loss, taunting him, reminding him of the bloody mistakes he had made. Haddi had been indentured for thirteen years but had never felt as enslaved as he did now. He was a prisoner in his own body, ashamed of the things his hands had done and his heart had felt, useless to save those he loved.

It was that burden which fueled his flight, that yoke which drove him up the side of the Scalas, crashing wildly through *kurz* shrubs, scaling the slated mountainside. It was that bondage of spirit which found him clinging to one of the enchanted rock faces that formed Praeceps – two vertical granite slabs rising parallel to one another about a thousand feet into the air, depending on whose feet were used as reference. The twin cliffs sat nestled into the mountain range about a third of the way up, like two guards at their posts. The rock formation Praeceps was the only point of entry to the upper Scalas.

The ever-changing walls on either side had mesmerized Haddi– clearwater spouts erupted forth from newly formed fissures in the surface of the rocks, only to disappear again into others. Footholds became smooth without warning. Slippery, see-through *klarmoss* crept over the surface in unexpected places. A clear mind and fine-tuned spirit were crucial assets for such a feat. Haddi had neither, and the question of whether he intended to live at all was as precarious as his perch a few hundred feet from the top.

He could never do it the way Shia had, by choice, boldly facing her death and walking forth into it willingly. Though he had surely *wanted* to die at that moment, had almost waded in after her, the thought of their infant son had stayed him. What kind of father could he ever hope to be to Amar? The baby would be better off without him. He could grow up free from the looming specter of a mother who left him for the temptation of death. He could live a life without the constant shame brought on by a murderous father who had also failed to save his mother from her own despair. Another history could be woven for Amar, one that told of parents who gave their lives selflessly for him rather than selling their souls for their own desires.

But that's not how it would go. As the boy grew, there would be no way to shelter him from the reputation of his parents. No, the only way Haddi could protect Amar would be to remain alive, raise him in exile, and hope that one day he might be made to understand, and not repeat, their failings.

Now able to navigate neither up nor down Praeceps, Haddi's renewed determination to live had been replaced by a sense of panic. His fingertips had grown numb as he gripped the surface of the slick *gelb* stone, his stability weakening as the force of adrenaline subsided. Fear was just beginning to take hold when a wrinkled hand, decidedly not human, clamped down on his own, wrenching him upward and out of the turmoil that consumed him.

By the fire, in the mud, watching the two creatures to which he now owed his life, Haddi shifted once more against the tree. He narrowed his gaze at the flames, where Shia's image danced before him, wild – pale, straw-like hair and olive skin in contrast – and he begged it to consume her, to rid his mind of these painful visions. The woman that had waded into the Malú was not the same one he had loved and married. She was nothing more than a shadow of his Shia. And her loss was doubly devastating, for she had taken with her any hope of a family, hope they had fought so hard to hold onto, hope she had not been able to convince herself to feel as she clutched the blood-stained memory of the child that had perished in her womb before Amar. Haddi had failed them all.

"Haddi?" A gruff voice broke his concentration. "You eat. I feel no warmth from you. Eat, then sleep." The giant pressed a grainy loaf of bread into Haddi's palm before straightening to a height twice that of an average man and lumbering back around to the other side of the fire to his oddly-matched companion – a stout Irdish woman named Trude.

"I am of the *ancient* trollian clans, not the rebels," Trude informed Haddi as she introduced herself, though he had no idea what the difference was.

No Alterran had been known to come in contact with such creatures since Partitus and most, including Haddi, had believed them to be the stuff of folklore. Haddi gnawed on the coarse bread, crumbs clinging to his beard.

"*New* ways," Trude grumbled to herself, rising to stoke the fire. "Don't ever want t' be confused for one o' those back-stabbers, ye know, goin' on and on about their new ways of livin'. I like the old ways," she said, turning aside to spit out her distaste on the ground. "I miss Irden 'round these times." Trude squatted next to the fire. "Warmer down there about now. None of this white fluffy fallin' business. Just green and rain. Such a happy thing, rain."

"I like this snow," the giant grumbled back. "Makes tracks clear."

"Psh, not if it's fallen fresh. Just get closer to the ground, ye big oaf, n' maybe you'd have better luck with your trackin'."

"Where did you two come from?" Haddi asked, his voice hoarse and far away.

"He speaks," the giant chuckled under his breath, his bushy eyebrows raised to a jutting forehead as he deferred to Trude.

"Jeg here is o' the Tor," she began, keeping a sideways eye on Haddi while she spoke. "They live up o'er the Caligo Peaks, a few days hike from here. But ye wouldn't ever find it on ye own. Guarded with magic, 'tis. My home also, though not so well protected as our northern home was. The old magic was stronger there."

"Why did you leave it?" Haddi asked, grateful for the momentary diversion that learning another's story could bring.

"We had no choice," Trude sighed, taking a seat on a rock nearer Haddi, placing her wide, leathery hands on her knees. "The elders were betrayed. Betrayed by one o' our own and a man… if ye can even call him that. He ain't from Alterra."

"Orville…" Haddi concluded.

"You know him?" Jeg asked from across the fire.

"I do," Haddi responded as he massaged an aching knee and thought of Shia. His new companions did not need to know the extent of his relationship to Orville Zaide. "Came across him a few times as a boy. People seemed to like him a little better then. Lots of promises to help us with our problems."

"Ha! That man couldn't help himself o'er the edge of a cliff if he wanted," Trude huffed as she leaned forward and pulled her broad shoulders to her ears.

"Perhaps not," Haddi almost smiled at Trude's indignation. On another day he might have even laughed, but his mind proved incapable of such emotion. "So, what are you doing here? Why aren't either of you with your people?"

“Orville…” Trude began. “Well, he’s got some business goin’ on that’s hurtin’ these mountains, messin’ with the magic in ‘em.” She paused for a time, and Haddi resisted the urge to press her, lest she chose not to say more. He always found it remarkable what a person might say if left for a time in their own silence. “We weren’t sure what our purpose here was till we found you stuck on the side o’ that cliff this mornin’,” she went on. “Now we know.”

“What is the purpose?” Haddi asked as he extended his stiff legs in front of him, allowing the blood to flow freely once again.

“You know, Haddi, the old faith says that *ai ôwpo apío tov eós*, a gift from the Universe, will come t’ restore balance t’ the worlds, rejoin what was once united, remake what was torn apart. She has appeared to some in dreams as a child wearing a crown made of gold. Now, ‘tis also said that another must make way for her, a guide, *ai haddi*… and that’s you.”

CHAPTER 1

The Game

The manhunt players were just seven in number – uneven teams – and Dottie Noles' well-worn black Chuck Taylor was the last shoe drawn from the center and thrown into one of two piles.

"Hell no," Hudd complained from across the circle.

Dottie looked down at her hands, hoping to avoid Hudson Mead's trademark sneer.

"Put Dinky Dot's shoe in the other pile," Hudd said. "I'd rather have three against four than deal with her tagging along tonight."

Dottie felt a flush creep into her cheeks. A dozen half-constructed comebacks played through her mind, stinging retorts that she could use to defend herself if she could actually get a word out. She looked for backup from her older brother, Jack, but his face signaled indifference.

She turned away, angry tears welling in her eyes. *Dinky Dot.* Hudd had been calling her that ever since her family had moved to the neighborhood. She was just nine then, slight, scrawny, but not about to hang around with the other little girls playing dolls or house. She wanted to be in with the boys, to find somebody to play a game of catch with her.

"Dude, chill," Ben said. "I threw fair. The teams are final." Ben Rutledge was fifteen, older than Dottie by only a year, but a firmly clenched jaw and a pair of dark circles under his eyes seemed to add a few more.

"Ha!" Hudd scoffed. "Being on a team with Dot isn't fair no matter who's throwin' the damn shoes."

Dottie tried to ignore the mocking laughter in his voice. It didn't matter; the night's round was about to begin, and she wouldn't have to talk to anybody else for a few hours. As she turned to make her way toward the back of the yard, Penny Tackett sidestepped in front of her.

"Don't listen to Hudd," Penny said, placing a graceful hand on Dottie's shoulder. "He's just trying to get a rise out of you."

"Yeah, I… uh, thanks," Dottie stammered, uncomfortably aware of the hand on her shoulder and her own awful ability to make any social interaction awkward.

Ben's voice, bellowing from behind Dottie, saved her. "Go!"

The girls jumped into action at the sound of his voice. Dottie broke out into a run, heading in the opposite direction from Penny, glancing back briefly to see that nobody was following before she slipped into the trees.

The rules of the game were few and loosely interpreted. They had a five-minute head start. The hunted ran, the hunters sought. The perimeter for a round was predetermined. If any of the hunters caught one of the hunted, the captive was brought back to base and held under guard. The hunted teammates were responsible for keeping each other out of jail with the ability to "tag-out" their captured companions. The round was over once they caught all of the hunted team members. Then they would switch sides.

Dottie passed through a thin stretch of trees between her own yard and the one next to it. Wild blueberry bushes crunched beneath her feet. The sunset faded and a grey dusk enveloped her passage. She picked up the pace as her momentum carried her downhill into the adjacent street. Shoving her hands into the pocket of her hoodie, she braced herself against a cold gust and crossed the exposed cul-de-sac. Dottie knew one of the hunters was likely to have seen her, so she took a sharp left turn at the edge of the woods. She walked about fifty yards along the tree line before heading in deeper and doubling back in the opposite direction, seeking anonymity in the growing darkness.

She had half an hour of solitude as she wove in and out of the spindly pine trees, with nothing but the sounds of the forest floor beneath her feet and the humming that forced itself spontaneously from her chest. The rising moon barely lit her path as she got in deeper. The hair on her arms rose with prickling goosebumps. She couldn't shake the feeling that something was sneaking up behind her.

"Get a grip," she whispered as she stomped through leaves and pine needles, inhaling the sharp night air to steady herself. Fear. Weakness. She had too much of both, as her mother was constantly reminding her. Dottie paused on the outskirts of a backyard the next street over from hers and observed the warm glow of the porch light. The yard had one of those little playhouses. Not the fancy wooden kind, just a plastic Fisher Price that little kids seemed to like better anyway. She could hide there all night if she wanted. But this yard wasn't part of the designated play zone. Though who would ever know? She could stay there for an hour or more, wait for the call to go out, and then make her way back to base. *She* could be the last one standing.

But her sense of fairness stopped her from slipping into the little house, and she continued on her original route back in the direction of the base. After three summers playing the game, she had found it best to loop out, then double back close and find a good hiding spot. It left her vulnerable for a longer period, which sometimes backfired, but if she could make it into hiding, then she was within earshot of everything going on and could make better decisions.

Some of the older and faster manhunt kids could outrun the hunters and take greater risks – remaining more out in the open, luring the base guard away from the porch if any teammates were in jail, then betting on winning a footrace to free them and make it to safety. Meanwhile, Dottie found a cozy nook in a woodpile in one of the designated backyards where she could hide and wait out the round.

Dottie was tall for having just turned fourteen, yet she seemed to shrink as she rounded her shoulders, pulling her knees tightly to her chest. A rebellious golden curl escaped from behind her ear and fell into her eyes. She reached up to tuck it back into place. The decaying leaves crackled under her slight shift in weight. She held her breath for a moment, listening carefully. Not a sound. She slowly exhaled and vowed to be more careful, to keep her gangly limbs from giving her away.

Some kids tended to pair up to find the best hiding spots and avoid capture, but Dottie wasn't much in the mood for company. She felt like she always managed to say or do the wrong thing…or she said or did nothing at all, which was even more awkward.

Dinky Dot. Hudd's teasing voice replayed in her mind. It was as if she was nothing more than a period at the end of an incomplete sentence. It was almost as bad as when her grandmother used her full name. Hunched there behind the woodpile, she couldn't help but roll her eyes as Grandma's sing-song voice filled her head. *Dorothy May.* Dottie's grandmother didn't believe in nicknames. The aged woman's slender fingers would be interlaced elegantly in her lap, her posture flawless in spite of her eighty some odd years as she sat, crisply pronouncing each syllable.

Dottie secretly blamed her parents for choosing a name that made her sound like she was from her grandmother's generation, one that led to a nickname that only highlighted the vulnerability brought on by her already insignificant appearance. Not to mention the litany of *Wizard of Oz* references she had endured all these years.

A boy on the bus the other day had asked her if she was "off to see the wizard." And was she Dorothy, or perhaps the cowardly lion? She must be the lion. After all, her frizzy hair was basically a mane. Dottie had just sat there composing stinging retorts in her mind while her mouth stubbornly refused to open. The culprit laughed at her discomfort and retreated to his circle of sniggering friends. *Bully.*

She shifted her weight again, careful not to make the leaves crinkle this time, and stuck a half-asleep leg out in front of her to let the blood creep back in. She wasn't sure how long it had been – an hour? More? One thing was sure: this was a boring round so far. It was never as much fun with such small teams, too easy for the hunted to remain hidden. But then a twig snapped directly in front of her. She braced herself against the logs and peered out into the dark forest. Dottie held her breath as she waited to discover the source of the noise, heart pounding, her body tense and ready to jump.

"Dottie?" Penny's whisper came from the opposite direction as the twig, but Dottie nonetheless breathed a sigh of relief. "You back there?"

Dottie poked her head around the side of the woodpile, searching the darkness for the other girl, curls bobbing wildly.

"Geez, Penny, what're you doin? You tryin' to give me a heart attack?" She couldn't shake the feeling that somebody else was nearby.

"Sorry, Dottie," the other girl huffed as she slumped down next to her behind the woodpile. "It's just that I wasn't able to keep up with Hudd after Ben tagged us out of jail, and I don't like being out here by myself."

"How'd you know I would be here?" Dottie asked.

"Well… you hide here a lot," Penny said with a shrug. "Loop up around past the other street then on down to the Coffman's woodpile."

“I’m that predictable, huh?” Dottie laughed under her breath, shaking her head at her uncanny ability to be exceptionally dull.

“Don’t worry, I won’t tell any of the others,” Penny said with a sheepish smile.

Though she would never admit it to anyone, Dottie envied Penny, with her soft manners and sweet smile. Penny had a slender face with dramatic dark brown eyes and naturally long lashes. She was always smiling. It was never excessive or fake, just a genuine, approachable, *I-care-about-you* kind of smile. Dottie felt like anything she did around Penny came off as coarse. It took all of her effort to battle the perma-scowl that her mother warned was “going to get stuck like that one of these days.”

“Well,” Dottie said after a few moments of quiet, “we should probably try to find a less predictable hiding place. You good to move?”

“Sure,” Penny replied. “As long as we don’t go too far from the street?”

Dottie rolled her eyes at the trepidation in Penny’s voice, even as she noted the goose bumps on her own arms. She rose to her feet, brushing pine needles from her legs and glancing over her shoulder. Convinced they were alone, she beckoned Penny and started into the trees.

They trekked into the woods, crossing over a shallow ravine. When Dottie scaled the small ridge on the opposite side, Penny halted.

“Dottie, I really don't think we should go any further than this. Nobody will be able to hear us so far out,” Penny said, her voice quivering.

“Yeah, Penny,” Dottie replied, feeling a pang of guilt. “You're right. We’ve gone a little too far. Climb on up and we’ll double back toward the top of the street and down by the McKerrin’s, okay?”

Penny looked only mildly relieved, but the concession spurred her into motion and she quite capably hiked the incline to join Dottie. Penny brushed her hands together to rid them of dirt. As she straightened up, the familiar, calm smile was back on her face. She fell into stride next to Dottie as they started off back toward the road.

They had only walked a few yards when a dog barking nearby halted them. *Ari*. Dottie's barrel-chested, thick-headed pitbull had an unmistakably deep bark. *What was he doing so far from home?* She turned, locked eyes with a no longer smiling Penny and reached out impulsively to grab her companion's hand just as the ground beneath them began to shake.

CHAPTER 2
The Sorcerer

Orville Zaide sat forward in the creaky wooden chair, his leather shoes planted in front of him. Sweat glistened on his brow. He watched Ruya bend over the logs burning in the bell-shaped chimney, gently stoking the coals to bring life back into the dying flames. The old soothsayer deftly stomped out a few rogue embers that had jumped onto the floorboards. Light danced off the barren walls of the single-room apartment as shadow played in its wake. Her black hair cascaded like a curtain alongside her face, dangerously close to the fire, but Ruya neither flinched nor moved the hair out of the way.

It was a strong blaze, and Orville wore heavier clothing than Ruya. He told himself that the additional layers and too much wine were to blame for the relentless warmth, rather than acknowledging the impact of *her* presence. He wiped his sweaty palms on the legs of his pants and balled his hands into fists, steadying himself against a sudden rush of torment. He remained torn between his resentment of her rejection, self-loathing that she still made him weak, and an overwhelming desire to be near her. He would never let on. No woman, nor man for that matter, was allowed to hold sway over Orville Zaide.

Yes, it was the wine and his clothing that caused him to sweat so profusely. No matter how many years he had spent in Alterra, he refused to wear the layered cotton and wool tunics common to the people, preferring slacks and a suit coat. His servant, Amaya, had not understood the necessity of such "restricting dress" to begin with, but was dumbfounded when he insisted she iron out the wrinkles of his clothing with hot stones.

It was all about *presentation,* Orville had tried to explain. With his more sophisticated language and scientific jargon, his foreign hobbies and solitary lifestyle, Orville had created both a literal and figurative division between himself and the people of Lower Alterra. He kept dogs as pets, while the people viewed the animals as menaces – though he secretly loathed the slobbery creatures and left them in the care of his servants. He spent months secluded in his compound northeast of the city walls. He kept paper and a writing quill with him at all times to take notes, while the majority of Alterrans were illiterate. Orville's attire was just another way to emphasize his superior socio-economic status, paving the way for him to achieve the thing he so deeply craved: *influence*.

Orville met Ruya early on in his time in Alterra. She was mysterious and capable but didn't vex him needlessly like other women. He loved her then, though never so much as after she turned him aside and left him…for what? Her own pride and nothing more. It was some solace that she had never found a replacement for him.

Over the years since, Orville's visits to Ruya became fewer and farther apart, each one driven by an increasing desire to fill her with regret. Yet, around this same time each year – when the Kauon tree burned with an autumn red that reminded him of things he would rather forget– he felt an almost innate need to seek her out, hear her raspy voice recite the words one more time. He always attempted any number of ploys to put off his participation in the ritual, even now still hoping to resist it entirely. Whether he took leave of the city for a time, or engaged the counsel of one of Alterra's many other seers, he was somehow involuntarily compelled to Ruya's fireside before season's end.

Orville watched Ruya complete her familiar divination, blending the clearwater and neodymium powder into a paste in a wooden bowl, repeating the well-worn prophecy as he smiled back confidently.

With the prophecy told, Ruya rose and busied herself, prodding with agitation at the fire before turning to face him.

"Have you nothing to say, Orville?" She frowned, looking down at him over the ridge of a prominent nose. The angle of her gaze magnified the creases that played around her mouth and eyes, a face still pleasant to look at despite her age.

"And what exactly is it you expect me to say?" Orville countered, careful to keep his tone and manner light. It was cruel really, the way she never acknowledged the sacrifice it took for him to come to her, the humility it required.

"I suppose I don't know what else I expected," she sighed. "But the message remains unchanged, the clarity of the trails grows more pronounced as time moves past… when will you heed the words?"

The words. Words had only hindered his life. Orville believed that a great man derived his life's meaning from something within, not from a mere cluster of letters strung together weakly. Words were only as strong as the actions that backed them. Words were no more than rhetorical tools used to engineer a desired outcome. Words, like drugs, tricked the mind into believing them an absolute necessity and sole contributor to one's self-worth. He wondered how many false words had led to the downfall of lesser men.

He found strange comfort in the morbid original foretelling: *Your life's passion will be your end if you do not set it aside.* These words foretold his failure, and yet, he thought, *I am still here. The work that is my life is flourishing, as is my body and mind.* And then there was the part about the girl with golden hair. If not for this child who haunted him, both in the prophecy and in his dreams, he might never have invented his leaves.

Orville absentmindedly retrieved a small chess piece, a pawn, from the pocket of his suit coat and rolled it back and forth between thumb and forefinger. *Never be the pawn,* he thought, *never make the first move.* Ruya was still standing over him, waiting for his acknowledgement, but he remained silent, tired of so many weighty *words*.

"Do you believe you alone write the rules of life, Orville?" Ruya waved her hands in exasperation. "All others, the Universe, faith, all are obsolete?"

"Oh, why do you press me, Ruya?" he huffed. "If you have something important to say, say it. I'll not stand for being questioned in such a way. Not by *you.*"

"You will not succeed," she said. "And yes, I know, I've said this before." She paused to adjust the waist of her tunic, which only highlighted her figure.

Orville rolled the pawn back and forth, keenly aware of its flawed but familiar surface.

"The strength of the tarnish trail that represents the golden girl, it so deeply parallels the ancient salvation prophecy…."

"Ah, yes," he said with a sigh, "but you have mentioned this similarity before? Why have you not sought more clarity on this relationship?"

"You think I have not pursued answers? The Universe has not seen fit to shed further light on this for me, Orville." She pursed her lips at him in frustration. "But you will not be able to stop her. You will *not* succeed. There is no *if* in her portion of your foretelling."

"You threaten me, woman," Orville growled. She had gone too far, telling him that he was not in control of the outcome of his actions.

"Never," Ruya stated more calmly.

Orville watched as she set the divination bowl down on the table and sank back into her seat, placing her forehead in her hands. Back-and-forth went the pawn.

"You must stop what you're doing, Orville," Ruya pleaded, lifting her gaze to meet his. "Shut it down, or all you hold dear will be destroyed. You may not be able to save yourself from the girl, but you can still save others…."

"Twice incorrect," Orville snarled, more to himself than to Ruya.

"How's that?" Ruya asked, her voice like gravel.

"There is nothing in this world that I hold dear." Orville pushed his chair back from the table and rose to his feet. "And I alone control my destiny."

"Then why come see me at all? Why do you even bother if you know yourself to be beyond the rules of fate?"

"It entertains me," he retorted, taking a step closer to her. "*You* entertain me. At least you used to. I have no other purpose for you or these visits besides entertainment!"

Ruya stood as well, grabbed the divination bowl off of the table and flung its contents into the fire, sending a rush of heat and silver light into the cramped room.

Orville reached out on impulse and grasped the wrist of her outstretched arm, pulling her in toward him. His head spun from too many glasses of wine, heat, temptation.

"Put fate to the test, if you dare," Ruya muttered through gritted teeth as she pressed her forearms against his chest, breaking his hold and putting distance between them once again. Orville watched her chest rise and fall with a breath quickened by their sudden contact.

He turned to the fireplace, trying to regain his composure as he stared at the impressive metallic silver blaze that now engulfed the logs. Once the flames returned to their normal hue, along with the color of Orville's cheeks, he turned his attention back to Ruya.

“Where exactly might I look for her?” He breathed the question with a sigh, some of his agitation having left him. He did not wait for an answer, for he knew she would not have one.

He looked down, tucking in a loose flap of his shirt that had become disheveled, buttoned his jacket, and smoothed the legs of his trousers. He took two swift strides toward the door. “This girl…” he began, resting his fedora on his head and pulling it down in front. “Let her find me.” He placed his hand on the iron handle and let himself out into the alley behind Ruya’s home.

The thought repeated itself as he walked, desperate to rid himself of this nervous energy, needing to leave behind the dismal apartment and the stifling aroma of burning neodymium. *Let her find me*.

Orville watched Isaac pace the room in front of him. The servant was tall, lean, and kept his head entirely shaved. He wore the floor-length tunic and canvas shoes that were the trademark of the city’s indentured class. Yet here he was, a member of an oppressed people, pacing back and forth in front of a roaring fire in the great study of Gemma, Orville’s compound.

Soaring three stories high, the cavernous ceiling and wood-paneled walls formed Orville’s favorite space in the worlds. The brick fireplace that occupied the northwest corner was large enough to fit a dozen grown men, and housed flames that danced just as high. It was an odd time of year in Alterra, one Orville had never become quite accustomed to, where warm days gave way to freezing nights, and a room with such high ceilings was damn near impossible to heat when the darkness quickly settled.

The extreme weather also made it difficult to keep crops alive, so the Alterrans subsisted off whatever stores they had been able to accumulate during the last growing season. Gemma’s harvest had been less than robust, and Orville ate no more than a plate of seasoned potatoes and pickled cabbage for supper most evenings. His belly growled audibly, but would soon be soothed by copious amounts of wine.

Orville rested comfortably in his navy winged back chair, heels placed atop an ornately carved wooden table. Isaac paced anxiously back and forth, hands clasped behind his back, head bowed forward in deep thought. A dog most closely resembling a greyhound shadowed Isaac's every step. Orville disliked the look of the lithe creature. Two servant girls, one about nine or ten and the other in her late twenties, stood vigilant along the wall near the fire, doing their best to keep warm until they could be of use. The older of the two, Zaila, shifted anxiously from one foot to the other as the fire threw shadows at the opposing figures of servant and served.

Ignoring Zaila's fidgeting, Orville's gaze lingered on Isaac, waiting for the younger man to speak. Isaac had been in his late teens when he was caught trying to sneak into Gemma. He had told the guards he must see for himself the man he had heard whispers of in the back alleys. He was one of only a few who had dared to approach the compound in those earlier years, and Orville decided he liked the boy. In reality, he was consumed by curiosity about Isaac, who even then was devoid of mirth and possessed an abnormally sophisticated intellect for his age and standing.

Now, it was sometimes the case that exceptionally bright or well-equipped children from the Lower Half were partially bonded as apprentices in such roles as priests, scholars, or even placed within the Judiciary. Perhaps young Isaac had been destined for one such vocation. Yet, in the eighteen years since he came to Gemma, the stoic Alterran had disclosed nothing of his past. He had simply done Orville's bidding, acting as his strong right hand throughout the city and carrying out the tasks his master preferred to avoid. After all, murder was an unpleasant thing, though necessary on occasion, and in this area, Isaac was both skilled and utterly devoted.

Isaac slowed his gait and halted momentarily, back turned to Orville. "While there is likely no merit behind the old woman's words, sir, I wonder if we should be taking any chances. I do not like the supposed connection to the ancient salvation prophecy. That is one foretelling in which all Alterrans believe. If Ruya speaks of this to anybody else, it will spread like wildfire throughout the Lower Half."

"You worry too much about the people in the Lower Half, Isaac." Orville brushed away his concerns with a wave of his hand. "They are but gossiping hens who must have their entertainment. They are no threat to me. And yet, if there is still some girl who intends to foil me, I suppose we should do something to prevent it."

"I think if anybody is stupid enough to try something like that," Zaila interjected crossly from her post, "they won't be too hard to stop."

"Ah, my Zaila," Orville replied, "misinformed and unprepared such a person may indeed be. Nevertheless…let us not be caught sleeping."

The girl folded her arms and glared back into the fire as if it were the one who meant him harm.

"Isaac, speak with Garrett," Orville said. "Have him shore up the night guard, put them on extended shifts and see if he can't get a few more feet on the ground in the Lower Half. If anybody in Alterra catches wind of Ruya's most recent supposition regarding my foretelling, this should be sufficient to deter them from acting… impulsively."

"And what about this girl, sir?"

"I have reason to believe she is not amongst the people of Alterra." He would not disclose more just yet. "I'll handle her… for now."

Isaac gave a curt nod and left the study, the dog slinking out the door behind him.

"Tacita," Orville called to the younger of the two servants. "Come here. I have something I need you to do." The girl was rather difficult to look at – a gaunt face and coarse, yellow, straw-like hair. A jagged knife scar began at her left ear and trailed down to her collarbone, a wound that had left her unable to speak, which was a significant benefit to Orville. Isaac had brought the girl to Gemma a year ago, after she was rejected by the *bonders* and abandoned to care for herself, deemed physically and mentally unfit, even for the *Innova.* Often mistaken as being of simple mind, Tacita was perfectly suited to be Orville's eyes and ears throughout the Lower Half, where dark whispers circulated with ever-increasing ferocity. The girl with piercing grey eyes moved to the side of the table opposite her master and stood awaiting his instruction.

-

Once all his servants had gone, Orville rose to pour himself another glass of mulberry wine and stood swirling it absentmindedly in front of the fire. He was not sure he would even attempt sleep, so unsettled was he by the interaction with Ruya earlier that evening. He cared little for the foretelling itself, but the woman who delivered it was another thing entirely. To be sure, the essential, rehabilitative effects of a good night's sleep had evaded him for years as he succumbed to worsening insomnia, with or without Ruya's influence. Isaac urged him repeatedly to try a remedy for rest often prescribed by the Alterran healers, but Orville refused to take their reeking herbal concoctions. These remedies never failed to remind him of Aggie, and he wished to think of *her* about as much as someone might hope to recall the uncomfortable details of a particularly awful bout of food poisoning.

He and Agatha Polson had worked together closely many years ago, along with her then flame, Levi Hill. She was pushy, and there were few characteristics Orville detested so vehemently in a woman. She continually undermined his assertions and poked holes in his arguments. Orville believed her to be deliberately cutthroat, disrespectful, and too blunt for a female, regardless of her educational standing or success. Levi was no better, but at least that level of competitiveness was *normal* for a man in science. Levi enabled Aggie, encouraging her to speak up and question anything she felt necessary, even his *own* work.

Orville shook his head as his bitterness tainted the wine he drank. Then there was the matter of her work…countless hours spent studying, observing, and breaking down the healing rituals of ancient tribes from around the world, attempting to, as she put it, "harness the power of healing inherent to our natural surroundings." Aggie wanted to make these natural remedies "accessible" to the average person, to peddle her sugar pellets and nonsense to uneducated fools, who would then forego *real* medical care.

They had argued about it frequently. In fact, they had argued about a lot of things. Aggie and Levi seemed to have it out for Orville from day one. He cringed as his mind returned to that last day in the lab when he and Levi took part in a heated debate on the existence of a parallel dimension.

"We've picked it up in readings, Levi! You cannot deny that a foreign and contrasting magnetic field exists. You've seen the data yourself!" Orville had shouted across the table in the on-campus lab, Aggie shaking her head at them from behind her microscope.

"It was an anomaly, Zaide," Levi had shot back. "It's been two years, and you have yet to recreate the original outcome." Levi believed in the ethics of scientific research with an almost religious zeal, and this necessitated the ability to replicate results. "You've spent two years chasing a blip, running in circles after your own damn tail!"

"Watch yourself, Lee," Orville warned, enraged at the allegation that his findings were invalid. "I haven't been able to replicate the results yet. But you better be damn sure I will, and you'll wish you had supported me on this one instead of undermining me. That goes for the both of you!" He gestured accusingly at Aggie, who sat back from her specimen with a sigh, eyebrows raised and arms folded, awaiting the onslaught she expected from her belligerent peer.

"You!" Orville continued ranting. "You've done nothing but patronize me about this. Time and again you've ridiculed my work when it suited you. You just watch..." His hands shook as he backed towards the door of the lab, unable to remain in the room a moment longer. "You'll both wish you had taken this seriously."

That was the last time he had seen either of them. It was that very day that he made up his mind to prove them wrong, all of them...Aggie and Levi, the other members of their cohort, his professors, and his doctoral panel. The latter had penalized him for staying the course on research that they stated could not "hold water." They were all so short-sighted.

He had left the lab blinded by rage and damaged pride, but as the anger subsided, determination took its place. He had spent the year prior charting a map of the identified “hot zones” of competing magnetic forces and believed he had narrowed down the origination of the so-called “blip” to a roughly twenty-mile radius in Tennessee. He would have to conduct his research unfunded and on his own with no backing should anything go awry, but he was confident that would not be the case. In the end, he told himself, he would not have to share the glory of his success with any of his close-minded doubters, and that suited him just fine.

CHAPTER 3
The Seer

Ruya's neighbors always looked forward to Orville's yearly visit. It reignited their curiosity about them, with the news of his arrival circulating the Lower Half and providing fresh gossip for weeks. Ruya pressed the heel of her left hand to the small of her aching back as she watched him stroll down the dank alley, unaware of the many pairs of eyes that followed his path.

Forty years since the first reading. None of her other *sights* had taken so long to come to fruition. The night's chill and too many hours on her feet were wearing on her. Worry had settled into her chest. She could go back inside, fall in a heap onto her warm cot by the fire, but Garrett was expecting her. And the well-worn reading, coupled with Orville's unusually brash behavior and the parallel context of the ancient prophecy, had her nerves frayed. No, Ruya would not sleep tonight.

She waited for Orville's outline to disappear around the corner at the end of the long row of stacked homes, then reached back through her door and grabbed a wool blanket from a peg, securing it around her shoulders. Ruya pulled the heavy door shut behind her and pushed on uphill against a gusty draft that slipped down between the buildings, making her way in the opposite direction from her guest's retreating form.

Orville's visits were always variations on the same scene. A taunting declaration that, after yet another year, Ruya's prophecy had not come to pass, followed by an ever-increasing confidence either that she was wrong, or that he possessed the supernatural ability to thwart fate entirely. Many times she had entertained the idea of simply turning him away, saving herself some grief, but what she knew about him was dangerous, and this meant that he was also dangerous to her. She did not dare deny him another round in his own game. And this was all indeed no more than a *game* to Orville Zaide.

So, forty times he had sat across her table as she mixed the silvery paste of neodymium powder and *clearwater*. Forty times the mineral powder, poured out into a bowl, tarnished and formed dark lines as it followed the path of least resistance. Forty times Ruya had closed her eyes and recited the ancient words, asking the Universe to reveal to her the fate that lay before her guest. Forty times, the same, two-part message. The first – his passion would kill them all if he did not let it go. She had always felt grateful for that *if*, that single word giving her hope. His experiment would not save them, nor would it bring him power, as he believed. And yet, the second part….

Ruya had loved Orville once. She had been intrigued by him immediately when he came into Sum. Something about him had mesmerized her – his piercing blue eyes, the way he spoke about a better and more pure society. Little had she known the harm he was willing to inflict to procure that end.

She would never forget the way he explained he was twenty-three years old when they met. How strange it had seemed to her then that anybody would bother to recall the exact date of their birth – bonded Alterrans did not keep accurate records of their births, the number of years indentured being a more valued measure of age. For eight years, they had made a life together, shared their dreams. But in the end she left him for another, a man who showed her how truly dangerous Orville was, who tempted her with his vision of uplifting others through something he called "enlightenment." In every way, he was a man who was the exact opposite of Orville Zaide. She had loved Theo, loved him still despite the sixteen years that stood between the end of that relationship and her current journey to Cairo's pub.

The sound of the city gong brought her mind back to the present, the six loud clangs signaling shift change. Cairo's pub was only a short distance from her home, but she moved quietly, averting her face – these meetings were always a risk, and she did not wish to bring danger to Cairo's door. She wound her way in and out of the back alleys, hoping to lose the attention of any curious eyes and waiting for the bustle of the shift change to subside. As the sun fell, patches of firelight from nearby homes lit her path just enough for her to make her way along the earthen corridors, down serpentine stairways, and around a handful of the street youth huddled in a back doorway.

Ruya wove first north, then east through the city tenements, before heading back south toward Cairo's. The hubbub from the main road kept her company. The highways circled like rings around the outside of each half of Alterra, with stairways placed periodically along the way to take commuters up to or down from the eight-story-high roads. The residents of the Lower Half worked in opposing day and night shifts that found the main roads humming and full of commuting workers every evening and morning at six. Most traveled on foot, but a rare few had wooden carts drawn by donkeys. Members of the Lex, the city's militant guard, changed shifts at opposing windows – midday and midnight – so that they might stand guard, with their dogs at their sides, while the bonded people trudged past them.

Men, women and children alike made their way north to the Belt as Ruya moved through the alleys below. They crossed over into the Upper Half to work the night in any number of service-based vocations. Some were employed as house servants or kitchen staff who kept fires alive, washed laundry, cleaned, and prepared meals for the following day – many of the affluent preferred these tasks were accomplished at night so as not to feel emotionally burdened by seeing them done during their normal waking hours. Other workers were in service to the merchants at the Bazaar and worked the night peeling and slicing potatoes to be cooked in oil and seasoned, stocking vendor booths with an array of pickled vegetables, and maintaining the Upper Half's extensive common areas.

The city of Alterra dated back thousands of years. Ruya knew there were parchments in the Gallery that contained the city's history but had never seen them with her own eyes. Alterra was made up of two circular sections divided by the Belt, a wide corridor with guarded entrances on all four sides. Two walls formed the city's perimeter, with about fifty feet of floodable pathway in between them. If the city were ever under attack, a rerouted and dammed-off section of the Holt River could easily be opened, directing water into the space between the two walls to create a formidable moat. The city's hourglass shape and dual perimeter allowed for a secure city that was relatively easy to defend, while still leaving the center accessible to traders and travelers, though there had been few of either in recent years.

Ruya came around to an eastern section of the Lower Half, moving away from the noisy main road and down into a residential pocket of the city. She descended a narrow flight of stairs and came to a peculiar half-width door with no handle, lying sunken a couple of inches into a stone wall. Holding the blanket-shawl in place with one hand, she squatted down, dug her fingers in behind a small ridge between the door and the adjacent wall, and pulled. The door came open just far enough for her to stand and sidle her way inside.

She secured the door firmly behind her before turning down a narrow passage. The walls, ceiling, and floor were all made of ancient sandstone. A small urn sat on the ground at the end of it to light the way. About a decade or so her junior, Cairo lived a solitary lifestyle. He had been wanted by the Lex for twenty-four years for refusing to pay taxes on the wine he smuggled and sold. Cairo had not set foot outside his pub and living quarters more than a handful of times in just as long. Despite the lack of sunlight, the scrappy barkeep was darker than most Alterrans and kept his coarse black hair trimmed short.

"Good evening, my dear Ruya!" He greeted her as she ducked under the threshold of the pub's entry. "A little late today. I was about to send Brac out to look for you." He gestured to the giant of a man standing to his right behind the bar. Brac did not appear to hear him or to notice Ruya at all.

Ruya shook her head at the twinkle in Cairo's eyes. Brac was quite useful for breaking up fights and ridding the pub of non-payers, but the poor man was unable to see more than a few feet in front of him and lacked the wit to adapt to his physical handicap. Ruya had found him wandering hopelessly lost through the alleyways a time or two.

"No need for such measures on my account, Cairo," Ruya said as she took a seat at a small wooden table in the corner. "How's Laila?" Cairo's sister had been ill for the better part of the last year. She experienced phantom pain and weakness in her legs, but the healers in the *Innova* had been unable to find the cause.

"Ah, no real change, I suppose," Cairo said as he leaned forward onto the high stone counter. "The pain in her legs comes and goes, but she has not risen from bed in weeks. Hungry?"

"I'd take some *pan* if you have it to spare," Ruya replied, making a mental note to visit Laila during the daytime when she could. Might do the poor woman some good to hear a happy fortune. Ruya believed in the power of positive thought for physical healing. Though perhaps a less than honest practice, she sometimes used her vocation to plant the seeds of hope.

Cairo emerged from behind the counter a moment later with a cup of wine and a hunk of the sweet and salty *pan* on a curved wooden plate. He set the food and drink in front of Ruya, took a seat on the other side of the table, and leaned in to relate the most recent bits of juicy gossip circulating through the Lower Half. The Lex had raided a pub on the south side the evening before, taking dozens of protesting city servants into custody after they hadn't shown up for work. There was talk among the vendors and day-workers of building a tenement for the city's urchins outside the walls, hoping to motivate the Lex to actually enforce the anti-vagrancy laws and relocate the scoundrels. They could forage in the mountains just as easily as they begged in the streets and they had been wreaking havoc in the markets in the meantime. A group of older boys had made off with the majority of a vendor's food supplies that very morning.

Ruya listened for a time, sitting in the company of a second old friend that evening, though this one gave her far less anxiety than the first. She glanced around the room. Candles on each table provided dim lighting. Two worn out day-workers sat in silence, having a drink at stools up at the counter. A smuggler laughed heartily at a joke told by her male companion. A young and colorfully dressed couple sat sharing some tonic, fruit, and conversation in a cozy corner. Traditional Alterran clothing lacked dyes of any sort, but some of the youth of the city had begun coloring pieces of their garments to label themselves as unique members of society. Ruya thought it silly to spend one's precious time and resources on something so trivial. Nevertheless, she felt endeared by the young couple so deeply absorbed in each other, and she envied them the freedom to represent their particular cause.

"Oh! I almost forgot," Cairo said suddenly, leaning in towards Ruya and lowering his voice as she brought her full attention back to the conversation. "The most important thing, my dear, yes – the *leaves* – they're said to be increasing throughout the Lower half, down by the docks and even out toward the Scalas. The Lex were seen trying to destroy a cluster and all officers involved ended up badly burned!"

"Are you sure of this, Cairo? Your source…" Ruya felt her heartbeat quicken.

"... is a trustworthy one, I assure you. I'd hoped that this bit might be helpful for your meeting tonight?" He sat back in his chair and crossed his arms, pleased.

"Yes... yes it may indeed be," Ruya replied, placing a hand over her mouth absentmindedly, pondering the news. They sat in silence for a time, Cairo relieved of the burden of his secrets, Ruya absorbing the weight of the information.

It was well into the night when Cairo's began to clear out. The day-workers were the first to stumble out. Ruya imagined them making their way down empty alleys, dragging their feet into empty homes and falling into similarly empty beds, their wives likely gone to work the night shift. Sometime later, the young couple staggered out, happily drunk. The smugglers were the last to leave, hassling Cairo about the total of their bill. After Brac came around from behind the bar, they appeared to think better of employing their scam, dropped a few *commeri* onto the counter and grumbled their way out.

Ruya sat patiently, sipping from a second cup of wine and picking at the cooled *pan* in front of her while Brac and Cairo silently cleaned up the pub. She had started on a third cup when Brac retired to his living quarters for the night. Cairo helped himself to a bit of leftover *pan* and pickled beets.

Ruya's head spun from the warmth of too much wine as her thoughts drifted back to Orville and the prophecy. She had been the first to approach Orville when he so suddenly appeared in Alterra some forty years ago, and to this day, she was the only one who knew him for what he truly was…a man, and nothing more. She had warned him then, as she tried to warn him still, to be content. Leave the worlds be. His life's work would hurt them all. He would not succeed, she assured him. Her insights served only to fuel his passion; he was determined to prove her and her foretellings wrong and did not appear to understand, in spite of her efforts, that *fate is fate*.

The pub door suddenly creaked open and heavy footfalls echoed off the stone floors of the entry passage. She looked up to see Garrett stooping to enter. He was of middle age and unusually fair for an Alterran. Her heart warmed at the sight of him. He smiled broadly as he crossed the room to meet Ruya, placing a firm hand on her forearm and planting a kiss on her cheek before taking the seat next to her. She thanked the Universe that he did not hesitate to show her the affection befitting their familial relationship. For a short time, in this place of safety, they could simply be in each other's company without guard or hesitation, and it allowed Ruya to breathe a little more easily.

“I’ll just be in the other rooms,” Cairo said, speaking softly and offering a friendly nod to Garrett before taking his leave.

“How are you, Garrett?” Ruya asked. “You do look well. Sleeping enough?”

“Not really,” he replied with a sheepish smile, “but my hours are my own to set, so I guess I have no reason to complain about a lack of sleep.”

“You work too much,” she chided.

“There is too much that needs doing, and nobody else that Orville will trust to see any of it through,” he asserted.

“Cairo spoke of some altercation between the Lex and the leaves?” Ruya asked.

“Yes, Orville is furious,” Garrett replied as he shifted back slightly in his seat. “Another such incident happened a few days ago out in Idem. Tensions are growing between my guards and the officers, yet I lack the freedom to handle them.” He furrowed his brow. “Orville wishes to ignore the Lex, but I believe they are a legitimate threat as long as we stand in opposition to their desires.”

“He came to see me this evening,” Ruya said.

“It’s about time,” Garrett replied. “He’s been fighting it for weeks.”

“He looked tired,” she continued. “How has he been?”

“He’s rarely sober.” Garrett shrugged his shoulders. “Though perhaps now that he’s finally seen you he’ll ease up a bit.”

“He needs to think more clearly.”

“I’m not sure whether his mind is more clouded sober or drunk,” Garrett said. “Either way, a man cannot function on so little sleep and so much wine. He just drinks, paces, reruns his numbers and stares at the damn chess table for hours on end, then goes on rants at inanimate objects that he doesn’t remember the next morning.”

“How is NEM?” Ruya changed course again, staring down at her cup of wine with a small pang of guilt.

“She’s improving, but far from ready. She needs more trials, more time, but Orville’s getting anxious. I worry that he may jump too quickly, before the time is right. He’s becoming paranoid. Tonight he went on some tangent about someone who means to foil his plan, said that he must execute the entire thing *now* or never at all. Then he just kept repeating the salvation prophecy, the girl with golden crown….”

“Damn,” Ruya cursed under her breath. She had hoped being transparent with Orville about the reading’s growing similarity to the ancient salvation prophecy would act as a deterrent, not a stimulus.

“I wish I could just convince him to hold off. Perhaps I should suggest….”

“If you press him too hard he’ll dismiss you,” Ruya interrupted. “We need you to do whatever it takes to remain in his good graces. Stay even-tempered, support him and his actions… no matter what type of lunacy the man thinks up.”

“The plan is not lunacy,” Garrett countered. “The work is quite genius, in fact.”

Ruya cringed as she saw a glimmer of something akin to admiration in Garrett’s expression.

“He is too confident in NEM,” she said. “She’s a machine, first and foremost, and he can’t properly test her.”

“This is true,” Garrett allowed. “I do fear he’ll act prematurely if I do not somehow prevent it.” He shook his head and placed his open palm on the table in front of him.

“We can do nothing right now,” Ruya stated, patting his arm gently. “Garrett…” She paused and waited for him to look back up at her. “Could there be a reason to justify placing a personal guard on him at all times? Even two perhaps…”

“Many reasons could necessitate such precautions. Though I'm not sure how much good a guard or two might be if Orville makes up his mind.”

“Ah, perhaps not much,” Ruya conceded. “I hope that the guards might be more… preventative. You and I both know that

Orville is more measured and composed when he believes himself to be on stage. It would be best if you placed guards that were prominently born, sons of the Upper Half. Can this be done?"

"It absolutely can." Garrett glanced around the empty room, perhaps already searching his mind for a pair of guards that fit the description.

"Good," Ruya said in a low tone, contemplating. "It's a start."

"He has his girl, the silent one, Tacita, on some errand down here right now," Garrett added after a time. "She left Gemma shortly after dark, which seems odd to me."

"Yes...yes. Interesting." Ruya frowned, her mind churning. "How much time do you think we have before he loses his grip entirely?" There had been a time when such a question about Orville would have been made in jest. He had not always been so unsteady, so volatile. His judgment had become increasingly clouded in recent years, along with his obsession with NEM and his paranoia of others' intentions.

"Days, weeks, it's impossible to know," Garrett replied. "I'd say sooner rather than later."

"Waste no time with the new guards. Perhaps it will buy us a few days." Ruya paused for a moment. "I have an idea. Somebody that might be helpful to us with Tacita. I'll look into it at first light."

Ruya and Garrett filled the remainder of the dark morning hours with less formal conversation and easy silence, each, in turn, nibbling at bits of cooled *pan* or dozing in their chairs.

May your path be calm. The traditional Alterran farewell from Cairo replayed in her head as she stepped out into the dewy early morning light, a hunk of last night's *pan* heavy in the pocket of her tunic. Her path would be anything but calm today, yet it was one she knew she must walk. That's where she needed to start, with just walking. If she tried to focus on much more right now, the weight of it all might break her. She didn't have quite as much fight left in her these days. Many of her age were settling into their golden years, moving in with a family member, helping to care for the children too young yet for bond, or perhaps enjoying the rejuvenating company of the sisters at the *Innova*.

But Ruya had no such luxury – her children had been taken from her years ago, one by greed and the other by darkness – and she wasn't about to become a burden on some friend or obscure relative. So she walked. She walked through the narrow alleyways toward the South Market. She walked with purpose and with care. She walked with all the strength left in her and a determination that she intended to hold onto until her last day. The gong sounding six times to signal the morning shift change kept her company for a few paces. Shortly after, a hum carried over from the highway as night and day workers moved against each other around the Lower Half.

Before long she could smell the frying potatoes and coffee from the vendor carts, and her mouth began to water. She spotted a mangy streetcorner boy lurking in a flight of stairs with three others just north of the market and whistled for his attention. The boy's face lit up when he heard her, a toothy smile flashing under a layer of dirt and grime, though he only intermittently made eye contact, his gaze trailing along the ground and up the wall alongside her as he walked to meet her. She had known Lowell for almost twelve years, had been present at his birth. That was a date she would never forget.

"You know better than to slink around here right now," Ruya scolded as Lowell came closer. "Especially with what I hear happened yesterday. Did you know those boys?"

"Some of 'em," he shrugged as his gaze flitted upward to the building behind Ruya and back down. "But…" he paused, a smile creeping across his face. "I wasn't with 'em."

"Oh, what would Lin say?" Ruya asked the sky, placing a hand over her heart.

"She'd tell me…not to get caught."

Honest, Ruya thought. *Too honest*.

"But I thought you just said you weren't there," she countered.

“Well, then…I wasn’t,” the boy said, raising his hands, palms forward, in defense. “Promise.”

“Well, look, I've got a job for you,” she said. “Interested?”

He flipped his head to one side to move the hair out of his face. “It’ll pay?”

“Food only. I don’t have any *commeri* to offer you.” She pulled out the loaf of bread Cairo had given her and broke off a chunk. “This to start, more later.”

Lowell tilted his head, considering Ruya’s proposition as he rocked side to side, his body as incessantly active and uninhibited as his mind.

“Would you rather…” he began, still swaying in place, eyes flitting between Ruya’s and somewhere over her right shoulder. “Forget everything that has happened in the past… but remember everything in the future, or…forget everything in the future, but remember the past?”

“That is quite the question,” Ruya replied, amused by the riddle. “I suppose if I forgot everything in the past, I wouldn’t know how to do anything, would I? However painful a past might be, it most certainly is useful.”

“Is that your answer?” Lowell asked.

“It is,” Ruya replied.

“Well, that’s the right answer,” Lowell said, “but not for the reason you think. You see,” he paused, searching his mind for the previously rehearsed response. “You can’t forget the future because it hasn’t happened yet, the future becomes the past as each moment moves, as time moves always. So, if you remember the past, you remember everything.”

“A tricky question indeed! I am glad I did not choose incorrectly lest I forget this moment in particular,” she teased.

“Deal,” Lowell replied bluntly.

“What deal?” Ruya asked.

“The job.” He snagged the bread from Ruya’s hand and wasted no time sinking his teeth into the semi-stale *pan.*

“Oh, right.” Ruya smiled. She had to stay on her toes in a conversation with Lowell.

“So, what is it?” he asked through a full mouth.

“You know the girl named Tacita, the silent one that serves Orville? I believe she used to be on the street with you.”

The city’s street youth were almost always boys. Perhaps boys were just more likely to be rebellious by nature, restless in their own skin, seeking adventure to escape the steady pace of indentured life. Perhaps girls did not feel the same strain of bondage at such an early age, for their true oppression began once they reached womanhood. Perhaps even the youngest girls were more keenly aware of the dangers that threatened their kind, preferring the familiar menace over the unknown peril. Regardless, it took a particularly fierce girl to choose the life of an urchin and resilience to hold her own on the streets, for she would immediately become a target.

“Yeah, I know her,” Lowell said, slowing his consumption. “A mean one, that girl.”

“It won’t matter if she’s mean or not,” Ruya continued. The boy may be anxious for whatever reason, but she needed him to do this. She knew he was hungry enough to accept, regardless of his fears. “The girl is on an errand in the Lower Half. I need you to ask around, find out why. Then report back to me. It needs to be soon, a day at most. I’ll have more food for you after. Can you do that?”

“That’s quick,” the boy responded, looking up at her shoulder from under a furrowed brow.

“We don’t have much time,” Ruya explained.

"Alright, a day,” Lowell agreed, though his dubious frown remained. “Meet at Cairo’s?”

Ruya nodded. “And stay out of trouble,” she warned as the boy backed away towards his companions.

“Always,” he replied with an oddly forced wink.

Ruya couldn't help but chuckle as she walked away. That wink, where had he picked that up? And how many hours had he spent practicing it and observing others doing it with the hope that he would use it in the proper social context? Some people move to the beat of their own drum, but Lowell moved to the beat of another instrument entirely, one that was both primitively rooted and more sophisticated. His senses were heightened, but his ability to process was disorganized, his mind able to recognize the most intricately woven patterns and connections, but his physical self far less obedient. Ruya said a silent prayer to the Universe to protect the boy as she headed toward the din of the market.

The market took up the largest open space in the Lower Half which surrounded the southern entry to the city. The number of regular vendors had decreased over the years as permits from Subjugation became more difficult to come by and operative taxes increased, but it remained a bustling hub, especially during shift change. Husbands and wives, parents and working children, and groups of friends would meet here for a cup of coffee and a meal in good company.

Ruya made her way around the outer ring of vendors, sharing morning greetings and bits of conversation. The grocer at a produce stand insisted Ruya accept a crisp apple, a thank you for some help she had been able to provide his wife the week past. The poor woman had been in the *Innova*, expecting her first child after years of waiting. Unfortunately, the baby came too soon. Ruya was able to provide a bit of closure and hope through a foretelling. She predicted that the woman would have multiple children and that the soul of her baby had already reached Mundabi.

After offering her condolences for their loss, Ruya humbly accepted the apple, promising her future service and devotion. She eventually made her way around the market to the south entry. With only rare traffic from the south port, the gate was left open for the majority of the day. Halting as directed at the *muniat* station, Ruya named her reason for exiting, stating that she intended to visit the *Innova*.

She was permitted to pass and greeted the Lex officers at their posts as she did, though they offered no acknowledgment in return. The concept of *familiar* had been drained from them during their Gulley training. Their dogs replied for them with low growls and snarls. She had known these officers since their days in the *Innova*, where they had clung to their mothers' knees and gained nourishment at the breast. Choosing to focus on the memory of such peaceful times, rather than what the families of these men had lost, she passed through the gate and crossed the drawbridge over the empty moat. Ruya felt a bit of weight lift as she left the city's chaos – and the ghosts of men at their posts – behind her.

CHAPTER 4

The Quake

There was no time to think. Dottie and Penny gripped each other's hands as the ground quivered beneath their feet. Rolling energy churned the earth below them. The waves surged harder as the ground pitched and swayed, yanking the girls up off the ground, where they hovered momentarily before another pulse knocked them down. They rode out the quaking in the dark woods, remaining disoriented after it stopped, reeling from the aftershocks.

An eerie hum filled the air. The vibration permeated their bodies down to their bones. The suffocating silence was interrupted only by the sounds of Penny's hysteria and an unsettling, high-pitched whirring. Trees were torn out at the roots, turned upside down in the liquefied soil. Cloud cover and a chilling downpour began as the aftershocks waned, leaving the young girls paralyzed by an all-consuming darkness. Dottie was almost grateful for the storm– the sound of the rain muffled the unnerving buzz of static that surrounded them and it seemed to lull Penny into a less volatile state.

Was it finally happening? The catastrophe that her mom had always prepared her for? They had gotten into an argument about training that very night. Mom had wanted her to stay behind to help prep some radio and review what to do if an EMP hits, but Dottie had just wanted to get to manhunt. She'd had enough talk of death and survival, enough of what-if scenarios.

A garbled voice from a megaphone reached the girls during the height of the storm. Dottie yelled in response, screaming for help as loudly as she could. She considered leaving Penny to find its source. After stumbling only a few yards in the darkness, she accepted that she had no idea where the sound was coming from or where she was. She had completely lost her bearings. She released a mess of frustrated gibberish and repeatedly punched the black air until her fist collided with the meaty muscle of somebody's chest.

"Watch it, Dot!" Hudson Mead's voice yelled back at her as his hands firmly gripped her shoulders, bringing her flailing to a stop.

"Hudd?!" She shouted back, straining to make out more than his outline in the unending darkness that surrounded them. Even still, she knew him by his voice, and relief filled her.

"Who else, dummy?" He drew nearer to her.

Dottie dismissed the name-calling, but could not ignore the flutter in her chest brought on by their closeness. "How did you find us?"

"I saw Audrey chasing Penny up the street before the quake hit," he said. "I was trying to find them when I heard you screaming like a maniac."

"Penny's just over there," Dottie said, gesturing behind her. "But we haven't seen Audrey. The megaphone…."

"Military, but they're already gone."

“Military?” She echoed, her voice becoming more audible as the rain slowed its pace.

Hudd released her and stepped back. “Yeah.”

“Why?”

He did not reply, but moved past Dottie towards the growing sound of Penny’s sobs. He knelt beside her and whispered something that appeared calming.

“What do we do now?” Dottie asked as she approached the others.

“Wait till morning,” Hudd answered.

Dottie joined Penny on the ground under an unidentifiable mass of Earth, seeking what little shelter it could provide. She dozed on and off for the remainder of the night until a sliver of pink sunlight signaled the end to the nightmare. Cold, stiff, and utterly exhausted, Dottie rose to greet the day and the changed world it brought.

Her breath rose up before her in a steamy cloud as she stood in the completely silenced woods. The humming had stopped at some point while she slept. All around her were the remnants of chaos–mud, broken ground, uprooted trees–and the earth that hung above her head was filled with dangling roots. The combined odors of rain, frost, dying leaves, and burning wood assaulted Dottie’s nostrils. Penny lay in a muddy puddle at her feet asleep, or perhaps unconscious, but still breathing. Hudd was awake as well, watching her from where he sat next to Penny.

Dottie had dreamed of being in an earthquake when she was little, but it was nothing like what she had just experienced. The sound that occurred during the event and the silence that followed were details she had never anticipated. Her dream had taken place inside a library, books raining down on her as she tried to navigate the aisles. In it, she had been looking for a specific title that she never found, but had continued to search undeterred by the onslaught of paperbacks. The reality she faced was much worse. Penny woke suddenly, gasping, eyes wide in terror as she scooted backward in the mud until she came in contact with the upturned earth.

“We…we’re alive,” she stammered, looking from Hudd to Dottie.

“We are.” Dottie was aware that she should probably find something more reassuring to say, but other than being grateful to still be alive, she felt assured of nothing herself.

“How?” Penny asked, tears welling in her eyes.

“Luck?” Hudd suggested.

“When did it stop?”

“Not sure, maybe a few hours ago?” He replied. “Earthquakes don’t normally last that long. Then again Rhode Island isn’t supposed to get Earthquakes at all.”

“I’ve never actually been in one,” Dottie said.

“Neither have I,” Penny added. “Everybody else is okay, right?”

Dottie looked down at Penny for a moment, wishing she could put the other girl’s mind at ease, but she didn’t have a good feeling about what they would find once they made their way back home. Hudd remained silent.

“I don’t know, Penny,” she said. “I hope so. Did you guys hear that noise even when the shaking stopped? Reminded me of going through a car wash.”

“Yeah, I heard it,” Penny replied. “Felt it, too.”

“Same,” Dottie agreed, remembering the way the vibrations had caused the hair on her arms to stand on end. “We should go. We’re all soaked through, and I don’t know about you two, but I can hardly feel my hands anymore.”

“Go?” Penny asked as Dottie started off in the direction opposite the sunrise.

If she were right about where they were, now that she could see, they wouldn't need to walk far to get back to the street.

“Home,” Dottie said without turning to face the others. *Hopefully it’s still there.*

They left the woods in silence and entered a world that was almost unrecognizable. The street was split in two, large slabs of road rising into the air some dozen or more feet, broken and jagged. At least half the homes on Arden Valley Road no longer stood. Portions of foundations were exposed by the hard rain from the night before, which had washed away the charred remains of walls and roofs. The nearest house was still smoldering in spite of the downpour. They'd caught fire, but how?

The kids had to clamber up a segment of ruptured road to get a decent look down the hill. Penny's house still stood on the left side of the street. Dottie's, just ahead on the right, did not appear to be so lucky and she couldn't see Hudd's from where they were. The girls climbed down and broke out into an exhausted jog toward their homes. Dottie looked back over her shoulder only long enough to notice Hudd still perched atop the upended ground. Why was he so calm?

She slowed as she approached the remnants of her front porch, while Penny continued past, calling out for Audrey. Dottie's chest heaved as tears streamed silently down her face. One. Two. Three. She climbed the steps that remained, blackened, but intact. The same could not be said for the rest of the home.

What will you do? Her mother's voice suddenly filled her mind as she recalled the many conversations that started with that question, Janie's face flashing in front of Dottie as she struggled to stay standing.

What will you do, if the worst happens?

Dottie stepped forward. Something crunched under her feet. She looked down to see the charred remains of Jack's flip phone and reached tentatively to pick it up. He had just gotten it for his sixteenth birthday, only the second kid on the street to acquire the coveted technology. Body numb and heart racing with fear, she climbed over a fallen beam that blocked the entrance to her home, the front door she had painted purple last summer no longer there. Feet that felt detached from her body carried her down the hall and into the kitchen. She tried to call out, but her throat was tight. She must be in a nightmare. She had had these dreams before, the ones where she desperately tried to scream for help, but somehow could not make a sound. She would wake up any moment now… she had to wake up. Balling her hands into fists at her side, Dottie stomped her feet and shook her head from side to side. She wasn't waking up.

She walked toward the living room, or what remained of it, and fell to her knees at the edge of a mass of ceiling. The entire thing had collapsed. She let Jack's phone slip through her fingers and fall to the ground. Her parents would likely have been in there when the quake hit, watching *Sportscenter*. Had her brother run back in to find them when the shaking began?

"Mom," she breathed in a voice that was no more than a whisper. But the sound scared her more than any scream ever could, for it ended her hope that she was simply experiencing the most terrible of dreams.

"Dad!" Dottie was able to get a little more force behind her call this time and followed it up with another while clawing desperately at the charred debris. She dug at wood and ash, and tugged on heavy beams, bracing herself with her feet against one and pulling with all her being on another. It was no use. Nothing would budge, and nobody remained alive to hear her. Defeated, Dottie sunk into a heap in front of the immovable mountain of rubble.

What will you do," her mother's memory prodded, *if I die, if dad dies?*

"I don't know," Dottie whispered to the memory.

But you have to know, you have to be prepared.

"Prepared for what?" She asked aloud, tears streaming down her face.

Anything, the worst. Don't fear, but prepare. If you expect the worst, nothing can surprise you. That's why we practice.

Her mother had failed to mention how the worst would be so incredibly paralyzing.

What will you do if you are alone?

"Find you."

But I'm not here.

"You're in the living room."

I was. But now I'm not.

"Where are you?"

I am nowhere that you can find me.

"Then I'll find help."

Don't accept help from anybody you don't know.

"I'll call somebody I know."

The phones are dead. You won't be able to use them.

Dottie rose on unsteady legs and stumbled to the telephone that had been knocked off its shelf on the other side of the kitchen but had somehow escaped the fire. She grasped at the receiver, raised it to her ear, and heard nothing.

What will you do?

"I'll stay here, wait for somebody to find me."

You'll be a sitting duck. The woods.

"Like camping?"

Like surviving. Trust yourself. You know what to do, where everything is, how it works. Find it. Use it...remember what I taught you. Stay hidden until you know it's safe.

"Where's your family?" Hudd's voice behind Dottie made her jump. She hadn't heard him enter.

"In the living room, I think," she replied without turning to face him. What was he doing here?

"You didn't look for them?"

"I…" she paused, still facing away from him. "I couldn't get through, and I don't think I could see it anyway."

"Dottie…" Hudd's voice was grave. "What if they're still alive?"

Oh, God. I assumed they were...how could I just assume?! She had been so focused on her mother's voice instructing her to go, move on, do all the things they had planned for should something like this happen, but she hadn't made sure. She had been conditioned to accept their deaths her whole life, but never had the possibility of them surviving with her been discussed. A sickening feeling of guilt knocked her to her knees like a physical blow.

"We need to look," Hudd continued in a whisper.

Rocked by apprehension, Dottie struggled to get back to her feet and staggered around the corner toward the living room. She pushed and pulled at the debris with renewed determination and Hudd dropped in alongside her. She dropped to her hands and knees, making her way forward through a crawl space that opened up underneath a pair of crisscrossed fallen beams. She had to sink to her belly and drag herself down to get through a gap in the rubble, kicking and pushing until she could move no further.

Horror at the thought of her family trapped and dying collided with overwhelming claustrophobia as she remained wedged in the debris of her burned home. She looked up, searching the darkness for signs of them. Just as Dottie was ready to retreat, she saw it. The singed corner of her mother's favorite floral pajamas.

She strained forward, blinking frantically to clear her eyes of the dust and ash. Tears streamed down her face. A sheer golden ray filtered in through a slit in the rubble as the sun made its way across the sky, casting just enough light for Dottie to make out the outline of three bodies. Her father lay curled around her mother, enveloping her, his face buried in her shoulder, and her mom was reaching for Jack, who lay sprawled face-down a few feet away.

She could not see their faces. Had they died in pain? In fear? Had they had time to wonder where she was? She would never know. She pressed her eyes shut, remembering them, embedding every detail she could recall about their faces into her mind before they became lost to her. Her mother's angular face and prominent nose; her father's startling blue eyes that so clearly revealed his emotions and the way they crinkled at the edges when he smiled; and Jack… for some reason, she had a hard time remembering Jack as he was now. Try as she might, she could only picture a younger version of her brother. But perhaps it was better that way. They hadn't gotten along very well in the last few years. Maybe she just wanted to remember him at a happier time.

"Dottie?" Hudd's voice boomed behind her. "Dottie, what do you see? Are you stuck?"

She had nothing left inside. Dottie lay frozen, wedged in the wreckage of all she had once held dear, staring at the faceless dead bodies of her mother, her father, her brother. No amount of training could have prepared her for that image. Firm hands grasped her ankles, pulling her back through the crawl space as if ripping her heart from her chest.

"No!" She screamed and kicked back at Hudd, clutching desperately to the mess of half-burned wood in front of her.

"Dottie, calm down!" Hudd yelled, though she could hardly hear his voice as he pulled her from the morbid cocoon. She fell to the ground, thrashing hysterically. A torment of grief overcame her. She sobbed, screamed, swung her fists at Hudd if he came near her, or pounded them against the chunk of flooring on which she sat, a futile protest against her new normal.

"Dottie," Hudd said quietly as she started to calm down, "You saw them?"

She did not, *could* not respond, but inhaled sharply as her mind answered the question.

Yes.

"Did you see them?" He asked again. "Are they…"

Dottie's voice rattled in her chest. "They're dead."

"I didn't mean to make this harder on you," Hudd said as he sat a little closer to Dottie.

"No," she responded. "I needed to see. And you were right, what if they were still alive in there? What if I had found my way back last night? I could have saved them."

"No, Dottie. With the way that room collapsed in and enveloped your family, they would have passed from the smoke inhalation before anything else."

"How do you know?"

“Because the same thing happened to my family, Dot. Because there was nothing I could do to save them and I was right there in the damn yard. I couldn’t find a way in.”

Dottie searched Hudd’s face, noticing the bloodshot eyes and drained expression. It made sense now, why he was here with her rather than searching for his own loved ones, why he hadn’t seemed so eager to find his way back. She reached her hand out and placed it on his, surprised at the ease with which she made the gesture. In that lowest and most isolating moment, she felt connected, and she vowed to cling to that lifeline with whatever she had left in her.

CHAPTER 5
The Outcasts

Ruya delighted in her visits to Nobi, Haddi and Amar's camp. It had been decided long ago that she would continue to live and work in the city to avoid prosecution from the Tri, and that Amar would remain with his father in the Scalas foothills, though coming to terms with this arrangement was more difficult than she had admitted then. The boy would be nearly sixteen now, around the same age his mother was when she met and fell in love with Haddi. It had been months since Ruya had last seen the boys, wrapped her arms around them.

After exiting through the South Market, she took one of the travelers' roads east toward the *Innova,* then cut through some of the old herding pastures that were once filled with livestock. When her mother was a little girl, the unbonded children of the Lower Half would play amongst the sheep, cows, and horses. But the days of flourishing trade and agriculture had disappeared before Ruya was born, and with them, the general use of these grazing lands. The morning fog that crept in from the ocean overnight and settled well into morning gave the deserted pastures an eerie feel, but Ruya welcomed the invigorating feeling of cool mist on her cheeks.

The dewy grass squished beneath her feet as she walked along a decaying wood fence, moving over the uneven ground with practiced ease. Once she reached the colorful Kauon, its leaves emblazoned with fiery red, orange, and yellow hues this time of year, she entered the woods and tracked further east into the base of the hills. The only one of its kind in Alterra, the tree was said to have sprouted thousands of years ago and had since grown wider than any of the various breeds of *hoch*, though not half as tall. While the old tree had once inhabited Alterran folklore, such stories were now rarely recalled. Kauon seemed almost to sag in its spiritual neglect.

Hiking up the skirt of her tunic, she plodded through a sparsely wooded area, strewn with overgrown paths. The footpaths had been well-worn back before the Tri-Commission imposed the external curfew, but it was now rare for anybody to be outside the city walls, let alone wander this far into the foothills. The recent generations of Alterrans, Lower and Upper, master and servant alike, had all become so much more disconnected from nature. The elite prided themselves on being able to manufacture anything they might need, and the indentured peoples no longer had the luxury of leisure and exploration.

Ruya arrived at Nobi just as the sun peeked through the clouds over the Scalas, dissolving the last of the morning dew and fog. From the outside, the camp appeared peaceful, unchanged since her last visit. When Amar was just a baby, Haddi had built a roughly eight-foot wall around the little clearing using boulders, mud and *hoch* needles, completing it with a gate made of woven *kurz* branches. It was sturdily built, if a bit unnecessary.

She had spent most of her time with them in the early months of Amar's life. The *muniat* didn't know the difference between that and the time she would have been expected to spend with Shia in the *Innova* after the birth of a first grandchild. So she had stayed, holding, rocking, and caring for Amar, funneling all of her love and distilling her grief while Haddi worked obsessively to secure Nobi. Haddi said the wall was to keep out unwanted wildlife, but Ruya knew he was guarding against another kind of predator.

She wrapped her hand in the loose fold of her tunic and dug for the thorn-peg which secured the gate. *These men and their secret doors,* she thought, remembering Cairo's the night before. *Don't they know that if somebody wishes to harm you, a door will not stop them?* Malicious minds are never straightforward.

As she entered the courtyard, she took a minute to breathe in the familiarity of the place: the musty odor from the two-room canvas tent, held together with leather strapping and staked into the ground with hefty *kurz* thorns. Ropes tied from the ceiling frame to the trees kept the structure erect. Ruya had once tried to convince Haddi to build a more permanent dwelling, but he would hear nothing of it. Even now, so many years later, the man lived ready to run.

Along one wall sat a wooden table stacked with cups, bowls, and a few utensils, all items that Haddi had either made himself or had Ruya smuggle to him early on. Drying herbs hung by a string along the wall behind the table and a small trapdoor underneath led to a cellar-box where Haddi stored their food. She let her gaze wander. The tent, the kitchen, the walls, and at the center of it all, a magnificent fireplace made of plaster and slabs of *gelb*. A wooden carved *pi* hung from the top of the bell-shaped hearth, where a warm fire danced. The intricacy of it was out of place in such a humble dwelling. Haddi had built the structure specifically for Shia for their union ceremony before the darkness had descended, touching all their lives.

Unions between bonded peoples were not recognized as legally binding in the eyes of the Tri. There were laws protecting indentured maidens and mothers from the wandering hands of Lex officers and members of the elite. For those women who lost their purity but had not yet conceived a child, there was nothing written to protect them from the desires of more powerful men. It was known that the Judiciary would not punish men for having their way with these young brides, so their unions were discreet affairs. An exchange of words in front of a few family members, a promise and a prayer to the Universe for guidance.

The ceremony usually took place in a home, but Shia had wanted theirs to be out here, not wanting to whisper her love for Haddi in some stifling room. The ritual was sealed when each of them threw a handful of neodymium into the fire before speaking their oaths in front of the dazzling silver flames. Haddi had snuck out into the woods every evening for weeks before the ceremony to build this fireplace. Ruya recalled how annoyed Shia had become with his unexplained absence, and then how radiantly her daughter looked as she stood in front of it, lost in the eyes of her beloved as they recited the ancient scripture.

Each a point in the eternal circle, the Universe our most perfect center, complete.

An iron kettle began to whistle over the fire and Haddi emerged from under the flap of the tent, dressed like Orville in the pants he had fashioned long ago. She understood their practicality but seeing it bothered her nonetheless.

“We had hoped we’d be seeing you soon,” he said, looking both surprised and pleased. “I was just about to make some coffee. Have some?” He gripped her forearm and embraced her as Garrett had done the night before.

“Please,” Ruya replied.

“Go head on in, I’ll be right there,” Haddi said, gesturing for her to enter the tent.

It had been too long since she last slept, and she felt a constant ache and chill in her bones. Another cup of coffee, especially the kind Haddi concocted, would do her some good. Ruya took a seat inside on one of the seed-filled leather cushions strewn about on the floor. Shelving constructed from a felled *hoch* bordered the main room of the tent, leaving sitting space for no more than two or three people. Glass vials and wooden bowls lined the shelves, filled with numerous minerals, herbs, and roots.

Ruya was settling down in the cozy room when Haddi appeared through the tent flap with two steaming mugs.

"Amar should be back soon," he said as he handed her a cup. "He'll be glad to see you."

"What is he up to?" Ruya asked.

"You're not gonna like it," Haddi said with a sly smile. He brought his mug to his lips and blew on the steaming liquid. "If I had known you were coming, I would have kept him home just to avoid telling you."

"Goodness, what has he gotten into?" Ruya asked, wide-eyed, though only mildly concerned. She could not imagine someone as *good* as Amar getting into much.

"I'll let him field that question when he returns," Haddi said, raising his mug in salute.

"I have been too long away." She held her clay mug between her hands, deeply inhaling the rejuvenating scent of the spiced drink. Closing her eyes, she allowed herself to simply be present in the moment, away from all the worries and burdens of life, in the company of the only person with whom she could be truly transparent and unguarded. She felt her mind center itself as she sipped the hot beverage, its warmth trickling down into her chest. The coffee Haddi made was far from ordinary. He drew his water from the base of the Klar and crushed herbs into the grounds. Ruya felt a happy hum along her scalp. She opened her eyes to a room with colors that were brighter than they had been a minute before. And there was Haddi, smiling back at her from the cushion on which he sat.

"You really should take some of the blend with you, Ruya," Haddi suggested. "It won't be as pure made with the water from the Holt, but should still bring you some relief, some peace."

"I wish that I could," she sighed, "but the Tri has been cracking down on substance limitations, more frequent raids. I can't afford to get caught up in that right now."

"Well then, you'll just need to visit more often," Haddi replied. "This is good for you, Ruya. You need to take the time to care for your body and spirit or you will be of no use to anybody."

"Yes, I know," Ruya said grimly, "and yet, if I cannot do what needs to be done immediately, there will be nobody left to need me anyway."

Haddi raised his eyebrows at her cryptic statement. For a fleeting moment, she entertained the idea of confiding in him about Orville's recent divination but thought better of it. Haddi would not be happy to know that Ruya still allowed Orville's visits.

"Don't mind me," she said, waving away any concern she may have raised. "Just the rantings of an old woman."

"You've earned your ranting," Haddi said, lifting his mug again in a respectful toast.

"How is my grandson?" Ruya asked.

"He's well," Haddi answered. "I feel as if he has grown a foot or more since you last saw him. We can hardly pull together enough food to sustain the boy."

"I remember when you ate that way," Ruya said. "Always hungry, never still."

"Exactly," Haddi laughed. "The boy never stops moving. There's a specific type of mushroom that grows along the Klar this time of year, and I believe we can trade it at the Belt for a substantial amount of goods…blankets, a bigger pot, a sharper knife. Amar has been harvesting them."

"You'd chance trading at the Belt?" Ruya asked, her voice lowering with concern.

"Amar does well with the traders," Haddi assured her. "Now, our business first. What do you need to restock?"

Ruya shook the image of her sweet grandson peddling rare mushrooms amongst the hardened traders at the Belt and relayed her mental list: *amarus*, a bitter, purple-tinged root that calmed a racing mind; *dulcifer,* sap collected from the stringy *alba* trees and used to sweeten tea and soothe a sore throat; *uvam*, a sour leaf that eased an upset stomach and curbed its rumblings if hunger arrived prematurely; a bladder of *clearwater,* and a vial of *magié milk* would complete her stores. Haddi nodded at each request.

"I have the first three," he said with a grunt as he rose to his feet and began searching through the unmarked vials on the shelves. "I only have a half-bladder of *clearwater* to spare and will need to make another trip up the mountain for the *magié milk*. How urgent is the need?"

"I have enough *milk* for a few more weeks at least," Ruya replied, "and the half bladder of *clearwater* should hold me over just as long."

"The *Innova* has asked for more milk as well," Haddi continued. "Certainly enough need between you both to warrant a trip up the Klar. I'll go in the next few days as the weather allows." He placed the three vials and the half-full bladder into a canvas sling and handed it to Ruya before returning to his cushion on the ground.

"Perfect," she said with a smile as she tied the laces of the pouch around her belt. "And now that you've reminded me, the *Innova*… I need to get over to see Basira. I haven't been summoned to a birth in weeks."

"The woman… Basira," Haddi began, jabbing at the small fire with a green stick, "she is completely blind?"

"Yes," Ruya responded, "but her other senses more than make up for the lack of the one."

"I've only met her once," Haddi went on. "She didn't seem to like me much," he added with a wink.

"You're an acquired taste," Ruya teased in return. "Basira possesses dual strengths in prophecy and healing that are amplified by her loss of physical sight. Quite impressive, in fact." In spite of Basira's indisputable talents, she had been sorted as "moderately impaired" as a young girl and sent to live out her years in the *Innova*, training the next generations of seers and healers.

"And she uses such talents to help the women of the sisterhood?" Haddi inquired further. "How?"

"The women of the *Innova* experience their world as one," Ruya explained. Life inside the Sisterhood was not discussed with the men of Alterra. Though Haddi no longer fell into that category, it felt strange to Ruya to tell him about such things. "The women, we celebrate life together, mourn death together, walk through the trying early stages of womanhood and motherhood together; we use our unique skills and training to contribute to the greater whole of our little village for whatever chunks of time we reside there." She paused to sip her quickly cooling coffee. "We work plots of land, look after livestock, make and repair clothing, cook meals, provide remedies for ailments both physical and spiritual. Basira does indeed use her talents to help the other women, as the rest of us do, yet she has this subtle way of teaching the rest of us to help ourselves."

"Eldress wisdom perhaps?" Haddi asked with a mischievous smile.

"Perhaps," Ruya chuckled. "Be careful who you call eldress, now. I'm not too far behind her."

"All the more reason I insist you drink," Haddi teased, nodding at the cup in Ruya's hand.

"Indeed," Ruya couldn't help but laugh at Haddi's boldness. He had never been one to contain his thoughts. She loved that about him. "Now, what can I bring back for you?"

"We should probably increase our food stores before the snows start," Haddi replied as he scratched at his beard. "I suppose anything preserved, except for cabbage. Can't stand fermented cabbage."

"You never could." Ruya smiled to herself, staring down at her coffee and drawing a finger along the rim. "Shia asked me to serve it to you when she was mad at you once. Pure mischief, that one..." She trailed off, realizing what she had said.

A sullen look darkened Haddi's face, the corners of his mouth sinking as his eyes became dull. Ruya should have known better. She knew Haddi had no interest in revisiting old memories.

“Kauon,” Ruya began, searching for some bit of small talk to employ, “I feel like it has changed colors earlier than normal this year.”

“It has,” Haddi stated as he glared into the fire.

“I wonder why… perhaps we will have a colder winter.”

“It is not what’s coming,” Haddi growled, “but what has been going on for years that has changed the color of the leaves too soon.”

Ruya frowned across the fire at her melancholy companion. “What has been…”

“The Scalas, the Klar, the *force* that gives them life is waning. We no longer have enough of the resource to keep it balanced. It has been stolen.

“You mean what Orville has taken?”

“I do.” The dark circles under Haddi’s eyes seemed more prominent as he spoke. “Though I expect you already know that. After all, you use only a pinch of the substance to see, while Orville uses substantially more for his *work*, and you must know he has to be mining it from somewhere?”

Ruya knew that Orville was getting the minerals from the Scalas. The neodymium drove the energy and lifeforce of all Sum. But she had hoped his work would not be significant enough to affect the universal energy.

“For one who can *see*, you are blinder than Basira,” Haddi said, his words hitting Ruya as painfully as a stinging blow.

Her heart ached in the silence that followed. It ached for the accidental words that she’d spoken, reminding Haddi of what haunted him. It ached for the future she had not been able to see, for her years of blindness to Orville’s sinister schemes. But most of all, it ached with a longing to be free of the weight that rested on her now.

There was no bringing Haddi back when his brooding became this severe. She knew his bouts of gloom well, and she also knew it would be through by the time she returned, the bright and peaceful man she so adored present once more. She placed a kiss on the top of his head and patted his shoulder before making her way out of the tent.

Ruya waited patiently by the fireplace for Amar to return, and when he finally did, it was with a bag full of mushrooms and a heart-warming grin for his *Avia.*

"Why are you standing out here?" Amar asked, embracing Ruya with all of the warmth she had been craving desperately.

"The tent was beginning to feel a bit crowded," Ruya replied, a flush creeping into her cheeks as she looked down at her hands.

"Is he bad?" the boy asked with an understanding smile.

"Oh, not *that* bad. We all just need a little space now and then."

Amar tilted his head to one side, a playful smile on his face, accentuating the dimples in his cheeks. "What did you say about my mother this time?"

"How she once asked me to serve fermented cabbage to your father when she was angry with him," Ruya replied, her heart growing lighter in the cheerful presence of her grandson. "They were not much older than you are now. She knew he would eat it out of respect for me…and would hate every bite. And I was none the wiser until years later."

Amar chuckled and shook his head. Ruya watched as he moved closer to the hearth to stoke the flames. He was indeed growing up quickly, was already taller than his father. He deserved to be amongst youth his age, getting into trouble, making friends, falling in love. And yet there was no way to change the truth of their circumstances.

"I've missed you," Ruya said. "I cannot believe how you have grown."

"Grown right out of my shoes," he said with a wink, raising a foot to show off two bare toes poking through the canvas front.

"Well that won't do," Ruya said, frowning at her grandson's foot.

"I'll be going to the Belt for some trading in a couple of days…"

"Yes, I've heard about this," Ruya cut in.

"You don't approve?" he asked, his expression amused.

"I have concerns," she admitted.

"I'll be fine, *Avia*," Amar reassured her. "Besides, we need supplies for winter, and you know as well as I that father can't show his face at any of the trading posts."

"I suppose you're right," Ruya conceded. "And unfortunately, I also suppose that I best be heading back to the city myself." She couldn't go much longer without checking back in with the *muniat* at the gate, as there would be no record of a call to the *Innova*.

Ruya reached out to hug Amar, who now had to bend noticeably to return the embrace.

"Take care of your father," Ruya said as she released him and patted his arm, blinking away tears. "Help him remember where he is and what's important *here*."

"I will, *Avia*," Amar replied, blue eyes sparkling.

He had Shia's blue eyes, though without the darkness. The zest for life that shone from them, that was once Haddi's. He was becoming more like Haddi as he grew up and this relieved Ruya. While she longed for glimpses of her daughter's brilliance, she would not wish the torment that came with it on anyone. And Amar was filled with the quiet confidence and self-assuredness that comes from an unburdened life, by the freedom of knowing what you know and not having to explain it to anyone. If nothing else, what Shia and Haddi had endured and what Ruya had suffered on their behalf had at least given Amar a life unbonded. She held tight to this thought as she made her way back to the city.

As she passed Kauon not long after, Ruya caught sight of an unusually agitated cluster of Orville's leaves. She had never been able to convince him to reveal their ability or purpose, and the metallic gold leaves appeared to move of their own free will, rising and falling though the air was still. As she made her way through the pasture, the numerous clumps of shimmering leaves began to split apart and regroup into one giant mass, like a swarm of bees surrounding and protecting their queen. This was behavior she had never before witnessed.

Ruya froze as an eerie hum filled her ears and the swarming leaves became further agitated, churning in the air like the waves of the Malú. The buzzing rose to a climax, the leaves climbing higher into the air than should be possible. She clutched the canvas satchel of tinctures at her waist. The clamor ceased abruptly, and the disturbed horde of leaves plummeted to the uneven ground that was now swaying precipitously beneath her feet.

The ground heaved under her for minutes uninterrupted. It took Ruya a few attempts to regain her footing once the shaking stopped. She raced back to the city as quickly as her wobbly legs could carry her, hurrying through the south gate, noting that the Lex officers and the *muniat* were no longer at their posts. The market was in chaos, but thankfully not riddled with the devastation she had feared. Ruya navigated through the clutter of broken down carts and strewn produce, making her way through to the back alleys that would lead her home. Plumes of smoke rose up from the rows of tenements. As she passed, confused masses spewed forth from Triplica – a series of three buildings joined together to form a tower, a triangular courtyard at its center.

"*May their paths be calm*," she intoned, a brief plea to the Universe to protect the families affected by the fires. Ruya was grateful to see no substantial damage on her route home, though her heart went out to a brood of raggedy children huddled together in the doorway of an abandoned workhouse.

Ruya barely managed to stumble through her back door to her bed before collapsing into an exhausted heap. She had not stopped moving for days, had not slept, had eaten very little. Haddi was right about one thing: if she wanted to be of use to anybody, she needed to start taking care of herself a little better. And for what she was about to do she would need her wits about her. Orville had crossed a line. The first part of the prophecy left no room for error. He would fail in his endeavors. There was no saving him. But the rest of the foretelling – there was an "if" in those trails that caused Ruya to hope, an "if" that meant her most important mission was just beginning. It was a mission she knew she would not live to see the end of, but she needed to put what little life she had left into it nevertheless. Her limbs felt numb, tingly, disconnected from her body. The room around her spun, and visions of swarming golden leaves filled her thoughts as she succumbed to a heavy sleep.

CHAPTER 6
The Circle

Haddi perched on a narrow ledge at the top of Praeceps, his heels wedged into the wall across from him to keep steady. He let his arms fall limp at his sides to rest the burning muscles before the last, and thankfully easiest, leg of his hike. Who knew how many times he had scaled the enchanted cliffs in the sixteen years since Jeg and Trude first pulled him up. The climb was different each time, yet he no longer questioned his ability to tackle it. The Universe, it appeared, wanted to keep him around for a while. That didn't make it any less unnerving when something in the surface of the rock face altered unexpectedly, threatening to throw him off entirely.

Haddi had climbed many a sheer surface, and while Praeceps was neither the longest nor least navigable, its ever-changing face meant that one was allowed no breaks. Having recovered from the hard sprint up the tandem granite cliffs, Haddi bouldered his way up and out of the top of Praeceps to a precipitous, but flat, footpath along the mountainside. Just a bit farther and he could rest. To stay where he was would have made him a sitting duck for the scarce but aggressive predator that called this area of Scalas home. He'd had only one previous run-in with the black mountain lions, but hoped never to repeat the incident.

Like a prodigal son, Haddi entered the clearing where he had found himself saved the day Shia took her own life, where Jeg and Trude had placed upon him a weight to which he expected never to become accustomed to. He sat on the ground with his back against the very same spiny *hoch* tree and looked over the still-stacked stones that had formed the firepit at center. Breathing in deeply, Haddi closed his eyes and let his mind wander back to that night.

-

"Why me?" Haddi asked Trude, unable to imagine why he would be worth the trouble to the *Universe* to send such impressive creatures to save him from his own stupidity.

"'Tis written in the sacred Gelb," Trude answered, though her voice sounded oddly far away as a buzzing filled Haddi's ears. "*The purest of nature is only for the purest of heart and broken in spirit. It is for the least among us*. This is something ye must never forget, Haddi." Trude's voice was low and steady as she kept her eyes focused on the blaze.

"Wait," Haddi said, shaking his head. "How *do* you even know my name? You've both said it… but I never told you."

"We've always known yer name," Trude replied. "We just never knew when you'd be comin'."

Haddi stared at Trude, both in awe and, in a way, with amusement at the absurdity of it all.

"I… I don't understand," Haddi stammered. He lifted his hands to his head, pulled the strip of leather free from the tangled mess that had become his hair and ran his fingers through and down, rubbing his eyes and face in an effort to bring feeling and clarity to them.

"There is one t' come who will heal the Universe of division," Trude explained, "bring together all the creatures, even the men. But there is also one who must come before to pave the way. One who will act as guide into the spiritual realms."

"I think you have me confused with somebody else," Haddi replied. "I'm pretty sure I'll end up in Incendi, not any higher realm of the spirit."

"*It is for the least among us*," Trude repeated.

"No more now," Jeg cut in. He got up from the log and lowered himself to the ground with more agility than Haddi expected.

"Jeg's right," Trude said firmly. "Enough for tonight. You'll learn more tomorrow. You need to get some sleep."

Haddi didn't put up a fight. He still felt drained from his near-death ordeal and his mind was a noisy place. Protective magic, Irden civil war – conflict between clans of creatures he hadn't even thought were real – betrayal precipitated by Orville, giant Tor, obscure messages… and he was expected to play some role in all this?

The purest of nature is only for the purest of heart and broken in spirit. It is for the least among us. Broken in spirit he may indeed be, but pure of heart he most certainly was not. He had killed men, beaten them senseless with his own fists then left them to die in pools of blood. No… Trude must not have meant those words for him, or perhaps she thought him to be somebody he wasn't. *Or maybe*, a voice in his mind suggested, *there is more to you than you believe*. With that, Haddi slipped into a fitful dream-filled sleep.

He walks through a forest at night. Had he risen from near the fire without realizing it? No, no... There is no fire nearby, not even the smell of cinders. This forest doesn't just smell different, it is darker in hue, more bland, as if the color in everything has faded. The hoch-like trees are smaller, lackluster. The dewy purple moss that lines the floor of the Scalas has been replaced by decaying fallen leaves.

He looks up into the sky through sparse tree branches, but can only find one moon, lacking the iridescence of the silvery moons he'd known his whole life. He walks on, unsure of where his feet are taking him but feeling compelled forward nonetheless. He hears leaves crunch ahead of him. He slows his pace, coming closer to the edge of the tree line. A young girl appears. He sidesteps behind the trunk of one of the frail trees to get a better look. She seems to be alone. She sits on the ground with her back against a large stack of chopped up wood.

The girl is oddly dressed, wearing fitted clothing that covers all four limbs with holes at her knees, holes that appear strategically placed. Her black canvas shoes are strapped together over her feet. He knows he has seen similar dress before, but where? He marvels at the wild ringlets of golden hair that pop out of her head at any given angle.

He shifts his weight to get a better look. A twig snaps under his feet. He remains still as the girl's eyes immediately move towards him, piercing the place in which he stands. He opens his mouth to speak, but no words come. He stands there, transfixed, as the girl's amber eyes bore through his chest.

-

Haddi jolted upright, breathless, next to the now smoldering remnants of the night's fire. Sweat trailed from his brow as a forceful shudder ran through his body.

"What did you see?" Jeg demanded, hovering so high over Haddi that his attempt to meet the giant's gaze sent Haddi into a violent spin.

"I… a girl. It was a dream," Haddi muttered. "It was just a dream." Yet, he searched the night sky for the two familiar moons and did not breathe easily until he found them.

"There ain't no such thing as just a dream, Haddi, not at Atrofi" Trude said as she came closer, kneeling down in front of him.

"Atrofi?" Haddi asked, eyes wide, feeling his body tense against another foreign word.

"'Tis where you are," Trude explained. "Dreams received here are messages from the Universe Herself. A girl… what did she look like?"

"She was dressed oddly, her hair…," Haddi paused, making a spiraling motion with his index finger. "Like rings, golden rings."

"A one with golden crown," Trude muttered.

"A one with… the ancient salvation prophecy?" Haddi looked from Trude to Jeg in a desperate plea for understanding.

"'Ay, 'tis written," Trude stated, as if those words alone could explain the sheer insanity of it all.

"I don't understand."

"Beyond the Caligo Peaks, the old magic remains," Trude explained. "The most ancient of truths are carved into the Gelb there. These things are but a whisper of ancient history for your kind. For us… the Tor, the *magié*, the ancient clans of the Irden, all the other creatures of the realms, 'tis what we live by."

"Who wrote these things into the stone?" Haddi shook his head in a last vain attempt for clarity.

"'Tis said the first of each lineage met at a great council there, thousands of years ago. The elders o' the Irden, the King o' the Tor, the leaders o' the other scions that existed in greater unity then. The old magic was alive in more than just the *magié* and the Klar in those times. 'Tis said the Universe herself was present and carved the truths into the Gelb to remain there for all creatures to learn and know. But there were some at the council, your kind, who felt these truths should not apply to them. They resolved to distance themselves from the old ways, believing this move exempted them from the *universal law.* What they did not understand was that only in the light of the truth could they truly be free."

Trude paused, remaining silent for a few moments. Perhaps she was giving Haddi a chance to ask questions before continuing on, but it seemed to be a retelling that drained her more than regular conversation.

"The men turned on one another," Trude added after a time.

"Partitus?" Haddi asked for clarification.

"As ye know it, yes."

As slivers of morning sunlight slipped up and over the top of the Scalas, Haddi could finally make out more than the immediate space around the fire. There was not far to look – a couple hundred feet of woodsy landing between the side of the mountain and the cliff below, Praeceps just to the south of their location. All around them the ground was lightly dusted with a layer of snow, except for the place in which they stood and a ring that stretched about twenty feet radially from the fire.

"Stand up," Jeg instructed.

Haddi complied, though executing the act itself proved to be more difficult than he anticipated.

"Look at the ground," Jeg said.

Haddi again looked in all directions, down at the dry dirt ground that so abruptly turned to snow in a perfect circle.

"Ye are standin' in a place known as Atrofi," Trude explained. "The weather ne'er touches this place."

"Now look at your feet," Jeg ordered Haddi.

Haddi did as instructed, looking down and noticing a dark line in the soil running directly between his feet. His head tilted to one side as he considered the change in mineral, yellow and black swirled together. The line extended from the place he stood to the center of the fire and behind him still to the outer ring.

"Take two steps to your left," Jeg commanded next.

Haddi took two steps left, then another two, then shuffled backward until he toppled rear-end first over the fallen log on which he had rested the night before. As he moved, the line followed, the ground around it giving way obediently. It followed him under the log and to the other side, where it settled underneath him once again. He reached out a hand to feel it, its surface warm and humming with a vibration that made him feel alive in a way he had never known before.

"Ye are the compass," Trude said quietly. "I told ye last night… ye are the guide. Ye will lead us to the one who will complete the circle and unite us all again. And we… well, we must move quickly, for there is one more thing ye need to see."

CHAPTER 7
The Gang

Dottie rounded her back against the mess of living room debris, pulling her knees to her chest the way she had behind the woodpile the night before. Hudd's shoulder pressed against hers as he sat in silence next to her and she allowed herself to lean into him. She couldn't decide whether she was angry with or grateful to her mother for all the years of preparation.

Dottie's mom had always possessed the combined tendencies of a conspiracy theorist, a doomsday prepper and a wilderness survivor. She certainly never shied away from the discussion of her own mortality, working to prepare Dottie for the worst-case scenario. It had been frustrating growing up. She doubted other kids her age were at home talking about imminent doom, death, and survival on the weekends. But Dot had also been grateful for it. She learned skills that none of her peers possessed, and she knew the world held all sorts of threats, natural or otherwise. She was living that now. Yet, none of her mother's training had prepared her for the debilitating pain of what "alone" really felt like.

Damn you for making it all sound so easy, she cursed her mother's memory. *Did you leave this part out on purpose?*

Regardless of her mom's accuracy in anticipating what would actually happen, Dottie was now faced with the decision to either lie down and mourn the lost or to *use* what she had learned.

The basement. Everything was in the basement.

She put her head down and pushed up against Hudd and the dead ceiling.

"Where are you going?" Hudd asked, falling in step behind her as she headed back to where the basement door once stood and where the foundation was now exposed.

She didn't respond. Best just to show him. She was able to walk straight down the unfinished wood stairs. The fire had charred the top few inches of the walls. A foot or so of water flooded the basement floor. Gritty light streamed in through the windows that lined the walls and from sections missing from the floor above.

Dottie sat down on the lower steps. She removed her shoes and socks and rolled the cuffs of her muddy jeans up over her calves. Hudd followed suit. She dipped her toes into the water. It was cold.

"Dot…" Hudd's voice came hesitantly behind her. "What the hell is this place?"

She turned to face him, anticipating the look of surprise on his face. She followed his gaze to the other side of the basement where rows of floor-to-ceiling utility shelves held enough tools and supplies to last a family of four at least two years. Mattresses, sheets of plywood, cinder blocks, sandbags and bags of ready to mix concrete lined one wall, while school supplies, textbooks, and a full homeschool station ran along the other side. Dottie's mom had upped her game recently with concerns over Y2K, but the truth was that a majority of it had been ready to go for years.

“My mom liked to be prepared,” Dottie explained.

“Prepared, but… this is excessive. It’s like a bunker in here.”

Dottie answered Hudd with a shrug, not quite sure how else to respond. She scanned the basement again. She had never really thought of it as excessive, but it did give off a bunker-like impression. But to her, this was home. As she looked out into the room she saw Jack playing *1080 Snowboarding* on their Nintendo 64, leaning back in his chair with his feet propped up on the craft table. She saw her dad riding the recumbent bike as he flipped through his latest issue of *Golf* magazine. She saw herself pitching a softball into one of the old mattresses propped in the corner by the ping pong table.

Just yesterday her greatest worry was some bully on a bus and getting her curveball down. Today, she was surviving. Her mom had told her this, that it would all change in an instant, but again she felt cheated by the lack of preparedness for how gut-wrenching, nauseating, and terrifying it would all actually be. She dipped her toes into the frigid water again. This was happening. This was real and not just some bad dream. She slid both feet into the water, inhaling sharply as her skin adjusted to the temperature.

She wasn't sure how long they would need to prepare for, but she knew they needed to be able to survive alone, together, and with Penny. She still owed Penny. They wouldn’t be able to stay here with the way it was flooded. Penny’s house still stood. Perhaps that would be a short-term solution for them. Mom wouldn’t have liked that much. She would have wanted her to go into the woods and stay away from buildings and people. But staying at Penny’s would protect them from the elements and they could remain near the rest of the supplies if anything else was needed.

The hiking packs and a majority of the gear appeared to be intact, the flood water only covering half the bottom shelf, which contained mostly gallons of drinking water. She held her breath and eased forward in the chilly rainwater. She grabbed a couple of packs from a higher shelf, handing two more to Hudd before going back over to the craft table, unloading and checking the contents of each in turn.

“What’s with the math?” Hudd asked, pointing at the chalkboard propped up on the back of the table that was covered in half-erased algebra equations.

“That’s old,” Dottie answered. “My brother was always trying to teach me stuff.” Jack would sit her down for hours with the chalkboard, running her through lessons as she pretended with all her might that she understood why A plus B equals C.

“Teach you algebra?” Hudd raised his eyebrows in question. “Considering that your basement is a bunker that almost seems normal.”

“Let’s pack up,” Dottie said.

“For?”

“Look, you said some military came through…”

“Right.”

“Why would the military be the first responders? And why hasn’t anybody been back since?” Her questions were met with silence. “The phone lines are dead. We need to be ready to travel or hide out for a time until we know what we’re dealing with.” She expected Hudd to laugh at her, tease her, but he just nodded in affirmation and followed suit as she began sorting gear: magnesium fire starters, iodine tablets, flashlights, multi-tools, and water bottles with built-in filters.

Dottie returned and moved on down the second row. She chose a small camping knife for Penny, then secured a rope, a travel-sized cook set, camp shovel, some twine and a hatchet and inspected a slightly intimidating Rambo-style Bowie knife for herself. She grabbed a tactical belt with a sheathed half-serrated switchblade, a holstered flashlight, a zipper pouch that held more fire starters, a compass, and another multi-tool. They found another camping knife and a hatchet between the bags and clipped them onto a belt for Hudd. Dottie looked longingly at the rows of gallon water jugs, wishing she had the means to take them with her. Instead, she settled for filling four water packs and hoping they could find other sources of water as they went.

“You think you can haul two packs?” She asked Hudd

"Easy," Hudd replied.

She'd have to carry two herself until they got back to Penny, but it would be worth having the extra fuel. Dottie grabbed a duffel and waded back along the storage rows loading up with food supplies: canned beans, chicken, tuna – they'd need protein – a stash of vacuum packed MREs, and the energy "goop" packs marathon runners use. There were even a few recently purchased bags of beef jerky and trail mix. Each of the hiking packs had a small first aid kit, but she grabbed a more comprehensive one off its shelf. Gauze, tape, butterfly strips, instant cold packs, warming packs, antibiotic ointment, numbing spray, liquid bandage, ibuprofen, tweezers and bandage shears… meticulously packed into this case were pretty much all the things one would hope *never* to need.

Back at the craft table, she unloaded the duffel and divided the food stores between the packs, purposefully placing the lighter items into the one she was assembling for Penny. She wondered what destruction Penny had found at her own home. *I'm not going to think about that now*. Finally, they checked and tightened the rolled up sleeping bags strapped to the bottom of each pack.

"What else?" She said, more to herself than to Hudd. "Water, fire, food, tools… toilet paper!" That was one luxury she didn't want to give up. Good thing her mom was always prepared with extra toilet paper, wet wipes, hand sanitizer and a mental map of any and all nearby bathrooms. Dottie found a couple of individually wrapped rolls of toilet paper in another plastic tub and added them to her stash.

"What about winter gear?" Hudd asked. "Boots, coats…."

Hudd was right. They were dressed for a few hours of fall chill, not days of travel and possibly snow. Unfortunately, her family's snow boots and winter coats had been in the mud room, which now lay under the mess of caved in ceiling upstairs. But on the bottom of the last row of shelves were tubs filled with hiking boots, jackets, utility gloves, and tarps. It wasn't strict snow gear, but it would do. Dottie added a tarp and more rope to one of the packs and Hudd even found a pair of her dad's old utility pants. He held them into the air for Dottie's permission.

"Might as well," Dottie said. Dad wouldn't be needing them. "Take whatever you think you can use."

There was one more thing: the radio, the one her mom had wanted to show her how to prepare for storage the night before. The metal ammo can that they had planned to use for a makeshift Faraday cage still sat on the craft table next to the loaded-up packs.

"What's with that?" Hudd asked as she removed the lid and the lining of aluminum foil from the rim of the can.

"There's a radio in here," Dottie explained. "This protects it from an EMP."

"EMP?" Hudd asked, eyebrows raised.

"Electromagnetic Pulse," Dottie said. She wasn't quite used to this non-teasing version of Hudd and felt hesitant to show just how much she knew about the subject. But an expression of real interest on his face prompted her to expand further. "Look, it's basically an explosion that jacks up the Earth's magnetic field and fries the entire power grid. Anything that runs off of batteries, magnets, electricity… zapped. All of this is supposed to protect the radio so that it can still be used."

"What can we even pick up with that?" Hudd questioned.

Layer by layer, Dottie unwrapped the radio that she pulled from inside the metal ammo can: cardboard, gallon Ziploc bag, aluminum foil, brown craft paper, aluminum foil, another Ziploc bag, more aluminum foil, a smaller Ziploc bag. And there it was, a portable Shortwave AM/FM radio ready to go.

"This thing can pick up radio frequencies worldwide," Dottie replied. "*If* it works, and if there's anybody out there broadcasting, we should be able to hear it. She pressed down on the power button and a surge of triumph accompanied the sound of radio static that filled the air around them. She pressed the scanner arrows and moved from one frequency to another, waiting, *nothing.*

"We should go," Hudd said after a time. "I'm worried about Penny. We can try this thing again later, okay?"

"Yeah." The radio was still working. That was the most important thing. They sat on the steps and put on the fresh wool socks and hiking boots. Hudd hauled the packs to the top of the stairs two at a time, somehow knowing that she needed a moment to bid farewell to the memories that filled the room.

She said goodbye to the Christmas ornaments made from beads and pipe cleaners that still decorated the craft area from last year. She smiled to herself as she recalled dragging Jack up and down the street with her to sell them to neighbors for twenty-five cents each "or five for a dollar." She said goodbye to the hours of lessons, training, preparing and organizing at the behest of her mother. And she said goodbye to the childish fear she'd always had of this basement, a fear that paled in comparison to the daunting and uncertain path that lay in front of her. She turned and ascended the stairs for what she expected was the last time.

"I'm glad you were here," Dottie said as she joined Hudd at the top. He did not respond. She didn't want him to. She shouldered her own pack and the one meant for Penny and followed Hudd back toward the front door.

This was no longer *her* home. The happy scenes that she recalled so clearly were no longer *her* memories. They belonged to someone else, someone childish enough to think her life was hard, someone naive enough to believe her family was off-limits to tragedy.

"Goodbye," Dottie whispered as she placed her hand on the skeletal frame of the front door, feeling the grain of the wood under her fingertips. Her now extra-frizzy curls bounced as she lifted each pack over to the other side of the fallen beam before climbing over herself. She hauled a pack onto each shoulder, faltering under their combined weight. Determinedly gripping the straps at her shoulders, Dottie walked away from the burned remnants of her home, her family, her life.

Loaded up with four full packs of supplies and outfitted more appropriately for the impending winter weather, Dottie and Hudd emerged into the mid-morning sunlight. They walked along the dried-out wall of wild blackberry bushes that bordered Dottie's yard, the air cooler than it had been the previous few days yet eerily calm. They followed the same path Dottie had taken just two nights prior at the start of their game and passed over the crunchy blueberry bushes.

She tried to steady herself against waves of anxiety mingled with pure dread. But with each step a force stronger than her resolve bubbled to the surface, churning her stomach until she doubled over in violent heaves. Grief coursed through her as she sank forward to her hands and knees. The packs dropped to the ground. Her clumsy fingers clamped down on the dry leaves, soil wedging beneath her nails. Sobs passed through her like the cruelest of waves, wreaking havoc on her body and mind.

She let the grief consume her, submitted to it. What if she just stayed here, admitting defeat and refusing to move? She imagined the ground opening up and swallowing her whole. It wasn't an entirely unpleasant thought.

Dottie had started to drift away when her vision suddenly began to refocus, and her shoulders eased away from her ears and relaxed forward, rounded. She breathed. Shallow, raking breaths at first that slowly grew more steady. She tentatively shifted back onto her heels, lifting clumps of dirt in her still-clenched fists. She released her grip and watched the leaves fall back to the earth, crumbled now and slightly moldy after being so long separated from the trees that once bore them. She began to hum absentmindedly – a low, familiar tune, a lullaby her mother sang to her as a child – as she rocked herself slowly back and forth, back and forth, allowing her arms to fall limply into her lap, palms up in a prayer of desperation.

The haze of grief gradually waned, and she became painfully aware of a stream of snot and tears running down over her mouth and neck, soaking the collar of her sweatshirt. But what did it matter? There was only Hudd alive to witness the ugliness of her grief, and he had never thought much of her anyway. There was nobody else to hear the anguished, warbled lullaby hummed so low, no others but the ever-listening leaves of a dying autumn day, a shiny cluster of which rose in an enchanted swirl to greet her despite the fact that there wasn't even the slightest breeze.

CHAPTER 8
The Magié

Haddi worked his way up along the outer bank of the Klar, carefully stepping between rocks covered with Byzantium colored moss. The crystal-clear stream meandered its way down the mountainside, tumbling over boulders and fallen tree limbs. His scarred knuckles stared back at him as he gripped a small ledge and pulled himself up and over to a higher bank. Pausing for a moment, Haddi leaned against the massive trunk of an old *hoch*. Relaxed against the tree, he took a few measured breaths, adjusting to the thin air. He glanced up at the natural canopy above, wispy white clouds feathering the sky.

So strange to think that just the day before the world had been caught in such violent upheavals. He had been in Nobi, sitting by the smoldering remnants of the fire he had shared with Ruya when the ground began to convulse. The quaking caused their tent to collapse in on him. He had wrapped himself in the canvas ceiling, rolling his body back and forth in the dirt to douse the flames that caught his forearm, then rose on unsteady feet to find his son. Amar was in the center of camp, gripping the side of the *gelb* hearth to remain standing and Haddi rushed to him until it was all over.

They had spent the remainder of that day repairing their camp. Haddi set off the next morning for more *magié milk* and was relieved to see that the Klar and the *magié* pool remained undisturbed, especially after surveying the state of the lower Scalas – misplaced slabs of rock and fallen trees had made the sparse mountain terrain more challenging to navigate.

Haddi wore his mess of black hair tied with a strip of leather on top of his head, wild strands breaking loose and falling into his face as he scanned the tree line on the opposite bank. He rested there, closing his eyes and inhaling the heady and invigorating odor of *hoch* needles and *gelb* – a bright yellow mineral that ran like crusted veins in the ground and fused itself into ancient volcanic boulders lining the base of Brennen Peak. The combination gave the boulders a striking black and yellow marbled appearance. Haddi had seen marble once during his bond as a mason for the city builders. It had been brought over on a rare trading vessel long before Haddi was even born. The beauty of that slab of exotic rock came nowhere close to the dark majesty of the *gelb* slate.

Haddi steadied himself as he felt the distinct flutter of *magié* brush his cheek, but he dared not open his eyes. They were reading him, trying to determine his intentions. Driven entirely by intuition, the *magié* were unable to hold memories. Over the years he had found that they were more receptive if he took the time to calm and steady himself, breathing away any anxiety or tension, and allowing them to make their assessments unhindered. Should he arrive burdened or anxious, they seemed to have a hard time determining the source of these emotions and often pushed him back down the mountain. Down was a direction he could not afford to go today. The *milk* was needed, for Ruya, the *Innova*... and there were others, too. Easily flustered creatures, the *magié,* and they owed passage to no one.

After a time, Haddi no longer felt the *magié* against his skin. He breathed in once more, before opening his eyes and taking in the scene that lay before him. Iridescent and no bigger than a man's hand, hundreds of sparkling white *magié* fluttered inches above the Klar, which had been still and unoccupied just moments earlier. It was impossible to know where one of the fairy-like creatures stopped and another began as they moved in murmuration, riding a light breeze.

The sweetest sound, somewhere between a song and laughter, reached Haddi's ears. The music filled his soul. It quenched a growing desire to become lost in the harmony, momentarily erasing from his mind his intended purpose. He gazed at the slated cliff behind the fall. Mist drifted up from its base as towering columns of metallic stone reflected and separated the sun's rays into colorful ribbons. The rainbows played off the ridges of the cliff in time with the sprightly *magié* song. A shiver ran down Haddi's spine as he leaned back to gaze on the height of the falls where it sprouted from the clouds. He wished to hold onto this image forever. *At least,* he thought, *I don't have to share it with anybody else.*

Most of the Alterrans were too afraid of what folklore said about the upper Scalas to attempt this journey. Stories of hostile Tor were sufficient to keep most men at a distance, never mind their minimal basis in truth. Combined with the arduous hike to the clearing, and considering that Praeceps was the only point of entry, any others were easily deterred.

Haddi stood up, letting his eyes adjust to the brilliant silver light produced by the swarming *magié*. Thorny *kurz* lined the forest on all sides. The shrubs were too dense for passage, leaving him no choice but to follow the Klar up underneath the waterfall that churned over the top of Brennen Peak. Haddi sprang from rock to rock like a cliff goat. He balanced atop a boulder, poised to jump, when it suddenly rolled to the side, throwing him into the shallows of the Klar with a loud splash. The playful hum from the *magié* grew as Haddi joined in with a chuckle, rising slowly to his feet.

"Go easy on me," he told the now still stone as he patted its warm surface, "I'm not as young as I used to be." In truth, he had been feeling the years creeping up on him for some time now. His body ached for days after these hikes. He rested more frequently along the way. Haddi knew he would not be able to keep making this trip forever, yet he believed that somehow his soul would find a way to this place, even when his body failed him.

Haddi made it the rest of the way up to the falls without further trickery. Wading along the outer edge of the pool, he wound his way behind the falls. The roar of the water filled his ears and drowned out the *magié* music in the clearing. A musty odor greeted him, the crisp smell of *hoch* fading away. Haddi pulled himself up out of the water and onto a narrow ledge. As he sidled his way around a corner, the dank hollow opened, revealing an impressive cavern. Purple and red moss crept down the sides of the walls of the cave like a veil, draping the marbled Gelb. Condensation from the falls gathered on the surface of the smooth stone, making Haddi's path a slippery one. He took his time, carefully scaling a series of bouldered steps that led to the uppermost portion of the cave. His head rang with the drum of the falls.

Haddi spotted a few stray *magié* lingering above him as he neared the source of the great waterfall. He had to work his way through a crawl space to get to the pocket of the cavern where he had found the natural milk spigot, dragging his body along the bottom of the dark, narrow tube. It was only on these rare occasions that Haddi cursed his broad frame. He breathed a heavy sigh of relief as he pulled himself up and out of the tunnel, stretching his limbs.

Inhaling the perfumed scent of the little cavern, Haddi let his eyes adjust to the light that streamed in through a hole in the rocks high above. Milk-white veins mingled with the *clearwater* that spewed from a series of spouts in the cavern wall. The creamy strands were nature's most precious gift. The *magié milk* could nourish even the frailest of infants, sustain the elderly, and had done miraculous things for the women giving birth in the *Innova*.

This was how they had sustained Amar after Shia was gone when the baby refused a wet nurse and wouldn't accept the goat's milk they offered. Once thought to be a place of folklore, Haddi had discovered the fountain shortly after Shia's death when Jeg and Trude led him there from Atrofi.

The familiar sequence of memories flashed before him: the guards, so much blood, exile, Shia drowning – her back to him so far away, him running as fast as his legs could carry him across the open field as this shadow of the woman he loved waded into the swirling pool of black, lethal water. After it was over, he had returned to the *Innova*, to Amar, just weeks outside his mother's womb. He had climbed an old *hoch* just outside the walls of the Sisterhood and looked down into the courtyard. And there was Ruya, walking slowly back and forth, swaying side to side as she went, singing to Amar. The baby was in the best possible hands. Believing in that moment that Haddi could never offer Amar a better life than the one Ruya could give him, he ran. Oh, how he ran. As far into the hills as his body, fueled by anger, and his heart, worn down by grief, would carry him. He had almost given up, had almost joined Shia, when something–a sense of duty, the feeling of lingering love–overwhelmed him and convinced him to stay alive. That's when Jeg and Trude had found him.

When Haddi finally returned to the *Innova* and explained to Ruya all that had happened, she showed little surprise over Shia's death. Perhaps she had seen it coming in a reading and had prepared herself for the outcome, but the lack of emotion unsettled Haddi.

Ruya had told him that he was meant to find the clearing, that it took what happened to Shia, to him, to bring him there.

"Only the most broken of men could have found that realm," she had told him, echoing the words that Trude had made him memorize. At the time, he had believed himself too broken a man to care. Ruya had spoken of a "duty to the Universe" and an obligation to follow through with the quest it had gifted him. But Shia's death was no gift. It could never be turned into something positive. The old seer had then spoken of some overarching "good" that he could do for others, but at that time, when it was all so raw, he didn't want to hear it.

Good. Why should he put himself out for the good of so many others: all those who had judged him and Shia from afar, all those who had offered aid only from a place of self-service, all those who had failed right along with him to bring Shia out of the darkness…darkness so completely isolating it finally consumed her and left he and Amar to face the world without her.

In the cavern, a small glass vial of *magié milk* slipped to the stone floor, jolting Haddi from his dark memories. The nearby *magié* were becoming agitated. Haddi needed to take his mind off Shia before he got himself into trouble with the fickle spirits. He turned his attention back to the spout from which he filled a new vial, removing it as it became full, and placing a cork in the opening at the top. *Such a waste*, he thought as he looked down on the broken glass and puddle of liquid.

The substance these natural spouts omitted was pure, not cloudy. Like oil and vinegar, the *milk* and *clearwater* intermingled without ever blending into one another. It took time and patience to fill the vials he'd brought with him up the mountain. Not long after his discovery he had tried to find the source of these spouts and had spent hours picking his way up the outside of the great cavern. He had even felt he was getting closer to the origin of the hidden fountain when a swarm of *magié* blocked his path and pressed him down and out of the cave. They were protecting something, of that he was sure.

It had been sixteen years since Shia's death, the better part of two decades since Jeg and Trude had peeled a younger, more reckless version of himself off the side of the cliff. So many years had passed since Haddi first stumbled his way into the *magié* clearing. At that point, he had still been reeling from the rawness of it all, but over the years this had become his home. It was getting more difficult to leave it. Someday, he feared, he might not be able to resist the urge to remain here. The trees, the water, the stone, the very air was alive with something he could not completely comprehend, yet it was something his very soul craved.

Light glimmered off a chunk of broken bottle shaped like an arrowhead. Haddi picked it up without thinking, moving it around in his hand, testing the sharpness of its edge with the tip of his finger. He brushed it softly against the bulging veins on the inside of his left wrist.

"So many ways to die," he whispered.

A faint scream filled the little cavern, drawing Haddi once more from his dark thoughts as the glass sliced through the skin on his thumb. The handful of *magié* that had followed him to monitor his activity began to surround him. More *magié* streamed through the crawlspace, screeching furiously.

"Damn it," Haddi whispered, knowing full well he had been too careless with his thoughts. The *magié* felt his anguish, anger, and deepest desires more strongly than even he could. Because of these thoughts–regardless of his intent–the *magié* would demand he leave. But now too many of them were funneling through the narrow tunnel he had entered from, and the opening high above him was no longer even remotely accessible.

His panic rose as the *magié* pressed in on him from all sides. One fluttered up directly in front of him. Its wings and antennae were pearlescent, the body the white-blue color of the opal Shia had always worn around her neck. Pale eyelids flashed open, exposing fire red eyes.

CHAPTER 9
The Radio

Dottie stood in front of Penny's house, letting the two heavy hiking packs fall to the ground on either side of her as Hudd walked up the stairs to the front door. Penny emerged from her home with empty hands, still with an easy smile on her face in spite of the grim nature of their situation. She had been one of the first neighborhood kids to befriend Dottie when they moved here, though they had absolutely nothing in common. Penny didn't play any sports, always had her hair done, wore makeup, and knew all sorts of stuff about clothes and shoes. Sometimes Dottie felt like Penny was speaking a foreign language, talking about her Von Dutch trucker hat and Juicy something-or-other sweatsuit – and she was popular. She had always offered Dottie a friendly smile and was something of a safe haven in an otherwise hostile environment.

Dottie had been to three different schools in town since the move, four if you count that year of homeschooling. She didn't dress like the popular girls. She didn't talk like the popular girls. She sure as heck was not as pretty as the popular girls, one of whom made this clear with an extra hurtful comment, casually stating, "I can't tell if you're a nerd or just trying to look like a guy." Dottie had never been good at confrontation. No matter how damn smart she *knew* she was, she could not form even a single complete sentence when confronted, and "shut up" never seemed to have quite the effect she desired. *Sticks and stones may break my bones, and words will* always *hurt me*. She'd been completely caught off guard when Penny walked right in front of the mean-girl and took Dottie's hand.

"I really like your shirt today, Dottie," Penny had said. "Yellow's a pretty color on you. You should wear it more." She smiled her contagious smile and gave Dottie's hand a squeeze before turning and walking away with the other girls. At first, Dottie had felt angry at Penny. Was she mocking her? But no, Penelope Tackett did not have a mean bone in her body. She didn't have any ulterior motives. She was simply being kind.

I owe her, Dottie thought, not for the first time, as she watched Penny make her way down the front porch steps. This was her chance to return the favor of that gift of momentary inclusion. The other girls had not stopped teasing her, ignoring her, baiting her, but Penny never participated and Dottie hung on to that small gesture fiercely. She wondered if Penny knew how big an impact she had had on her, or if she even remembered the conversation. All Dottie knew now was that she could be useful here and try to keep Penny safe.

"Welp, there's nobody here," Penny said as she and Hudd walked back down the path to Dottie. "My parents were out at a work party, so they're probably still just trying to get back here. And I bet Audrey was rescued by whoever had that megaphone last night." She waved her hand to the side as if to banish any doubt. Jack had fallen head over heels for Audrey that first Summer of Manhunt. Though Audrey would likely never have known it, since Jack kept most things to himself, Dottie thought Audrey was the real reason her brother ever came out to play. If he hadn't been guarding the base, if he had been out in the woods with Dottie, he might be standing next to her right now. *I'll think about that tomorrow*, she thought, recalling her favorite Scarlet O'Hara line.

"What's all this?" Penny gestured to the packs on the ground.

"Uh…" Dottie hesitated, thrown off by the other girl's optimism. "They uh… they're hiking bags. We packed this one for you." Dottie gestured to the smaller of her two. "Did… did you put on makeup?"

"Just some gloss," Penny shrugged. "My lips were chapped. What's in the packs?" She asked, appearing only mildly curious, tilting her head to one side. Dottie couldn't help but note the likeness to a certain neighborhood cocker spaniel that did the same every time you said its name, but she squashed the thought immediately.

"Survival stuff, mostly," Dottie explained. "Food, first aid kit, some tools so we can cook if needed."

"Do you really think we're gonna need any of that?" Penny asked with a nervous smile.

"Well…" Dottie hesitated, "I mean, we hope not for long. But we have no idea what's going on right now. We haven't seen or heard another person all morning. Don't you think that's strange? We need to be ready."

Penny looked from her to Hudd, nodding, her eyes wide.

"Look Penny…" Dottie shook her head and looked down at her feet while she went on, "I don't know about your parents or your sister. Maybe it's like you say. But mine – my parents, my brother – my family is *dead*. Hudd's too." Fresh tears fell down her face. "They're all gone and it's just us now."

"You're wrong," Penny stated, her smile finally fading into a blank expression.

"I'm not," Dottie retorted sharply as she took a step forward. Penny flinched.

"We saw them, Penny," Hudd spoke softly, compensating for the rise in Dottie's tone. "We saw them," he repeated. "They're dead."

“I… I’m so sorry,” Penny whispered, tears filling her eyes as she gave Hudd a fierce hug then moved toward Dottie.

Dottie lifted her hands, palms forward, in an effort to stay Penny’s condolences. “It’s fine, Penny,” she heard herself say. “Everything is fine. Let’s just figure out what to do next, okay?” She tried to ignore Penny’s crestfallen expression. If anybody hugged her right now, even so much as gave her too long a look of sympathy, she’d crumble.

Just then, Ari’s unmistakably deep bark echoed forth from the trees, as it had the night before, a lifetime ago. Yet, this time, the Earth remained still. Dottie didn’t stop to think. She heaved her pack up off the ground and broke out into an awkward, hunched over run in the direction of the barking.

“Ari!” She called out to him, whistled, clicked and clapped for him. The barking ceased. She stood in silence in a small clearing, straining, listening for any sign of life. Branches rustled as Ari darted out from the woods in front of her, jumping up to her chest and knocking her backward onto the ground. She hugged his thick neck as he covered her face in slobbery kisses and nuzzled into her, grumbling with happiness.

Hudd emerged with Penny close behind huffing under the weight of her pack, but Ari darted off into the trees. Dottie scrambled to her feet and tumbled after him. Just when she thought she had lost him again, she would catch a glimpse of tail that drew her forward. Ari halted. As Dottie came to a stop behind him, her eyes trailed past to a massive fallen pine, under which lay a boy in a mess of mud and branches.

“Ben,” she breathed.

“Shit…” Hudd whispered over her shoulder.

In a dense patch of woods, Ben lay on his back with his lower body wedged under the fallen trunk of the pine tree. Mud and pine needles plastered his clothing and were caked into his hair.

“Oh my gosh, Ben!” Penny gasped, covering her mouth with both hands as she finally joined them.

“Hey.” Dottie dumped her pack onto the ground.

“You look like hell,” Hudd added.

“You're tellin’ me,” Ben replied. “Ready for Armageddon?” He asked, seeing the four hefty packs the others were hauling.

“Oh, shut it,” Dottie shot back, but couldn’t help but smile a bit in response. She hated being teased, but at least Ben did it with a smile and without the sting that others conveyed in their taunts. “Looks like you’re gonna need some of what's in these bags. Your leg broken?” Dottie asked. She’d broken her leg a couple years ago in a skiing accident. A triple spiral fracture that landed her in a miserable full leg cast for six weeks, and out of softball for much longer than that. She hoped that wasn’t the case for Ben. She’d have a hard time even figuring out a splint, let alone a way to move him.

“I don't think so,” he answered. “I mean, it hurts like hell, but I can move my toes, so I think that's good, right?”

“Yeah, totally,” Dottie said with feigned confidence. “Now the question is, how the hell do we get you out?” She circled Ben and squatted down, separating the branches and leaves to see exactly how his leg was positioned. Hudd knelt down next to her. The tree had broken off a few feet up from its base, the stump blackened by what Dottie guessed was a lightning strike.

“See anything interesting?” Ben called to Dottie.

“Dude…you got lucky,” Dottie replied. “This is actually kind of cool.” A thin slab of rock next to his leg had kept the full weight of the tree from crushing the bone. “You've got a pretty gnarly looking gash, though.”

“We need to get you out so we can get this thing clean and covered up,” Hudd added.

Dottie and Hudd started breaking away all of the smaller branches that covered Ben and his imprisoned leg. “Penny, we could use some help,” she called over her shoulder. Penny hadn't moved.

“Not if there's blood...” Penny called back as she took her hands away from her mouth and eased her pack down to the ground.

“You think Dottie would be so intrigued if there wasn't some blood involved?” Ben asked with a groan as a moving branch caught the open wound. “Yikes, Dot, take it easy!”

Dottie poked her head up over the top of the branches and scowled at him, curls bouncing furiously. “Serves you right. I didn't do it on purpose, but you deserve it either way.”

“Geez, sorry Dot,” Ben replied with a pained smile. “I was just teasing.”

Dottie stepped back from the tree.

“Yeah, uh, I know,” she mumbled hurriedly. “Look, I'm not sure how to do this. We’re not strong enough to lift that thing straight up, and lifting it from the end would put too much pressure on your leg. We could try to roll it, but I’m pretty sure that would crush your leg, too…”

“Sounds like some pretty great options,” Ben replied sarcastically. “You could use some kind of lever,” he suggested. “Get a thick branch and wedge it underneath, try to lift it just enough for me to slide out?”

“On it,” Dottie responded before disappearing into the trees again. She searched through a cluster of recently fallen branches for one big enough to handle the job, yet not so big she and Hudd couldn’t maneuver it together. She pulled the switchblade from her belt and whittled a bit of bark off a branch that fit the description. *Still green, this should work.* She hoisted the branch up onto her shoulder, teetering under its weight and made her way precariously back around to the others. Ari paced in a circle around her. Penny still stood where they’d first caught sight of Ben, shifting her weight from side to side and absentmindedly kicking at some dead leaves on the ground.

“How ya hanging in there buddy?” Hudd asked Ben.

“Been better. Glad to see a few familiar faces. What the hell’s going on out there, anyway?”

“I’ll get you caught up on that later,” Hudd replied, watching Dottie heave the lever back onto her shoulder. “I better help Dottie before she hurts herself.”

“I've got it under control,” Dottie grumbled.

“She’s got it under control,” Hudd echoed as he crossed his arms and shifted his weight back on his heels.

Dottie opened her pack and took out the bowie knife. She started to hack away the larger branches they hadn’t been able to break off easily with her hands.

“You’re sure that thing is for little girls?” Hudd mocked as she whittled a few chunks out of the bottom of the lever to form a wedge.

She rolled her eyes to herself, but the teasing didn’t bother her half as much as it would have a few days ago. She knew it was all some aloof persona. She had seen a different side of Hudson Mead.

“Let up already, Hudd,” Ben chided. “My leg’s killin’ me and at least Dottie is *trying*. Help now, heckle later, cool?”

“Hey, I’m here to help if she’ll let me,” Hudd replied, placing his hands over his heart in a feigned gesture of humility.

Dottie stood, wiping the blade clean on her jeans before sliding it back into its sheath. She glanced around, searching for a rock big enough to work as a hammer. Finding one, she returned to the tree and began to pound the wedge-end of the branch in between the slice of rock and the tree next to Ben’s leg. She knew that the ground on the other side would be too soft and would likely absorb the lever, rather than allowing her to work against it.

“I’ve gotta admit,” Hudd said as she stepped back to rest, the lever firmly wedged in its place. “I’m kinda impressed, Dot.”

“Yeah, nice job, Dottie!” Penny agreed.

“Thanks!” Dottie smiled breathlessly, hands on her hips. This was actually going to work.

“Problem is, you gotta be strong enough to pull the lever down,” Hudd said to Dottie as she gave it a test run. It didn’t budge.

“Maybe you could let Hudd help you with that part,” Ben suggested with a groan.

Hudd sauntered over to Dottie.

“Go slow,” Ben warned. “You don’t want to snap the thing on the first try.”

“On three, Miss Dot,” Hudd said as he grabbed ahold of the higher part of the lever.

One, two, three… they dropped their combined weight down and heaved the tree up a solid inch off the rock. It was enough. Ben groaned as he dragged his body along the ground until his leg was freed. Hudd and Dottie eased the tree back down.

“Ha!” Dottie danced a little victory jig. “I can’t believe it worked!”

“Simmer down there with the happy dance,” Hudd teased.

“Oh, just lay off her already and come help me,” Ben called from the other side of the tree.

Dottie and Hudd went over and knelt down near Ben. Getting him out from under the tree had aggravated the open wound on his leg, causing it to bleed anew.

“I need to stop the bleeding,” Dottie said, more to herself than the others. The light streaming through the trees fell dim as cloud cover moved in swiftly.

Then what do you do? Mom’s voice played in her mind, kicked up by the sudden chill in the air.

“And then find shelter,” Dottie replied aloud.

“We can go back to my house,” Penny offered, peaking hesitantly around the wall of tree branches.

Dottie looked up, the comment causing her to realize that she had lost her place for a second, forgotten where she was. “Good, that’s what I had been thinking. Come on over, Penny. Don’t worry, you don’t have to look at it. Can you bring the big first aid kit from my pack?” She turned back to the boys, surprised to find sober stares in place of their usual light-hearted smirks. “What? Neither of you gonna make fun of me?”

“Guess there isn’t anything to make fun of right now,” Ben said.

“I’m sure I could think of something if you’re feeling neglected,” Hudd chimed in. She shot a peeved look in his direction but felt a little proud at the same time. She stole a longer glance at him while they waited for Penny to find the first aid bag. Something had darkened in his eyes, cooled. The sparkle was gone, even as he retained his outward humor, and she knew what had taken it away. She returned to the task at hand.

A branch of the tree seemed to have torn right through the leg of Ben’s jeans and dragged across his shin. Dottie took her switchblade and cut the rest of his pant leg off below the tear. She opened up a large square of gauze and placed it on top of the wound, balling up the strip of jean fabric and using it to apply firm pressure. She repeated this a second time with a clean gauze pad and was happy to see that the blood did not saturate the second pad. Taking a bandage out of the kit, she wrapped Ben’s leg and secured the gauze in place.

“So, what's going on out there?” Ben asked while Dottie worked on his leg.

“Everything’s abandoned,” Hudd began. “Lots of houses caught fire right after the quake. No idea how. Some first responders, military…” he paused, staring down at his palm, picking at the dead skin around a callous. “Well, it looks like maybe the neighborhood was evacuated, but I'm not sure.”

“That makes sense,” Penny said. “I heard somebody with a bullhorn at one point, but everything was so crazy….”

Crazy indeed, Dottie thought as Penny trailed off. Earthquakes didn't happen in New England, at least as far as Dottie knew. And it wasn't just the ground that shook that night. It felt as if the air itself had raged with violent tremors. Charged waves had pulsed through her body and made her already wild hair stand on end. Her hands tingled at the recollection, and she fumbled with the metal closures for the bandage.

Dottie finally managed to secure the wrap on Ben’s leg and packed up the first aid supplies. She half expected some sort of taunt from Hudd about her rough first aid job, but he seemed to be absorbed in his own thoughts. She understood that. She kept sliding back into her own thoughts, too – a twig snapping, Ari barking. The old dog had come to rest his heavy head in her lap as she worked and she bent down to kiss the top of his snout.

The kids silently readied themselves for the short walk back to Penny's. Dottie carried two packs, Penny one. Hudd hauled the fourth while playing human crutch, stooping under the crook of Ben's shoulder, an arm around his back for stability. It was slow-going. What should have taken ten minutes took more than half an hour as the gang took frequent breaks to let Ben and Hudd rest. But they finally made it back to Penny's.

"Stop…" Ben whispered to Hudd outside Penny's front door, taking in the scene of the upended neighborhood for the first time.

∝

Dottie sat on the bottom step of Penny's walkout basement, removing her shoes and coat. Ari lay close by at her feet. A brown corduroy sectional surrounded a red brick fireplace. Three windows up high on one wall let in an adequate amount of sunlight, though Dottie knew it wouldn't last much longer as evening quickly approached.

"We should probably all try to drink a bit," she broke the heavy silence and pulled two water bottles out of the bags. "Don't want to get dehydrated."

"Dottie, seriously, where did you get all this stuff?" Ben asked.

"My mom," Dottie responded, shrugging her shoulders. "She always had this preparedness thing, a whole setup in our basement. I kinda thought it was dumb, or crazy, but…" the memory faded quickly as reality reared its ugly head. *I'll think about that tomorrow*.

"What was she so afraid of?" Ben asked.

"Nothing," Dottie replied. *Everything*, she thought. Dottie's mom had been the youngest of ten. Big Catholic family. Her dad led a Boy Scout troop and two of her brothers even made Eagle Scout. Preparedness was second nature for Janie. *Fear* was first.

"Do you know if she…" Ben began.

"She's *dead,"* Dottie said firmly as she walked over to the coffee table and laid out the first aid bag. "My family is gone." *They're just words,* she told herself, *they don't mean anything. I'll think about it tomorrow.*

"Did you see *my* house?" Ben asked.

Dottie felt a sharp stab of guilt in her belly. She hadn't even thought about Ben's family.

"It's still there," Hudd cut in. "Was your dad home?"

"Yeah…" Ben replied quietly, "but he was probably too drunk to know what was happening."

"Do you want one of us to go back and look for him?" Dottie asked, realizing even as she spoke that this unrealistic suggestion was driven by her own remorse.

"Nah, it wouldn't matter either way," Ben said, then continued before the others could press. "Hudd… what about yours?"

How could something like that not matter?

"*Gone.*" Hudd offered nothing more, nor did his tone leave the door open for further question. "I'm gonna go for a walk. Get some firewood." He rose abruptly and left, letting the front door room slam behind him.

Penny ducked upstairs "to look for something" while Dottie addressed Ben's leg again. Her clumsy hands betrayed her inexperience as she faltered her way through cleaning and rebandaging the wound. She cringed along with him as she poured some of the filtered water over it and used a clean gauze pad to rub away the dried blood. Numbing spray, antibiotic ointment, liquid bandage and butterfly strips followed in a less-than-perfect, but overall effective patch-job.

"It looks great, Dot," Ben tried to reassure her through gritted teeth as she sat back to assess her work. "Feels better now too. You seem like you know what you're doing."

"I really don't." She frowned at the floor. Blood stained the carpet around them. She should have thought to put a towel down, but if they all made it through whatever was happening, and if they were even still alive, she hoped Penny's parents would forgive her.

Ari had relocated to the couch to bury his nose under a throw pillow. Seeing him so cozy, Dottie had to fight the heavy onset of fatigue. She could go curl up next to him once they had a fire going. The storm door creaked open and closed again upstairs. Hudd descended with an armful of firewood and twigs.

"You could have just gotten it from the whole stack of wood out back," Penny said as she came down the stairs behind him, a large black garbage bag in tow.

"Well, *you* could have told me that sooner." Hudd unloaded the fuel next to the fireplace. "Dot, you got those fire starters?"

Ben hopped on one leg over to the couch next to Ari. Dottie retrieved the magnesium starters from her pack, while Penny pulled an array of coats, boots and winter accessories out of the garbage bag.

"You guys can help yourselves to any of this," she said. "Mom and dad won't mind."

Hudd made no move to take the fire starters from Dottie, so she took that as her cue to begin work on it herself. Everything was still damp from the night before and she wondered how dry it would all have to get to take a spark. As she laid them out to dry on the brick hearth, she noticed Ben frowning and holding onto his left arm.

"You okay?" She asked.

"Yeah, my arm just feels kind of funny." He pulled the sleeve of his sweatshirt off, sticking his arm out the bottom, as Dottie walked over to where he sat. She knelt down next to him to take a look.

"What the hell is that?" Ben blurted as he lifted the sleeve of his t-shirt, revealing an intricate tree-shaped burn running the length of his upper arm. Penny and Hudd appeared next to Dottie.

"I know what that is," Penny said, pointing to the feathery pink lines branching out from Ben's elbow, running up over his shoulder. "They're from a lightning strike," she explained. "You probably got hit by it when it struck the tree. I think Mr. Alves called it Lichtenstein, Lichtenberg, something like that."

"And I thought Dottie was the nerd," Hudd teased.

“It’s just cause Penny has a crush on Alves,” Ben chimed in.

“Oh my gosh, I do not!” Penny exclaimed as a flush crept into her cheeks. “The pattern is really interesting, though. It's something to do with the way the electrical current moves through your body. Does it hurt?”

“Not really.” Ben shrugged. “Itches a bit. Do you think we should put something on it?”

“No idea,” Dottie mumbled. “Maybe we just leave it for now, and if it starts to hurt or peel or something, we can try the burn cream.

Dottie couldn’t sit there any longer. Her skin was crawling from the unnerving tree-like marks on Ben’s arm. She dug in her pack for some of the MREs and handed them around before settling down with her own, Chili with Beans, and consumed the meal without tasting it. Dottie felt numb, chilled despite the warmth of the room, and resolved to get a fire going. Grabbing the hatchet out of her bag, she began chopping the branches Hudd brought back into more manageable lengths for firewood.

“Good thing my parents didn’t put in that gas fireplace with the fake logs,” Penny said. “Not sure we would have been able to burn anything.”

“That’s it!” Hudd yelled, rising suddenly to his feet and beginning to pace. “Dottie, what kind of fireplace did you have?”

“The kind you start by flipping a switch…”

“Same with mine,” Hudd said. “Ben?”

“Old fashioned, wood-burning.”

“And your house is still standing… I wonder if the fires were somehow related to the gas fireplaces….”

“You might be onto something, Hudd,” Ben said.

“Maybe we should try that radio again,” Hudd muttered and darted over to the packs.

“You guys have a radio?” Ben questioned eagerly.

Dottie just smiled and nodded as she sat down on the hearth. She took four large logs and leaned them against each other so that there was plenty of open space in between for air to flow through. She filled in the area in between with smaller branches, leaving an opening in the front through which she could slide her nest once she got it lit. On a small forked branch, she wove the leaves, bark, pine needles and small twigs Hudd had collected into a little nest on the split.

Hudd retrieved the radio and came to sit on the floor next to her. Ben, Penny and Ari watched from their spots on the couch.

He held it in his lap as if it were a crystal ball, gazing intently at the tarnished green metal, hands hovering over the crank. Static filled the space around them for the next few minutes as he tried different channels.

Dottie took out the magnesium fire starter and shaved some of the silver mineral onto the flat stone next to her, the buzz from the radio fraying her nerves.

She felt the gaze of the others at her back, watching her work, listening to the buzz of the radio. This wasn't just about lighting a fire, it was about proving her worth to them.

"Mass evacuations…" the two words burst forth from the radio so abruptly that Dottie jumped. She kept an eye on the radio over her shoulder, as if watching it would make a difference, while she struck her knife to the flint to send sparks flying at the magnesium.

"As far as Europe…" more broken words permeated the air. Hudd desperately tried to adjust the dials for better reception.

"No contact…" the voice was British.

"Millions… dead."

Just then, one of the dozens of sparks caught hold of the metal shavings and burst into flame inside the little nest.

CHAPTER 10
The Magnate

Orville stood in front of the ignition switch, his body trembling with the echo of his pulse. His pulse? No, *hers*.

Exhilaration, magnificence…immortality. Surely no mere man could have accomplished what he had, even given another forty years. Had he imagined it? The glass shattering. Who broke it? His hands shaking, sweating, pressing firmly down on the lever. Whose hands? It seemed so simple: just grip the handle and press down. His body was quaking with something more akin to desire than fear. But then the ground moved beneath him. He had imagined this moment thousands of times, played it through in his head, step by step, dreaming of the day *she* would be ready. And, there she was…NEM, still humming with residual electricity – and he, her creator, in awe.

To Orville, NEM was both mistress and master. Hundreds of tons of mineral precisely aligned into the largest and most powerful Neodymium Earth Magnet ever created – one able to generate an electromagnetic pulse powerful enough to destabilize the magnetic field that held two dimensions apart – his world, Earth– and the world that included Alterra, which the people called "Sum." Orville remembered from his undergraduate Latin that *sum* meant "I am," and had learned long ago that Alterran root words shared similar translations. Perhaps merely existing was enough for these people, but it could never be enough for him.

Orville loved NEM in a way he had never been able to love any creature of the flesh, safe to love *her* without fear of rejection. Human beings were messy, imperfect creatures, and more often than not, unworthy of his time and energy. But NEM was flawless. Her power and precision far exceeded anything a person could achieve. He was bound to her always.

After Orville made his final stand against Aggie and Levi so many years ago, he had resolved to prove them wrong. With equipment permanently "borrowed" from the university lab, he hiked for days before he reached an old iron mine in Tennessee. The abandoned mine was nestled deep in the Appalachian Mountains. Throughout the Second World War, it was rumored the government conducted experiments and tested new biological weaponry there. Once the war was over, the government called for a complete shut-down of the mine and surrounding areas. Regulators cited the need to protect some newly-endangered bat population, but residents and miners alike were paid a small sum to keep their mouths shut and move on with their lives somewhere else. It had remained mostly undisturbed since.

Orville had picked up his first set of relevant readings near the mine two years prior, the ones that Levi had called "a blip," and as he neared the opening, he once again registered volatile levels of electromagnetic frequency. He was able to follow the noise of his EMF reader straight through to the rupture, and from there he stepped right into another world. A world filled with a profoundly deprived people, magnificent terrain the likes of which did not exist on earth, and two glowing moons.

He had formed a plan for Alterra shortly after finding his way through the rupture, and he was finally realizing his goals. An irrigation system on the Earth side of the rupture redirected water from a set of streams into the iron mine. If he could just widen the rupture with NEM's pulse, the crude irrigation system could be rerouted into Sum and fed directly into the Holt River. There could even be opportunities for the Alterrans to draw from other resources that Earth had to offer, things that could help them prosper. The mine, after all, was ideally suited for discretion. They could camouflage the rupture and keep the second world completely hidden. At least until the time was right….

He had been tempted to expose Sum on numerous occasions, to prove he was right to his earthly doubters, but this other world was not yet much to boast of. Would it not be a sweeter victory to single-handedly create a world superior to Earth and place himself as leader of a newly freed and flourishing people?

With this end in mind, Orville had positioned himself squarely between the indentured people of the Lower Half of Alterra and the elites of the Upper Half. To the Lower, Orville was a magician, a sorcerer, one who could lift the people up from their depravity. To the Upper, Orville was a danger that threatened a coveted and protected way of life, someone who must be kept at a distance.

He believed the people of the Lower Half loved him. He was like a father to them, and as such, he knew he must shelter them as one would shelter children from the sharks in the ocean. Indeed, the Alterran Council had been too slow to respond to the formation of Orville's guard when it grew so suddenly a few years after he arrived in Alterra. By the time the Council produced an order to have the guard shut down, they had already lost their leverage. They were no longer a physical threat. Now, so many years later, Orville's guard and the Lex coexisted in a fragile truce, though Orville believed he truly had the upper hand.

Still, to keep the Upper and Lower halves in balance was like playing a game of chess against oneself: moves had to be made, but the goal was to make them with as few casualties as possible on either side. A solo game of chess was a favorite pastime of Orville's. He had carved each piece of his chess set by hand and regularly sat down to play on nights when sleep was elusive. With these games, his goal was not a checkmate. Rather, he sought the ideal stalemate, a position where neither side had any move to make, resulting in deference to the only one who was not required to play by the rules.

Like a puppeteer choreographing the dance between opposing sides of a civil war, he was the one calling the shots. He must not reveal too much. If the people understood what he was planning to do -- where he intended on taking this, once Sum became a more stable and resourced world -- it would only halt momentum. Orville believed knowledge was best when compartmentalized, reserved for a select few who could then take action unhindered, more greatly benefiting society. Making decisions free from bureaucracy or the desire to appease the masses made progress so much more fluid.

His belly churned as he recalled discussing this very dynamic with Ruya and Theo so long ago.

"Take the printing press." Orville argued. He knew Ruya incapable of comprehending such a machine, but Theo had been able to place the earthly historical reference. "The free dissemination of information was the worst thing to ever happen to the modern world. We were better off before information was so easily spread… so easily skewed."

"You would be surprised what worth others would offer you," Theo had replied.

"The Alterrans are a resourceful people," Ruya added then. "We would thrive on progress."

"Mass progress only ever served to put information in the wrong hands, uneducated hands," Orville had asserted. *Keeping people in the dark was for their own good.*

Ruya and Theo had tried to persuade him that the people had a right to know about NEM, to hear the potential risks, to have the right to weigh in.

Orville placed the palm of his hand on the warm side of NEM, who buzzed happily with the reverberation of the pulse she had just put forth. At this moment, he could simply *be*. He did it. It worked. *She* worked.

His rare moment of peace was broken by the abrupt opening of the door to his lab. Isaac marched across the dirt floor of the basement laboratory and straight to Orville's side.

"Master," Isaac began, his voice cracking like a young boy's, "what have you done?"

"What have *I* done?" Orville asked the question under his breath without opening his eyes or turning from his beloved NEM. "I have saved us. I have saved you."

"I don't understand," Isaac whispered back. "I thought she wasn't ready. Why did you not inform us?"

Orville sighed in frustration and pulled the dented wooden pawn from his suit coat before turning to acknowledge the servant whose remarks were most definitely above his standing.

"What exactly makes you think I owe *you* any information at all, Isaac?"

"I… I just mean that we were unable to ready any of our men, sir," Isaac stammered, dropping his eyes to the ground and backing away from Orville. "One of the corner towers completely caved in. We lost men. Substantial damage in the city as well from what we can see from here."

"A necessary consequence," Orville shot back. "It was time. I felt it. I don't owe anybody an explanation for that. Least of all you."

"Yes sir," Isaac responded with a modest bow. "I wasn't trying to suggest I was deserving of anything. I was just surprised. Sir, this rift, ripple…"

"Rupture," Orville corrected.

"Rupture?" Isaac repeated.

"I've decided it is the most fitting term," Orville rolled the pawn back and forth between his thumb and forefinger. "I suppose it does *look* like a 'rift,' but that term suggests something torn open or apart. But we know that the opening is a result of the worlds colliding, melding, moving through each other. Neither would 'ripple' be a fitting term," he continued, "as that would suggest some wavering in physical form, but in forty years, the opening between the two worlds has remained the exact same size, shape, location. No… it is neither a 'rift' nor a 'ripple,' but rather a 'rupture,' the result of a mass amount of force."

"Rupture," Isaac repeated.

"Though, for the sake of scientific methodology," Orville went on, momentarily forgetting Isaac's presence, "I suppose I should withhold final judgment on the overall accuracy of that label until I can observe its behavior post-electromagnetic shock."

"Sir…" Isaac hesitated.

"You want to know how the rupture got there in the first place?" Orville didn't wait for Isaac's reply. He reached into a dish on his desk and grabbed two small silver magnets. He held them up so that the servant could see them, first allowing them to attract each other, then flipping one magnet over to demonstrate opposing magnetic force.

"Our two worlds," Orville stated, "are divided by a massive magnetic field, held apart by the same oppositional force you see with these magnets. At some point in time, a powerful energy overcame the magnetic division, rearranged the lines of force and caused our walls to press together, fuse as one, and burst open."

"What could cause such a thing?" Isaac asked, breathless.

"It is hard to know for sure," Orville said with a shrug of his shoulders. "The mine where the rupture feeds into on the other side was believed to contain a large amount of unmined iron ore, while Sum hosts high levels of neodymium, both metals that can be magnetically charged given enough energy. They tested weapons there…"

"What do you mean they tested weapons?" Isaac asked. "Swords?"

"No, no," Orville shook his head. "Civilized societies have sophisticated weaponry… still, it's possible that something they tested put forth a powerful enough charge to cause all of this."

Once he had first navigated the rupture, Orville found himself a few miles west of Alterra. He soon discovered that the city was a resource-deprived and primitive society, having never reaped the benefits of certain discoveries and inventions found in modern cultures. They were a divided people, torn apart by a sort of pseudo-slavery – a system of indenture that restricted any opportunity for the bonded to become free, controlled by a disillusioned elitist class and a corrupt governing body. For reasons unknown to them, a once bustling trade route had gone dry, along with the river that supplied the entire city's drinking water. Holt River was dwindling rapidly when Orville arrived and had continued to lower incrementally each year.

Orville considered Isaac, softening slightly as he noticed the humbled posture of his servant.

"Well," Orville began, "I suppose I can understand you being caught off guard, but it's in the past now. We should be celebrating. The initial launch was a success."

"You've confirmed this, sir?" Isaac asked hurriedly.

"I don't need to," Orville replied with a wave of his hand. "My target coordination was precise, and there could only be so much variation in the concentration and effect of the pulse. It's all been controlled for." He walked over to the chalkboard that ran the length of the wall parallel to NEM, surveying for what must have been the thousandth time the precise algorithms he had spent forty years generating. "We'll get a team together to go out to the site of the rupture immediately," Orville said, more to himself than to Isaac.

"There is one more thing, sir," Isaac added, continuing cautiously. "Something I saw…someone."

Orville sighed and turned to face the servant. "Go on…" he said reluctantly.

"Garrett," Isaac said. "I saw him exiting a certain wine smuggler's underground pub this morning just after shift change."

"Perhaps he was just having a drink," Orville replied. "I don't care what the man decides to do with his free time."

"The barkeep, Cairo, is a known associate of a developing underground social movement," Isaac continued, "and it's not a place one just happens upon."

"What exactly is your concern here, Isaac?" Orville huffed.

"Cairo is no friend of ours," Isaac replied. "I cannot think of an honest circumstance that would have brought Garrett to such a place."

"You think his motive perfidious?"

"Sir?"

"Treacherous, dishonest, bad…" Orville clarified, reminding himself to choose simple words to communicate with his servant.

"Yes, sir," Isaac affirmed.

Orville watched Isaac for a moment. The man had never steered him wrong. Devoted. Loyal. Garrett, on the other hand, had indeed become more bold – disrespectful, questioning Orville's every move, even his very competency.

"Follow him," Orville concluded. "Better yet, have Rafi do it."

"Do you think he's the best choice, sir?" Isaac asked. "Rafi and Garrett are close."

"If Garrett is up to something, we'll need Rafi to step into his place," Orville explained. "And the only way our friend Rafi would agree to that is if he is given the responsibility of condemning Garrett himself."

CHAPTER 11
The Prison

Dottie took the smoking nest and carefully placed it beneath the frame of firewood, blowing into the flame as it grew, coaxing it, willing it into life. When the fire carried over to one of the logs she breathed a sigh of relief. *Finally.*

It was well into the afternoon, and while the basement had provided substantial warmth compared to outside, Dottie felt chilled, tired. What little they had heard over the radio had been mind-numbing. She suddenly had an overwhelming desire to sleep and sank down onto carpeted floor. Her eyes were closed before she had time to acknowledge her fatigue.

The moist dirt squishes between her bare toes. She looks down. A pool of milky water fills in her footprint as she steps back. The air suddenly becomes cold. She looks up at the sky. A shiver runs through her and goosebumps form on her bare arms, her hair standing on end. Her golden curls quiver in air that almost feels electrified. Slate grey clouds blanket the sky. They swirl hauntingly as thunder rumbles and lightning plays on the horizon. She turns around. She is alone.

A strange door looms in front of her. Firmly planted into a rocky, moss-covered mountainside, the ornate wooden door stands guard. Delicate fairies dance along the thick frame. Trolls with long beards wield axes and shovels. Giants lumber from panel to panel, hauling massive boulders. An indescribable glow illuminates from the carving on the door, so expertly and exquisitely rendered. Magic. The door tells an enchanting story. She takes a step closer, reaches out to trace the intricate carvings with the tips of her fingers. A creamy snowflake lands on the back of her hand. She is surprised that it does not feel cold. It begins to burn. She pulls her hand away from the door.

The sky is angrier now. Sinister. It crackles and shakes with a menacing force. Her hand still burns. She holds it up in front of her. A flaming red scar marks the flesh where the snowflake fell. A wiry, tree-shaped imprint. Panic surges through her as the burning becomes stronger. She searches for a patch of snow to cool her seared hand. It offers no relief. A cry rises in her chest, but she cannot force it past her lips.

Dottie gasped for breath as she bolted upright. Hudd was at her side, pressing her hand between his palms. Her eyes searched his, pleading for understanding.

“The fire shot a big ember at you,” Hudd explained, swiftly pulling his hands away. “Landed on your hand. You alright?”

“Uh… yeah,” she stammered, looking down at the flaming red circle on the back of her hand.

“Good. Next time, don’t pass out so close to the damn fire,” Hudd scolded, retreating to a corner of the room. Dottie stared after him, images of the enchanted door replaying in her mind.

“You okay, Dottie?” Ben asked from his spot on the couch beside her. “Want the burn cream?”

“Yeah,” she responded as she turned to catch the tossed tube. She applied the cream to her hand, picturing the tree-shaped scar from the dream snowflake. *It must have just been because of Ben’s arm*, she thought. *It was already in my subconscious.*

Dottie rose to throw the burn cream back into the first aid kit and snagged a bandage before returning to the fire. She stoked the logs as the room grew darker with the fading sun. A few feet away, Ben massaged an aching knee while Penny snoozed on the couch next to Ari, who still had his nose buried under a pillow.

Dottie’s mind was reeling as she recalled the fairy door. Her heart raced and her palms became sweaty while the strange storm replayed in her head. The apprehension she felt in her dream lingered. She would give just about anything right now to have some music, something to shift her focus. She would play the George Winston *December* tape that her mom used to put on while making dinner. Dottie closed her eyes, holding tightly to the memory of the soothing piano and recalling the way she would twirl carefree around their living room. She smiled to herself at the image of her childhood interpretive dance. Oh, to once again be free of the burdens of her new reality.

As daylight wavered, Dottie started to feel a little jumpy, and it seemed the other kids felt the same as they all gathered closer together around the fire.

“We’re on our own now,” Dottie began after they settled in.

“Cut the melodrama, Dot,” Hudd interrupted. “It's not like the *whole* world is dead… only millions.”

“Look,” Ben cut in, “this was an earthquake. That's a geographically specific event. So how did this affect so many people? The broadcast, that was BBC, he said ‘all the way to Europe.’”

“There's probably a good reason for all of this,” offered Penny. “We just need to search until we find an adult. They'll get us back to our parents, and we’ll all be fine.”

“Dottie and Hudd’s families are dead, Penny,” Ben reminded her somberly. “We heard what we did on the radio. This isn't as simple as just finding an adult…”

"And how the hell do we trust any adult left out here?" Dottie fired back at Penny. "Anybody who didn't evacuate stayed behind for a reason. I'd wager most of those reasons aren't good ones. That leaves us with a whole lot of people who shouldn't be trusted."

"We should try to walk into town tomorrow," Ben suggested. "We'll be careful," he added as Dottie began to argue, "but let's see what we find."

The gang stayed safe and warm in Penny's basement through the night. Dottie curled up at the edge of the couch with Ari, waking frequently to stoke and refuel the flames. It gave off plenty of heat and she let it burn low as the sun rose outside. The group downed trail mix and jerky for breakfast, readying themselves for the day ahead in silence. Ben and Penny got outfitted with winter gear, though the expected snow hadn't started yet, while Dottie and Hudd planned their route into town.

Ben was able to put a little weight on his leg and tested it out, hobbling around the room. Penny came up with the idea to use her old red wagon to pull Ben and a couple of the packs. He protested but was eventually convinced that it would be better for him to conserve his energy. They made their way slowly, quietly through the neighborhoods for most of the morning, at first stunned by the appearance of one upturned street after another. Eventually, it all began to blend together: some houses burned, some not; vehicles stacked on the shoulders of the roads and dozens of cars piled up in the center on the busier streets. And every single one still had keys in the ignition.

Hudd tried to jump in and start half a dozen in a row, but there was no turnover. All the batteries were dead.

Around midday, they stopped to rest outside the place that had been their favorite summer hangout spot. The little walkup ice cream hut, Josie's, sat eerie and abandoned at the edge of the town's main drag of businesses and restaurants.

"I need a break, guys," Penny said, perched atop a picnic table. "What are we even looking for anyway?"

"People..." Ben said through a mouthful of food. "Information. Useful supplies. Whatever we can find."

"Well, we haven't found any of those and I'm tired of walking." Penny pouted as she kicked at a loose nail on the bench of the picnic table.

"Why don't you and Ben stay here for a little while, Penny?" Hudd asked. "Dottie and I will head a little further into town and see if it's worth exploring more."

Ben didn't put up a fight. Dottie and Hudd remained close to the buildings, Ari at their heels. They stayed out of open view as much as possible. Maybe Dottie had watched too many suspenseful movies, but she had that feeling of being watched again. They passed the auto shop and computer repair store, a long row of office buildings, the Dairy Queen that was never as busy on weekends as Josie's just down the road.

As they walked past the courthouse and the old barber shop, a door creaked open at the gas station ahead. Dottie jumped back.

"Hide," she whispered to Hudd, grabbing him by the sleeve and pulling him behind her. They ducked around the corner of the building and into the adjacent alley. Ari followed. She held a finger to her lips as the boisterous laughter of two men filled the air.

"I still can't believe how easy that was, Greg," the first said.

"It was like somebody just flipped a switch for us and boom, open sesame!" Greg added almost gleefully.

"Those guards got what was comin' to 'em."

"All those years looking down on us...."

"Not a single one left to think they's better n' us now. Did ya see the look on old Joe's face with a pen stickin' out of his neck? And look at all this free shit we're gettin' to pick off!"

Dottie caught a glimpse from around the corner of bright orange jumpsuits. She reached behind her, desperately searching for Hudd's arm to grab. Not feeling him there, she turned around to find him with his knife drawn. He nodded at her belt. She slid the Rambo knife from its sheath and pulled a pocket mirror from the slip pouch at her waist to see around the corner. Ari's shoulders hunched and the ridge of hair that ran the length of his spine stood on end.

Greg and his pal were heading in their direction and the alley was a dead end at the side of an adjacent warehouse. She watched as Hudd dropped back and tried the two doors on either side. No good. Both were locked. He returned to his place beside her.

The convicts came around the corner and stopped, their smiles fading at the sight of two teens wielding knives and a big-headed pit bull.

"What's this, Mo?" Greg asked.

Despite her above-average height, Dottie only came up to Greg's chest. He wiped his hand back and forth over the wrinkles of his completely shaved head and glared down at her.

"Seems like we've got a couple of kids listening in," Mo responded. He was shorter than Greg, stockier, hairier.

"Hand over those shiny little toys you got there, eh?" Greg came toward Dottie, a hand outstretched for her knife. She took a few steps back, eyeing Hudd who shook his head.

"We didn't hear anything," she whispered, then repeated it louder. "We didn't hear anything."

Ari released a warning growl.

"Why don't you two just move on and leave us alone? We're no threat to you." Hudd tried to make his way in between Dottie and Greg. Mo came around Hudd's back, hooking his arms behind him and dropping him to his knees in one swift motion. Hudd's knife fell to the ground.

"Well then," Greg said, an evil smirk spreading up one side of his face. "What if I don't really care what you heard?" He reached a hand up to lightly touch Dottie's cheek, ignoring the knife in her hand. "What if there's something else I want?"

"You leave her alone!" Hudd yelled as he strained against Mo.

"I don't think I will." Greg's voice was too close to her. She could feel his hot breath on her face and all she could see was orange. She felt a hand come down on her wrist and she twisted it free, driving the knife forward. She heard Ari snarl and chomp at the back of Greg's leg. The blade hit a dense wall of resistance, a groan filled her ears, but all she could see was orange. She twisted the blade and pulled upward, just as she had been trained to do, and all she could see was orange, orange and bleeding red.

Dottie watched as Greg fell to the ground in a pool of blood, his intestines clearly visible.

"You killed him…" Mo muttered, releasing his hold on Hudd and coming for her. She ducked under his arms just as he was about to barrel into her, slashing the back of his thigh with the knife and shoving him forward into the brick wall behind her. He screamed, grasping at his leg while pressing himself into a sitting position against the wall.

Dottie felt heavy hands on her shoulders as Hudd pulled her around to face him, his eyes wide with terror.

"Don't watch them, Dottie," he commanded.

"Why not?" She heard a voice ask, but it was too far away to be her own.

"Because we don't need to see that."

She nodded and let herself be led away. She wasn't aware of much around her, except that they walked in the opposite direction from the way they came and that Ari was still at her side. Hudd dragged her stumbling through streets and alleys until they began to wind slowly back toward Josie's.

A loud buzz filled her ears as they passed under the pillared entrance of the courthouse. Hudd stopped abruptly. She followed his gaze to a cluster of shiny leaves out on the courthouse lawn. An ominous hum surrounded the strange, golden leaves swirling and buzzing like a swarm of bees. The world began to sway around her, but the ground was still firmly under her feet, and she felt herself falling.

CHAPTER 12
The Wolf

“Just trust me,” Orville said. “I know what I'm doing.” He couldn’t help but note the dark circles under Ruya’s eyes. They had grown more prominent in the last year. Apparently having babies could just about ruin a woman. Then again, Shia seemed to be particularly challenging. The first had not been nearly so difficult. Regardless, there was no justification for the lack of interest and concern Ruya had afforded him lately.

“It is not a matter of trust, Orville,” Theo spoke up from over his shoulder. “You wish to change the worlds with this giant… magnet. Yet you think yourself, similarly, to be a magnate, and in that lies your greatest flaw.”

Flaw.

“What do you mean, Theo?” Ruya asked.

“Magnate,” Orville responded instead, “sounds almost the same as magnet, and refers to a person of great influence, importance. As such, Theo is correct – I do believe myself to share such a nature with NEM.”

“No one man can be so great an influence on progress alone,” Theo countered, “lest such forward momentum be lacking in perspective. I have seen many years in each world, and if there is one thing I’ve taken away from both, it is that there is strength in collaboration, Orville.”

“I’ve heard enough,” Orville stated firmly. “Your years mean nothing to me. If anything, they disqualify you further. What progress have *you* accomplished with so many extra years? You may leave now.”

“But, Orville…” Ruya pleaded, leaning forward in the chair across from his desk. The two of them sitting there, she and Theo, a team newly formed to slow him down… there was something more going on here. His churning gut left no doubt.

“We’re not conspiring against you,” Theo insisted, as if reading his very thoughts. “There are others, people all throughout the Lower Half who wish to see Alterra rise. But like *us*,” he gestured to himself and Ruya, “these others will not follow you blindly. You have an opportunity to make allies.”

“Us…” Orville echoed, eyeing Ruya as she shifted uncomfortably in her seat. “You two would make quite the pair.”

“That isn’t what he means…” Ruya began.

“I don’t need *you* to translate what he means,” Orville shot back across the desk. “And I don’t need either of you -- nor these *others* of which you speak so confidently -- to raise Alterra from the dregs of its lowly existence. When I have accomplished what I intend, the people will depend on and praise Orville Zaide alone.”

Theo rose, body stiff, lips pursed.

“Ruya…” Theo turned to face her.

The way she looked back at him – had she not once reserved that look for Orville alone? That respect and admiration, that confidence…

"You do not need to stay in this," Theo told her.

"Leave," Orville growled.

"You have strength beyond this man," Theo urged.

"Leave." Orville rose from his chair. He would not allow some wolf in sheep's clothing to take what was his.

"Have you not already helped so many of the people?" Theo pleaded. "Have you not already contributed to the movement?"

"Ruya…" Orville warned as he walked slowly from around his desk.

"Your strength in prophecy is said to be greater than any prophet in centuries, in any class!" Theo was not backing down.

Orville moved in front of Ruya, blocking her from Theo's view. It was easy. The wolf was a small man.

"The things you *see*, they happen, Ruya! They *all* happen," Theo practically shouted over him. "The trade routes going silent, the river drying up, even the change in seasons…"

"Leave," Orville repeated, hovering over Theo. "Now."

Theo shook his head in resignation and walked to the door. Pausing in the doorway, he looked back over his shoulder to address Ruya yet again.

"Should you decide you are done wasting your time and talent on this lunatic, you have a place to go."

"Leave!" Orville bellowed, taking three long strides toward the door, reaching it as it slammed shut behind Theo. He moved just as swiftly back to Ruya, who stood in a defiant posture before him, her hands clenched into fists at her sides.

"How dare you," he accused.

"How dare I?" she replied. "How dare I try to help you? Try to connect you with others who also wish to see Alterra thrive?"

"You've gone behind my back," he shouted, heat rising into his face.

"I have not," she asserted calmly. Too calmly.

“And what is it about *him*, Ruya?” His hands were shaking.

“I don’t know what you mean.”

She was taunting him now, surely. “I saw the way you looked at him.”

“I have respect for the man.”

“There was more than respect in those eyes,” his shoulders dropped. “Have you been with him?”

“No.”

“Yet, you do not flinch at the question. Perhaps you wish to?”

“I wish to see freedom for my people.”

“And you know I am the man to make that happen,” he replied, calming slightly. This was not over.

“But why is it just up to one man?”

Damn this woman. She had given him more grief in the previous few months than all their years together combined. And she gave him so little of what he really wanted from her. He became suddenly aware of her body so near to his and wrapped his arm around her waist. She did not lean into him. He reached a hand up to her chin, lifting her eyes to meet his. There was a fire in them that was his, must always be his. He interlaced his fingers in her hair and pressed his lips firmly against hers, but she did not return his passion. She pressed at his chest with her fists, fighting off his advances.

“Stop,” she whispered.

“I will not,” he replied, pulling her in toward him again. But then there was the sound of sliding metal and the sensation of a cold blade at his throat.

“You will,” Ruya stated, her voice flat. “And you will never lay hands on me again.”

He could muster no other response to the current situation aside from laughter. When had she become so bold? He pressed forward into the flat of the blade and held her even more firmly.

“I’m leaving,” she said.

There were no tears. After so many years, did she not at least owe him regret?

"I'm taking my children. I'm taking my brother."

The knife was for show and they both knew it. He dug his fingertips into her back and pressed his face against hers. She twisted the knife just enough to draw blood. Orville did not flinch. He kissed her cheek, her neck, still firmly grasping her chin in his hand.

"Take the children," he stated calmly, slowly releasing her. "Your brother, on the other hand, will stay with me."

CHAPTER 13
The Train

"What are they?" Dottie whispered, resting in a crumpled heap on the ground, her back against Hudd's chest, the heavy weight of Ari's head in her lap.

"No idea," Hudd replied. "And if it weren't for the last few days, I'd be a lot more freaked out by them."

"How long have I been out?"

"Only a minute or so." He helped her sit forward. "How's your head?"

"Throbbing." She reached up and ran her fingers over a goose egg. She must have hit it on the way down. "But I'll be fine. We should get back to Ben and Penny."

"You should rest a second." Hudd shifted so that he was sitting at her side, one leg tucked in and the other extended in front of her. "Dottie… do you want to talk about what just happened?"

What just happened? All she could see was orange, orange and red and swirling leaves.

"We don't have to." He reached a hand up and placed it on her shoulder. "But, I… I think maybe we should try to."

Ari had jumped into Greg, pushing him forward into the knife. It was really Ari, not her own hand, that had taken a life. And he was just protecting her. She scratched his head along the back of his ears and he scrunched up his face in pleased response.

"Dottie…" Hudd prompted.

"Something happened," she said.

"Yes… something did," his voice had a sense of urgency. This had shaken him.

"But whatever it was, it's over now. It can't be changed," she said.

"No, I suppose it can't."

"So, maybe… maybe there's no point in talking about it."

"Maybe not right now, but maybe later." Hudd reached up and cupped her chin in his hand, pulling her face up toward his. He wasn't close enough to kiss her, though she'd be lying if she said the hope didn't cross her mind. No, he was simply trying to read her eyes. She wondered what he would find there.

In silence, he rose and helped her to her feet. In silence, they made their way past the Dairy Queen that was never as busy on weekends as Josie's just down the road, the office buildings, the auto shop and the computer repair store. And in silence, they walked back into Josie's outdoor picnic area to find Ben and Penny still perched atop the tables, arguing about the names of different ice cream toppings.

"They're called *Jimmies*," Penny insisted.

"Sprinkles," Ben retorted with an expression of mild amusement before catching sight of Dottie and Hudd. "Hey, you two. Successful trip?"

Dottie wasn't sure how to answer. While Ben and Penny were members of this small group, they didn't seem to really get it. *Ice cream toppings?*

"Not even close," Hudd growled as he stalked off around the corner of the building.

Dottie's cheeks burned, stung by the sudden and unexpected shift in Hudd's tone.

"Just try to ignore him, Dot," Ben said. "He's hurting, like the rest of us. He just doesn't know how to deal with it."

Dottie suddenly noticed the smile on Ben's face and the warmth of his hand, now gently touching her knee.

"So how did it go?" he asked.

"It was fine," Dottie's voice cracked. She thought about the men, the one she killed, the leaves. "It was fine," she repeated. *It isn't fine. None of this is fine.* Tears welled in her eyes, and she blinked hard to keep them from escaping. Dottie hugged her knees to her chest and looked up to find Ben frowning at her and Penny looking on with mild concern from the next picnic table over.

"What happened, Dottie?" Ben asked. "Something happened."

"We ran into some people," she whispered. "They're dead now." *Everybody's dead.* She turned away from Ben before she lost it completely.

"What the hell happened, Dot?" Ben pressed.

"It doesn't matter," she said. *It can't matter. If anything else matters, it'll break me,* she thought.

Ben grabbed her by the shoulders and turned her to face him. What was with these boys insisting she make eye contact?

"People dying doesn't ever not matter. That's not something you let yourself get used to, Dottie," Ben said.

"They were criminals…" Her voice wavered. "Bright orange jumpsuits. They'd escaped from a prison. We overheard them talking about how the doors all just suddenly burst open and how they killed all the guards."

"And they saw you?"

She nodded.

Hudd slowly came back over and stood next to a horror-stricken Penny.

"One of them," Hudd continued for Dottie, his tone softer now. "One of them got my arms behind me. Got me on the ground. The other one went for Dottie. Ari took his legs out and Dottie stabbed him in the stomach."

"He fell into the blade…" Dottie whispered.

"He didn't," Hudd argued. "You did it. And you did it well… as if you had done it before. Where the hell do you learn something like that, Dot?"

She looked up, staring in turn at the faces of each of her shocked friends, the last people she had in this world. How could they ever understand? The way she'd been raised, the things she had been trained to do. And yet, she was horrified at how easily she'd put that training into practice. She had anticipated such a thing to be much more difficult to execute.

"What was I supposed to do?" She glared at Hudd. "He said there was something else he wanted. Should I have given him whatever that was?"

Hudd shook his head, perhaps trying to clear the chaos that must now reside there in the wake of all they had seen.

"He said he wasn't going to leave me alone," she added.

"Sounds like you did what you had to do," Ben said. "But it also sounds like, maybe, Hudd's having a hard time with the fact that you knew how to do it…"

"... and that you are now so composed," Hudd added.

"Look, I told you guys my mom had this survivalist thing," Dottie said. "Well, it wasn't just like some hobby. She was scared… a lot, of people and government and nature. She made sure I knew how to defend myself." *But she never said how to deal with the aftermath.*

"Something like what you guys just went through is traumatic," Ben reassured them, "and people deal with trauma in all kinds of different ways, no matter how prepared you think you are. Dottie might just be dealing with this differently."

"Why don't we take a look at your leg?" she asked Ben, hoping this discussion could be left where it was.

"Yeah," Ben agreed, brow furrowed, "probably a good idea."

"How do you feel?" Dottie asked, grabbing the first aid kit and ignoring the continued stares from Hudd and Penny.

"I'm alright," Ben answered, "Feeling like garbage, but I guess I shouldn't expect any different. Leg's throbbing a bit."

Dottie unwound the bandage and lifted the gauze pad, careful not to pull the flap of skin away with it. She knew little about wound care, but she didn't like how the area around the gash was so red and inflamed.

"That looks like hell," Ben muttered.

"It's fine," Dottie said. "It's just healing." She tried to sound confident but heard her voice waver. She never was any good at lying. She struggled to keep her hands steady as she made another amateur attempt to clean and dress the wound. The harder she tried to be gentle, the more clumsy she became.

"You're doing a good job, Dottie," Ben reassured through gritted teeth as she finally secured the last clasp on the wrap. Sweat trickled down his forehead. "It didn't hurt at all."

"You're just trying to keep me from feeling bad." Dottie shook her head at him as she sat back on her heels.

"What?" Ben asked.

"You're just funny," Dottie replied. "You're in pain, and you're stuck with the least skilled nurse possible. You know what I just did earlier, what an awful thing I did. You'd be justified if you were angry or apprehensive with me even being near you, and yet you're worried about me, worried about whether I feel like I'm doing an okay job." She couldn't help herself. "I just… look, I suck at being positive. Like even when I try to tell myself to focus on something good, all I see is bad. You seem to be the complete opposite."

Ben looked down at his hands. "I guess I've had a lot of practice."

Dottie was glad for the quiet that fell over the group that afternoon. She needed time to think about the enchanted door from her dream, to retrace every line of the carving, wanting to burn each detail into her memory to shield her mind from the ones that now haunted her. As long as she could focus on the door, she would be okay. As long as she could picture the magical creatures, she could drown out the orange and red and swirling leaves.

It was late afternoon when they made it back to Penny's. One of the wagon wheels had busted and Hudd helped Ben hobble the rest of the way. The sun dipped down behind the trees and a wintery chill settled in. Ari led the pack. The group huddled near the fire in the basement with cans of beans and handfuls of Saltine crackers.

"You guys know Aggie Polson?" Ben asked at length. "She runs the science club." The other kids nodded. "I've known her since I was little. If she's alive, she won't have evacuated."

"How do you know that?" Dottie asked. She knew who Aggie was. The high-school science club met next to the theater where she went for drama club on Tuesday and Thursday afternoons, and Aggie was always waiting at the door for her students.

"She had this theory… a 'theory of mass exodus,' she called it. Basically, she figured that if there was ever a really big disaster, like what's happening right now, that the first wave of people leaving would be chaotic and dangerous, and she wouldn't want to be caught up in it. The second wave of evacuations would include people who needed a lot of assistance or those being forced to leave, and that wouldn't be much better. And the last wave would be like the guys you two met today." He gestured to Dottie and Hudd. "Ones she wouldn't want to cross. Her plan was to stay put, hunker down until everything settled, and she advised family and friends to do the same."

"How did she know something bad would happen?" Penny asked.

"I don't think she *knew* it would, just that it was possible. Either way, I think we should try to get to her." He glanced around the fire at the other kids.

"Well…" Dottie began. "It's a plan, and that's more than we've had for two days, so I'm in." She paused, getting used to the idea. "How far away is she?"

"Not far. I'm a little slow moving, but I think resting yesterday and today has been really helpful. I should be able to make it in one shot if we go slow. Plus, Aggie has a lot of experience with medical stuff. It would be good to have her take a look at my leg."

"I'm surprised you've stayed put this long," Hudd muttered.

"What's that supposed to mean?" Ben asked.

"Figured you'd want to find your mom," Hudd sneered.

"Watch it," Ben warned.

"What's he talking about, Ben?" Dottie asked. There was venom in Hudd's voice, something darker than Dottie had heard before.

"I'm talking about the fact that Ben's mom took off a while back," Hudd answered before Ben could. "You guys didn't know that? When was it, Ben, Christmas last year?"

"About then," Ben replied through gritted teeth.

"Guessing you think she might be with Aggie? I mean, they *were* friends."

"Doubtful," Ben glared at Hudd, ending the argument by rolling over on the sectional with his back to the group.

The night was frigid. The fire died out at some point while Dottie slept. Her eyelids felt heavy as she woke to silence in the dusky basement early the next morning. It was cold enough to see her breath rise as steam in front of her. She remained cocooned with Ari in her sleeping bag. Her nose felt numb from the cold, and her lips were raw from the dry air. *I could just stay here,* she thought. *Go back to sleep. Sleep until this is over.* She felt a familiar punch of anxiety in her gut and thought about sitting up. Over the last few years, Dottie had spent countless mornings curled up on her bathroom floor wrapped in a towel, unable to finish getting ready for school. She would lay there, waiting for the panic to subside. Why had she been so afraid? A bully? *Nothing.* The anxiety would hit her, unbidden waves of pure dread, making it impossible for her to move.

My God, don't you know this is too much, she pleaded now. *I am not strong enough for this.* She wasn't someone who prayed. She believed in God. She believed in Heaven and Hell and most of the things she'd learned from her Catholic upbringing. But despite this, praying was something she rarely did. *I am not tough enough for this.*

Dottie was cold. She was tired. Her entire body ached and all she could see was orange, red and swirling leaves. *If I move, this feeling will kill me.* Tears streamed down her face as the panic rose into her chest. Her breaths became short, sharp, her lungs painfully sucking in air. Her mind whirled from one painful image to the next: the burned down neighborhood, the unseen faces of her dead family. And that's when it surfaced – Greg's face contorted in pain, the knife sticking out from his mangled stomach. It took all the strength she had left to push away the feelings that were holding her body and mind hostage. She didn't want the others to know. *They cannot know how pathetic I truly am.*

"Dottie?" Penny's voice broke the silence at just the right moment. "Are you awake?"

"Yeah," Dottie managed to respond. Ari lifted his head and licked the salty tears from her cheeks.

"I think something's wrong with Ben," Penny whispered.

She had been unable to rise just a moment earlier, but hearing this spurred her into motion.

Dottie sat up inside her sleeping bag, limbs stiff and numb from the cold night and waning anxiety attack. Ari burrowed further into the corner in protest. The boys were sleeping on opposite ends of the U-shaped sectional, but Penny was standing over Ben, a blanket wrapped around her shoulders. Dottie couldn't get a good look at Ben from where she sat. *It's like pulling off a Band-Aid,* she thought. She took a deep breath, unzipped the sleeping bag, and stomped her feet from the cold as she went to Ben's side.

His face was ashen. Sweat gleamed on his forehead. His mouth contorted from his obvious discomfort as he slept restlessly. Dottie slid her hand out from inside the sleeve of her hoodie and felt his forehead. He was burning up.

"This isn't good," Dottie muttered. "We need to get him to Aggie's."

"How?" Penny asked. "Can we carry him?"

Dottie looked up at Penny. The usually timid girl was now stone-faced, calm.

"I can," Hudd's voice behind them made both girls jump.

"Good," Dottie responded. "Hold on. Let's see what we can do about this fever first." She jumped up and went to dig through the first aid gear. She found a handful of individually wrapped doses of ibuprofen. "See if you can sit him up," she directed. Hudd did as she asked without a single hint of the disdain he had shown the day before, making Dottie feel momentarily hopeful.

Ben grunted and strained to open his eyes. He tensed against Hudd, who used his own body as a wedge to bring Ben into a more upright position.

"It's okay, Ben," Penny reassured, dropping to her knees and placing a hand on his arm. "It's just a little fever. Dottie has some meds for you. You need to rest." Her voice was sweet, her smile comforting. Ben calmed immediately and leaned back against Hudd. *Penny's good at this part*, Dottie thought as she fought to pry open the packets. She finally got the slit in the package to split in half, and the two pills slid into her palm. Dottie placed them in Ben's mouth and Penny helped him drink some water.

They spent the morning trying to get warm while working to keep Ben's fever in check. Hudd rekindled the fire. Penny stayed next to Ben. The ibuprofen seemed to be helping. Dottie sat off to the side, whittling away the bark on a branch she's brought in to make a walking stick. She was grateful to have one of her Grandpa's pocket knives in her pack. Dottie's Grandpa had passed away when she was eleven years old. She remembered the countless walks they took together, hand-in-hand, talking about everything and nothing. She remembered thinking that losing him was completely unbearable, that the pain of it would kill her. She remembered lying on an air mattress in her grandparents living room the night after the funeral, while all the adults stayed up to talk. He had been with her, sitting there on the floor next to her, holding her hand. Whether she actually saw him, imagined him, or was just somehow willing him into existence, he was there. *Perhaps,* she thought, *he's here even now.*

Dottie was too nervous to try to unwrap Ben's leg. She wasn't sure what she would find and had no idea how to handle a badly infected wound. They had to get to Aggie. Ben said he could walk, but he was weaker now. The wagon had died along with so much else. They could try to create a make-shift stretcher, but that would take half a day just to build. With four packs and two people carrying a stretcher, they wouldn't get very far.

"Hudd," Dottie called across the room. "You said you could carry Ben… how?"

"On my back," he replied as he got to his feet. "We do partner carries in the off-season. I could try that with him."

Hudd was strong, Dottie didn't doubt that, but how far could they get with him hauling Ben?

"I guess we don't have any other options," Dottie said quietly, staring down at the ground. "Alright guys," she said as she rose to her feet. "Let's all get some food and water in us. Ben, you'll take some more ibuprofen before we go."

She opened the door to the backyard and stuck her head outside. Dottie looked up at a sky of dense white clouds. They'd need to dress for snow.

∝

Dottie had no idea how long they had been walking and hoped they were still moving in the right direction. Ben said that Aggie lived over behind the school. They decided they would cut down through the city-owned forest lands that backed Penny's yard. Dottie believed this would bring them to the top of Breakneck Hill, a steep, zig-zagging street that accurately reflected its name and overlooked the school.

Their progress was slow as they trudged through the woods. She took a water pouch and filled it for Ari, securing it on his back and over his chest like a harness. She'd been able to consolidate the rest of the gear down into three packs, rolling up the fourth and using a length of rope to tie it around Hudd's waist as a sort of makeshift seat for Ben. Though Hudd had been able to haul Ben much longer than she had expected, he still needed to rest more frequently as the afternoon waned. Dottie was grateful for each pause. The weight of the two heavy packs had set her lower back on fire.

"Why don't we all take a break," Dottie suggested as Hudd again halted, wavering under Ben's weight. "Time to refuel."

Hudd looked back over his shoulder and nodded somberly at Dottie before easing Ben to the ground. They sat in exhausted silence, snacking on the last of the trail mix and beef jerky. Penny was even able to coax Ben into taking a few bites.

"How much farther do you think we..." Penny began, before an eerie screech of metal on metal cut her off.

The high pitch of scraping steel sent chills down Dottie's spine. Her heart raced as metal crashed and silence followed. She held her breath, straining to hear more.

"Ben, Penny, you two stay here," Hudd said in a low whisper, a mouthful of beef jerky lodged in his cheek. "Dottie and I will go check it out."

"Ari…" Dottie hesitated. "Stay. Penny, keep him with you this time, okay?"

"Okay, Dottie," Penny replied, patting Ari's head.

Dottie watched as Hudd hurriedly chewed and swallowed the bite of jerky. She followed suit when he grabbed his hatchet off the rock next to him and rose to his feet. Rambo knife in hand, Dottie willed herself forward as she followed Hudd through the trees. Her stomach was in her throat. What would they find? More convicts, or worse?

They had hiked a couple of hundred yards or so when they came to the edge of the tree line. Hudd motioned Dottie closer so she could see what he saw.

It was more of the leaves they had seen the day before… and a train. The tracks meant they were closer to Breakneck Hill than she thought. But as fat snowflakes began to fall, it was clear they were not close enough.

"That's a Maglev train," she whispered to Hudd.

"A what?"

"A Maglev train. They're new," Dottie said, "My dad's company made the cars for this one. They're made out of fiberglass. Only the bases and tracks are steel, so they're lighter and more durable."

"Where are the wheels?" Hudd asked, noticing the way the strange train cars lay directly on the tracks.

"Well, they aren't supposed to be sitting right on top like that," Dottie explained. "They use something called *magnetic levitation*. It's actually really cool. Basically, the cars float along a guideway."

"So, these just aren't working?" Hudd asked.

"Yeah, exactly… I mean if the power's out everywhere, I guess it would make sense… no energy to create the charge?" She didn't remember much of what her dad told her beyond the "magnetic levitation" part.

"What do you think made that sound?"

Dottie scanned the length of the train.

"That car probably," she said, pointing at one that had broken away from the others. The lopsided car had rotated on its axis and slid off the tracks to one side. "Doesn't look like it will stay upright much longer." She paused, scared to voice her next thought. "Hudd… you think anybody is in there?"

"You think a train would be going somewhere without people in it?" he replied.

"Guess not," Dottie responded, pursing her lips at him.

"We should go look," Hudd suggested.

"You're crazy."

"I'm serious. We're still a few miles from Breakneck depending on how far in these tracks are. I think these are the ones that just got built by the country club, right?"

"They are," Dottie agreed.

"It's cold. It's snowing. It's gotta be late afternoon at this point 'cause the sun has already dropped below the trees. We could take some shelter in there overnight, then make the rest of the trek in the morning."

"If Ben makes it until morning…" Dottie said.

"He will," Hudd shot back, glaring at her. "And I don't wanna hear that shit anymore, got it?"

"Yeah, sorry." Dottie turned away from Hudd. She didn't want him to see the tears in her eyes.

"Alright then," Hudd said as he squatted down and grabbed a couple of small rocks that still stuck out from the fine layer of powdery snow.

Dottie stomped her feet on the ground to try and shake the chill that was beginning to settle into her bones. Hudd gave her a sly sideways smile.

"What?" Dottie asked, unable to keep from smiling back, despite the feeling of dread in her chest.

"You've got a good arm," Hudd said. "Throw these at a couple of the cars… make it loud."

"Now... *that* is something I can do," Dottie replied as she took the rocks from Hudd. She picked her first target. It was about the same distance as a throw from shallow center-field to home. *Easy enough*. Dottie stepped back, took a deep breath, and let the first rock fly.

CHAPTER 14
The Blade

Ruya struggled against Orville's embrace. The dagger slid across her sweaty palm, twisting slightly against his neck. He was calling her farce. She hoped he could not detect the fear and guilt that threatened to suffocate her. But he left her with no choice. Orville had helped her rise to a respected standing in Alterra and now she must act on the people's behalf. He had made her a mother, but she could no longer confine her children to the twisted life that he had engineered for them at Gemma. She willed her mind to escape somewhere else as he pressed his cheek against hers and kissed her face, but the image of a wooded trail could not mask the feeling of heated breath on her skin.

“Take the children,” he said, releasing her at last, taking a step back to perch on the edge of his desk. Out came the pawn from his pocket. “Your brother, on the other hand, will stay with me.”

“No.” She could no longer control the quiver in her voice.

“As far as I see it, you have no say in the matter.” A smile spread across his face as he saw her weaken. “You know as well as I that Sylvester will do anything I ask of him. Think of it as… a gesture of good faith on your part.”

“You do not trust me?” She had hoped… what had she hoped? That he would simply be heartbroken? That he would let her go without a fight? Orville believed her his rightful possession, she had understood that for years. All the more reason why she must remain strong. The longer she stayed, the tighter his hold on her would become.

“My Ruya, it is exactly the case that I do not trust you. Should you wrong me, should I find out that you’ve joined up with Theo and his movement, I will send your dear brother to you… in pieces.”

She took a step toward Orville, fighting off simultaneous urges to either embrace him or knock him in the head with the butt of her dagger. He had used her. Used her for her reassurance and insights. But she had failed him. Failed to somehow make him see that he was but another pawn in the game that would end in his own defeat. She could not save him. But she could still be of use to others, could try to remove her children from his influence. Ruya searched his eyes for any last glimmer of care for the world outside of himself. But it was as if he did not even see *her* standing before him. She turned and forced herself to walk away.

“You can walk out of here.” Orville’s voice followed her. “I will not hold you prisoner. But you will always belong to me. And when you realize that you are nothing without me, you’ll be back.”

∝

Ruya hadn’t seen Cairo in years, not since Orville came to Alterra and stowed her away. She stood in the doorway, taking a moment to let her eyes adjust to the dim pub. It was the middle of the day, but no sunlight found its way into the place. Yet, there were also no patrons to warrant more than a few sparse candles for light. Cairo and Theo sat at a table in the middle of the room, watching her.

Cairo rose suddenly to his feet. "I'd be lying if… if I said I thought I'd ever see you again."

He came toward her slowly, embracing her forearm and searching her eyes… for what was left of her soul, perhaps?

"Come, please, sit down." He ushered her to a seat at the table.

"Where are the children?" Theo asked, his voice calm.

Was he happy to see her? Angry with her for not leaving with him earlier? She couldn't read him.

"They, um…" she paused to take a desperate gulp of water from the cup Cairo placed before her. What must she look like right now? She hadn't stopped walking since leaving Gemma, had not even looked into a mirror to comb out the tangles left by Orville's hands.

"Are the children alright?" Theo asked, more firmly, but still without any of the judgement she believed she deserved from him.

"They're upstairs with Laila," she replied. "I shouldn't have left them…" she began to rise from her chair, but a spinning room brought her back to her seat.

"You should rest," Cairo said firmly. "You've only just left them. They are in good hands with my sister."

"What did you tell him?" Theo's blunt question shouldn't have caught her off guard. He was never one for small talk. And yet, she had not prepared an answer.

"That I was leaving, taking the children, my brother…"

"Where *is* Sylvester?" Cairo asked, brow furrowed.

"Orville wouldn't release him to me." Tears rose in her eyes and she blinked them away. "He's holding him in case I make any wrong moves."

"We can get him out of there," Cairo said. "This is why you must join our cause, Ruya. We can free Sylvester and then get to work on so many others."

"Sylvester will die," Ruya said, "if I join with you, if I help in any way, and Orville finds out.

"And what did you tell him about you?"

"That he would never lay hands on me again."

"And…"

"I had the knife…" she glared down at the table as if she wished to burn a hole in it. "He didn't care. He knew I wouldn't do it."

"What did he do to you?" Cairo asked, breathless.

Ruya came to her senses just enough to realize this was not a conversation she wished to have.

"Nothing," she said more firmly. "He just let me know that he would not be intimidated, not by me, nor by a blade."

"Are you hungry?" Cairo asked.

"No," she replied, "but thank you." She was grateful for the redirect.

The noon gong sounded in the distance and the three of them sat in silence until the twelve tolls completed.

Cairo rose from his chair. "I have to go meet with one of my suppliers. You two stay and talk. Help yourself to whatever you can find behind the bar."

Once Cairo had gone, Theo moved his chair next to hers. He leaned toward her as if planning to place an arm around her, but something stayed him.

"Did he hurt you?"

"Today?" She asked with a sad smile. "Or ever?"

"Both."

"Not this time, not like he has in the past," she replied. She could feel the warmth of his leg pressed against hers.

"I'm sorry," Theo said, folding his hand into hers.

"What do *you* have to be sorry for?" she whispered back. Was this man just as insane as the other? She looked up to find his face close to hers, yet not positioned in the haughty, condescending manner that Orville's had taken just hours before. There was a sad sort of smile, one corner raised just slightly and soft creases around his eyes. His grey topknot sat crooked on the top of his head, strands of silver hair framing his face. He was much older than she and yet put forth a vitality that she no longer possessed. "What do you have to be sorry for?" she repeated.

"I should have found a way…" he began. "I should have gotten you out long ago, you and the children."

"You know as well as I that I wouldn't have let you."

"Perhaps."

"Where do I go from here?" The words tumbled from her mouth unbidden.

"Forward. Upward. This man has controlled every aspect of your life and being for nearly a decade. It has, in many ways, become a crutch upon which you are reliant. But it doesn't have to remain that way. Eventually, you will learn to bear your own weight again."

"Where do I start?"

"Start where you are," he stated simply, as if it was obvious. "Start with trusting yourself, at least a little."

"How do I?" she asked, her tone a little sharper than she intended. "When I have allowed myself to fall to such a desperate place in life?"

"Our places of greatest despair are the breeding grounds for pivotal change." Theo leaned an elbow on the table, considering her thoughtfully. The hand that held hers provided reassurance. Such a strange feeling, this admiration and compassion from a man who had every right to discard her for her ignorance and fear.

"I have no options," she muttered. "Nowhere to live. I have not had my licensing reviewed by the Tri in too long, I worry they won't even accept it if I try to renew and I'll be deemed delinquent."

"It is when we believe ourselves to be out of options, that we learn to create more," Theo responded. "The movement, we need you and can also protect you."

"But how do I join with you when it means certain death for my brother? And even if Cairo can manage to extract him from Gemma, Orville will not just sit idly by and let us move on with our lives." Tears escaped from her eyes and slid down her cheeks. *Damn weakness.*

"Orville is a man to be feared," Theo affirmed. "But not because he is powerful or influential as he believes. He is a man to be feared because of his ignorant, selfish outlook on the worlds, his impulsive desires to possess and contain. While I understand your fear for your brother, doing nothing here… it's just not an option."

"I made the mistake of choosing sides once. I do not wish to do so again hastily." She was not giving him what he wanted. She couldn't. Not yet. She expected him to become frustrated, angry, but he gave her hand a reassuring squeeze.

"While I wish I could convince you otherwise," he began after a time, "I understand and will respect your desire to be kept… at a distance."

She looked down at their hands, still interlaced in her lap, his thumb tracing the same line back and forth across the top of hers.

"I… the children," he released her hand and looked around the room as if searching for the right words. "I could help with them. Care for them, protect them. And you."

"I cannot accept that, Theo." Or could she?

He sat back, cheeks flushed, and pressed his face into his hands.

"Forgive me." He leaned forward, taking both her hands in his. "My offer was out of place."

"I'm sorry," she muttered.

"You have nothing to be sorry for… I cannot begin to understand the life you have lived. To suggest that you need anyone other than yourself to care for your children, I did not mean…"

"No, no, I know," she tried to reassure him. "And it's a tempting offer, truly. I've spent many years now wishing to be rescued. But if there's one thing you have taught me, Theo, it's that I must be my own rescuer. I have something to prove to myself in all this."

"You are stronger than you know," he said. "Would you… at least be comfortable remaining a resource for Cairo and myself? Admittedly, and perhaps selfishly, I do not wish to see you go. But I understand if you need distance right now."

She hesitated. She'd had enough of selfish men. And yet, Theo's ability to recognize and admit his own selfishness – was that not, in fact, selfless? His transparency showed that he valued *her* over himself, even in this. Her shoulders sank as a wave of intense fatigue came over her. The day, and so many days and weeks before it, had been full of planning, strategizing, worrying. Could she go through with it? How would he respond?

"Orville is not here."

Theo's comment surprised her. Was she not the one with *sight*? He seemed awfully in-tune to her thoughts and emotions.

"You do not know him, what he is capable of…."

"All men are capable of evil, if we are truly honest with ourselves," Theo replied. "Some, more than others, allow themselves to be consumed by their own evil. But that man is not in this room. He is not here now. Loosen the grip that he has placed on you."

She focused for a moment on slowing her breathing, the image of being freed from Orville's chains clear in her mind.

"I will help," she said after a time. "I will help you, Cairo, the movement. But I do not wish to be known for doing so."

CHAPTER 15
The Dead

The hurled rock arced across the sky, landing on the side of the first train car with a satisfying clang. Dottie held her breath, waiting for a sign of life from inside the train. *Nothing.* She stepped to the side and chucked the next rock, hitting another train car. Dottie launched the last rock at a third car and waited for any sound or movement.

"You know…" Dottie began, "this was kind of a dumb idea. No offense, but it doesn't mean those cars are empty. Like the wrong kind of person would probably know better than to poke their head out to see what's up. And something… or some*one* had to cause that car to slide off the tracks, don't you think?"

“Yeah,” Hudd responded, shrugging his shoulders. “Still, the rocks make me feel better. Nothing wrong with a little false motivation.”

“Hey, at least you're self-aware,” Dottie teased.

“Well, look at you over here taking shots,” Hudd laughed. He took a deep breath and stomped his feet in the growing layer of snow. “Might as well get this over with. What do ya say, Dorothy? Off to see the wizard?”

Dottie shot a look at Hudd that wiped the grin off his face as his eyes widened in feigned intimidation.

“Kidding, kidding,” he said, palms raised in surrender. “Don't send Toto, I mean Ari, after me.”

Dottie rolled her eyes but followed him out into the open, bowie knife in hand. Her heart raced and her hands felt sweaty despite the cold and falling snow.

Hudd stepped up into the doorway of the nearest train car but moved away quickly.

“That was a passenger car,” he mumbled, “we don't need to deal with that.”

Dottie got the point and held her breath as she approached the next train car while Hudd went on to the third. This one had been some sort of kitchen/dining car, and it had fewer windows, booth seating, and a serving bar. Dottie couldn't help but note the resemblance to the club car from *White Christmas*. She and her mom had watched it together every year.

“*Snow... snow... snow...*” she sang quietly, *“it won't be long before we'll all be there with snow. Snow-O...”* She turned to find Hudd waiting behind her, an amused smile on his face.

“My mom loved that movie,” he said quietly. “Hey, so… the next train has quite a few people in it, too. And it doesn't seem to be as sturdy as this one. Plus, we might be able to break down that bar or the booths for firewood.”

“There are people in here too,” Dottie replied nervously.

“Yeah, there are probably a few in each car. We’ll have to move them out.”

“No,” Dottie asserted. “I can’t.” All she could see was orange and red and swirling leaves.

“Why?” Hudd asked. “With everything we’ve seen…”

“Seen… not touched,” Dottie tried to clarify, bile rising into her throat.

“You okay?” Hudd asked, eyebrows raised.

“Look, I just can't… I can't touch a dead body,” she repeated, looking away.

“Dottie, you’ve killed a man,” Hudd said firmly as he pushed past Dottie into the dining car. *There it was.* “I need your help.”

“There’s gotta be an empty car,” she protested. “I’m a wimp with anything dead.”

“We don't have time to search them all,” Hudd said. “Look, Dot… this is just one more hard thing, okay? And would you quit it with the negative self-talk?”

“Oh, I see how it is!” Dottie replied angrily. “So you can put me down whenever you feel like it, but I can't point out my own flaws?”

Hudd’s eyes widened. “Are you serious right now?”

“*Dead* serious,” Dottie responded, tilting her head to one side.

“Well aren't you clever,” Hudd said, rolling his eyes.

“I thought it was pretty funny.”

“Geez, you would.”

“What's that supposed to mean?!” Dottie shot back.

“You have *no* sense of humor, Dottie. It's terrible. Somebody teases you a bit, and you think they hate you. Stop taking yourself so seriously!” And with that Hudd turned around and climbed the last two steps up to the dining car.

Dottie did not respond, but stomped up the steps behind him, quickly forgetting what it was she was mad at him for as she took in what was waiting inside the train car.

There were four bodies. Two men, a woman, and a dog. Dottie and Hudd walked up alongside the first man. Dried blood trailed from his mouth.

"Grab his legs," Hudd directed.

Dottie stared at him blankly.

"Look," Hudd huffed. "Watch. You can do it without actually touching him. Use his clothes. Like this." He demonstrated by grabbing fistfuls of the man's shirt sleeves and heaving the body into a sitting position. "Grab his pant legs, and we'll drag him out."

Dottie knelt down and clenched her fists around the edges of the man's jeans. *It wouldn't be so bad if he had a story*, she thought. Ignoring the tears that streamed silently down her face, she heaved the man's stiff legs into the air and helped Hudd drag the body to the front of the dining car. *Dockers. He was a businessman. Single. No family left behind to grieve his death. He played basketball with his friends on the weekends.* She continued to create the man's story as they descended the steps and deposited the body on the frozen ground a few cars away.

The second man was older, in his sixties. *He's a professor at a university. He has grandkids that he sees every Sunday after church. They go to IHOP together. His granddaughter always gets the chocolate chip smiley-face pancakes. He likes to sneak bites from her and dab the whipped cream on her nose to make her giggle.*

"Almost there," Hudd said as they made their way back to the dining car once more.

The woman was next. She wore a sleek navy pantsuit and leather kitten heels. *She was somebody respected. A lawyer,* Dottie imagined. *A prosecutor. She gave her all for women and children so they could see justice done. She was ruthless to the accused but nurturing to the victims.*

“She was everything to somebody,” Dottie observed, without realizing she had said it out loud.

“We all were,” Hudd replied.

The dog was last. Dottie stared down at the scruffy little lap dog as Hudd wrapped a papery-thin blanket around the poor creature.

“Found this in one of the booths,” he explained. He cradled the swaddled body of the dog in his arms and left the dining car to place it next to the other bodies. *His name was Max. He loved peanut butter and tennis balls, just like Ari,* Dottie thought as she watched them go.

With the train car clear of the dead, Dottie and Hudd made their way back through the woods to Ben and Penny. The snow was falling more heavily now and blanketed the ground. Dottie felt the cold seep into her canvas shoes. The sun was low in the sky, slowly sinking behind the tree line. The loss of light made it seem even colder as they stumbled back into the section of woods where they had left Ben and Penny earlier that afternoon.

“Thank God!” Penny let out a relieved cry as Hudd and Dottie came into sight.

“We were really starting to worry about you two,” Ben said through clenched teeth as he tried to stand in the deepening snow.

“We found a place to take shelter tonight,” Hudd reported. “There’s a derailed train not far from here.” He went over to Ben and bent down so the injured boy could climb up onto his back.

“What we heard was one of the cars sliding off the tracks,” Dottie continued, “but the others seem to be more stable. We cleared one out for us to stay in ‘cause we’re still too far from Breakneck.” She loaded up two of the hiking packs and sheathed the Rambo knife. Walking stick in hand, she and Ari took up the rear of their traveling crew, Hudd carrying Ben in front, Penny in the middle. They trudged through the snow and decomposing leaves, heads bowed against an increasingly frigid wind.

They were almost to the edge of the trees when Hudd stopped suddenly, nearly causing a collision between the girls.

"Listen," he whispered.

Dottie strained against the wind for whatever sound had put Hudd on guard. Ari began to growl, the hair along his spine standing upright. A cluster of branches suddenly crashed to her right. A dusting of snow sprayed her face and clouded her vision. She could barely make out the shape of the man who emerged from the trees. Wild-eyed and growling like an animal, he ran at Hudd and Ben with a club-like weapon raised above his head. Hudd ducked out of the way, slipping in the snow. The two boys toppled to the ground as the attacker turned to swing at them again. Dottie rushed forward, swung her walking stick like a softball bat, and hit the man hard in the head. The club bounced off Hudd's shoulder into the snow as the wild man fell to the ground unconscious.

For a moment, time froze. Nobody moved. The kids stared at their attacker, taking in his shaggy, peppery hair, long hooked nose, and caveman-like club.

Dottie thought the man's clothing resembled a Roman toga with its layers of dull, draped fabric. But he had also tied long strips of fabric around his calves and forearms like bandages against the cold. She wondered if he had been attending an early Halloween party when the quake hit. *He must have been freezing out here in that costume*, she thought.

"Nice swing," Hudd said.

"Thanks," Dottie replied, still staring at their assailant. "Guess all that batting practice paid off."

"Dottie!" Penny scolded from behind her.

Dottie just shrugged.

"He's out, but it looks like he's still breathing," Ben said, pulling himself up out of the snow. "What should we do with him?"

Dottie unloaded the packs and searched for the length of rope she had packed. She turned back to the others with it resting in her hand. Hudd nodded. He cut the rope in two, tied the man's wrists together behind his back, and then tied his ankles together.

"He's like some crazy old hermit," Penny whispered from over Dottie's shoulder. She was right, Dottie thought. That's exactly what the guy looked like.

"We should just leave him," Hudd said.

"No..." Dottie whispered. She'd been responsible for one man's death already, possibly two if Mo had not survived. She wasn't going to add to that tally. "We should take him with us."

"Dottie, we can't haul an unconscious hermit..."

"So we just leave him here to die?" Penny interrupted.

"Geez..." Hudd ran his fingers through his hair. "I'm not going to fight both of you. But I don't like it."

"You don't have to like it," Dottie said. "And you can blame me if this backfires."

"Alright." Hudd shrugged his shoulders. "Ben, we're only a few hundred feet from the train," he said standing up from securing the ropes. "Think you can walk?"

"Yeah," Ben replied, "I got this."

"This might help," Dottie added handing him her walking stick. It seemed like the little kick of adrenaline had done Ben some good. His eyes were more clear than they had been the entire day and some of the color had returned to his face. *Maybe his body is fighting off the infection on its own*, she thought.

Dottie hauled two packs, Penny one. Ben hobbled along, leaning on the walking stick and occasionally on Ari. Hudd led the way, dragging the unconscious and raggedy old man along the ground, walking backward with his arms hooked under the man's armpits. The heels of the man's shoes bumped up the stairs of the train car now empty of the dead.

Dottie watched the glistening leaves rise and fall of their own accord, drawing nearer to the group as they climbed into the train. She went up the steps into the dining car and secured the door behind them. Little light remained inside now that the sun was so low. The ghosts of the passengers seemed to fill the air as they propped up the unconscious man in the far corner of the car, Ari standing guard over him. Ben held a flashlight for Hudd as he drove his hatchet into the table in the far booth, breaking it into firewood. Penny sat snuggled into one of the front booths, resting her head on the padded seat back, hugging herself and watching the boys.

Dottie searched behind the bar for food, but the only thing she found aside from alcohol were little bags of pretzels and peanuts like they hand out on airplanes.

The wood from the table was awkward to work with, but it would do. Hudd placed it directly under a hatch in the ceiling, which he opened to allow the smoke to vent.

“I’m gonna keep this thing small,” Hudd said. “It’ll still give off enough warmth so that we don’t freeze in here overnight, but I don’t want to risk setting everything on fire either. We’ve had enough of that.”

Once the fire was crackling and they were settled in a circle in the quickly warming train car, Dottie handed around the little snacks she had found along with the last of the jerky. Her stomach grumbled in complaint about the inadequate meal, but at least it was something.

“We've got an audience,” Hudd murmured, nodding his head in the direction of the hermit who now watched them intently from the corner. “Hey old man,” Hudd said through a mouthful of food. “What the hell did you attack us for?”

The man did not respond.

“We can question him in a minute,” Ben offered. “Let's finish our food. We all need it, and he isn't going anywhere.”

“Wonder if he knows anything,” Penny said quietly. “You know, about where everybody has gone?” She stared down at her half-eaten bag of peanuts, frowning. “I don’t even like peanuts.”

A low chuckle from the back corner of the train car interrupted her thoughts. Dottie turned toward the man, glaring at him. How dare he laugh?

“What are *you* laughing at?” she asked, her voice filled with venom.

“Such silly children,” laughed the man. “Such silly children Sylvester has been sent to see.” He spoke with a melodic cadence, eyes wild with merriment that fit neither their current predicament nor his own. Both his words and the tone with which he spoke made goose bumps appear on Dottie’s arms.

“Sent to see…” Ben repeated. “Who sent you?”

“Oh, but I can't tell you that,” Sylvester said with a wink. “That would be too easy. Silly children. But the leaves will let *him* know.”

“The leaves…” Hudd muttered. Dottie wondered if Hudd also remembered the strange leaves they had encountered the day before. “Let who know?”

“Two times is not the charm,” Sylvester chanted. “No, silly children. I cannot tell you.”

“Why did you attack us? Dottie asked, rising to her feet. “We did nothing to you.”

“It is not what you have done, little girl, but what you will do.” Sylvester tilted his head to one side, considering Dottie for a moment. “The hair is gold, indeed.”

“What does my hair have to do with this?!” Dottie said, unconsciously reaching for one of the golden-blonde curls that framed her face, heart racing.

“It has everything to do with this,” Sylvester sniggered, “and nothing. Everything… and nothing,” he repeated, before dropping his chin to his chest, laughing and muttering incoherently to himself.

Dottie felt her panic rise as she took a step forward. She wanted to shake the man out of his trance, question him, and find out what he knew. But Hudd’s steadying hands gripped her shoulders, allowing her to go no closer.

CHAPTER 16
The Urchin

Lowell crouched in a remote corner of the Hub, squatting back on his heels under a low-hanging beam with the backs of his hands pressed against either side of his chin. The room was long, and the ceilings were so low that one could only stand at full height in the center. More than a hundred men, women, and children in colorful garments were scattered about the room, reclining on their elbows or sitting cross-legged. Dozens of street corner boys like Lowell lounged among them. The pungent odors of straw, clay, and the many mingling bodies filled Lowell's nostrils. Condensation dripped down the muddy walls of the dugout. Lowell wiped the moisture from his palms onto his tunic. The hum of shifting, muttering, whispering children and babbling babies filled the silence as they all waited together, the people of the underground, the cast-offs of society. Lowell fought the urge to leave, overwhelmed by the combination of so many smells, sounds, *people*.

A street corner boy Lowell knew to be a *Lark* rose and walked to the center of the room, dressed in tattered garb. His eyes gleamed as he cleared his throat and began to recite:

"They look right through him,

The ones with places to be,

Those bound to one master or another,

They, who believe themselves higher than he,

Yet he is the one who is free."

The young orator spoke in low tones, his cadence purposeful, melodic, filled with the emotion of his isolation. Lowell envied the boy's poise and confidence. His own storytelling abilities did not warrant any recognition. Lowell tended to think more quickly than his mouth could move, leaving him stumbling and skipping over his words no matter how many times he rehearsed. Still, he relished the spoken word of others. They satisfied his desperate need to feel transported to another place. And so, he listened.

"They see him only to avoid,

The ones with places to be,

Those consumed by monotony,

They, who believe themselves happier than he,

Yet he is the one who is free.

They remember him as something to forget,

The ones with places to be,

Those drowned by the call of the gong,

They, who believe themselves freer than he,

Yet he is the one who is free."

The *Lark* finished his recitation, nodded his thanks to the spatter of applause, and took a seat amongst the crowd. Lowell listened intently as Jordan, the Uprisen's community leader, rose next to speak.

"To all those gathered here today," he began, "welcome! To those of you who have been united behind our cause for some time, we are ever pressing forward so that your time and energy will not be wasted." Jordan looked around as he stood in the center of the stage, hands interlaced at his chest, his rich blue tunic falling to the floor. "For those who are here for the first time, thank you. I would encourage you to reach out, to connect with somebody who's been here a while. Let them know how they can help bring you into the fold."

Lowell sunk deeper into his corner, hoping that no first-timers would feel inclined to reach out his way. He was thankful, at least at that moment, that few would be likely to confuse him for somebody warm and welcoming.

"Finally," Jordan continued in a lower tone, "I have a very important message for you tonight: The Tri-Commission has issued new sweeps throughout the Lower Half, even in some of the alley networks. We've had a few corner groups get caught up in the mix already. These are uncertain times for us all. *We must not become complacent. We must remain vigilant*. Know your call signs and your scripts. Stick to the Green Tunnels whenever possible. Now, more than ever, these means of communication and transit are crucial to our way of life."

Lowell had heard about the *Ravens*, the corner group in High Side that got picked up in a sweep just before the earth shook. Eight boys and one girl about his age all rounded up under charges of "loitering with ill intent," though Lowell had no idea where they had been taken – the nine of them existing in his mind as dashed tallies rather than faces.

"Now, for some lighter business," Jordan continued as he leaned forward. "Please, if you are not signed up for at least one committee, or a corner group for you young people, I'd ask that you work with our leaders to find a place for your specific talents and time allowance." He moved around the circle, animated by his passion for the cause as he continued. "Beautiful people of the Uprisen, we have come a long way in recent years, but I assure you it is not enough. *Never accept mediocrity*. We must each continue to give the best of ourselves to our cause, or we will not succeed." He slowed, again interlacing his fingers and flashing his trademark charismatic smile. "Thank you for your time tonight."

Lowell felt a pang of guilt. He had hung about the people of the Uprisen for the majority of his life and had benefited from their network and their resources, but hadn't really participated in their cause. It appeared he was more useful in his current capacity, though, and nobody seemed to miss him when he was away. Lowell had his own talents, possessing an artistic hand and something Hawk had referred to as a photographic memory. The old teacher had taken a particular liking to Lowell from the start, often encouraging him to arrive early for his group's lesson days to receive additional instruction. Lowell could look at any series of drawings or hear any number of words and precisely recall them hours, days, or even weeks later. This recently discovered talent had placed him smack into a central role within the Uprisen and its affiliated underground network, and being noticed made Lowell distinctly uncomfortable.

The woman called Troy rose next and walked to the center of the room. Troy was wiry, lean, and had red hair streaked with silver braided exactly eighteen plates down the length of her back. Lowell counted them each time he saw her just to be sure. She paced slowly within the inner circle. With hands clasped behind her, she stopped, planted her feet in a wide, confident stance, and lifted her head to speak.

"We are not a people rising…" she began, her voice reverberating through the otherwise silent hall. "No, my friends, we… we are a people *risen*!" Murmurs of approval circulated the room as she continued. "Risen from the dregs of the city. Risen by the Universe herself. While we appear as nothing, we act as the light-bringers to the enslaved and downtrodden. For *bond* is indeed slavery when the opportunity for upward mobility is suffocated, hope doused like the candle under its cap!"

The gathered beat their applause on the ground. Troy moved around the center circle, leaning in towards those seated around her, shaking her fist to the pulse of her own words. "We are all here as one relation. We were cast down, shrugged off by society as unworthy. Yet, my friends, I will tell you that today I am grateful for their indifference. For it is in their neglect that we have become enlightened." A broad smile animated her face, emphasizing the creases around her eyes and mouth. "I have also come here today to tell you that the time is near. The time for which we have all been working and waiting, the time to act." The gathered exchanged surprised looks and hushed words amongst themselves. "So, I now have a question for you, people of the *Uprisen*… are you ready to rise again?!"

A booming "Rah!" shook the hall. Fists and feet beat against the dirt floor, and Lowell felt every pulse in his bones. His palms sweated profusely as he sank back against the cold clay wall. That's when he saw her. The girl, Tacita, mouth clamped shut, pounding her fist on the ground by Troy's feet. Lowell barely heard Troy's call for military enlistment over the buzzing in his skull as he eyed her.

The rest of the evening, Lowell fought taut nerves and restless legs while the aspiring poets and storytellers of the *Uprisen* took turns at center stage. He watched Tacita closely. Ruya had tasked him to find this girl, learn what she was up to in the Lower Half. The job was to watch, remember, and report.

Abe was on stage now. He was older than Lowell. His shaggy brown hair was short and disheveled. Abe's cheeks burned red with the warmth of the *leaf* as he spoke.

"What's the difference between the Upper Half and the Lower Half?" he asked the crowd.

"Everything!" one voice yelled back.

"Money!" yelled another.

"We aren't lazy!" called a third.

"I'll tell you the difference..." Abe said. "The Lower Half has *all* the fun." He swung his hips in a circle as he delivered the punchline to uproarious laughter from the crowd.

Lowell leaned into his cozy corner in the Hub. He felt lulled by the warm, humming atmosphere of the gathering. The lighting was dim, the moist air cooling now as night fell, and he didn't mind all the voices and people so much this late in the evening when wine and entertainment worked to temper them. His eyelids became heavy and he let them close for just a moment.

When he came to, the people had largely dispersed. Only pockets of men and women remained, lounging and chatting amongst themselves. A few of the sit-in hosts shuffled around, picking up blankets and articles of clothing accidentally left behind. Lowell hurried to his feet, straightening his garments and repeatedly blinking to clear the sleep from his eyes. The girl was gone. At some point, while Lowell was sleeping, Tacita had left.

Panic and guilt at the lost opportunity weighed heavily on Lowell as he started off into the night. There was one person who could help him now, one who might know Tacita's whereabouts or at least have access to the information he needed to find her again. *The Gatekeeper.* Lowell wound his way through the northeastern part of the Lower Half, keeping to the alleyways, though the bustle of shift change had long died down. Those who worked the day slept soundly while the night workers were already halfway through their shift.

The Gatekeeper would have what he needed. The man had lived on the outskirts of the Uprisen since the movement began. Rumor had it he wasn't much older than Lowell then. He skipped bond, but rather than occupying street corners he had taken to smuggling wine through a series of unused underground tunnels. A clientele of various inn and barkeeps gave him access to a particularly useful network of hearsay and gossip. When the Uprisen movement began to take form, he helped the rebels navigate the underground. From that point, he protected all sorts of information and people related to the rebellion. The man also held a collection of scrolls and maps stolen from the Upper Half. The only edition ever created, it detailed every vein and artery, every trap door and hidden access point, and every last gritty detail of the intricate underground web.

It was well into the early morning hours when Lowell dug open the half-door to the Gatekeeper's pub. He walked the stone hallway, making his way with only the dim light from a nearby lantern to guide him.

"Lowell," Cairo said with surprise. "I wasn't expecting to see you tonight." Cairo tilted his head at Lowell in curiosity. "Trouble in the streets?"

"Not exactly," Lowell replied as he took a seat at one of the bar stools. "I've got some information for you if you've got *pan* and coffee to spare?"

"Coffee now?" Cairo asked with raised eyebrows. "Since when do you drink coffee, my young friend?"

"Tonight," Lowell responded, rubbing his face with his hands, trying to feel more awake. "I won't be sleeping anytime soon and hear it helps with that." He glanced up briefly to see Brac had just joined them, ducking into the room under the cellar doorway.

"Coffee it is, then," Cairo said as he placed a kettle on the stove and plopped some *pan* and an empty cup in front of Lowell. "So, what information do you offer me in trade?" Cairo had a well-established barter system. As Gatekeeper, he valued information as much as money. A patron could, if they liked, pay for food and beverage with *commeri*, but Cairo accepted information and gossip just as readily.

"The tone," Lowell began, "is changing in the underground." He paused to bite off a hunk of *pan*, speaking mostly with his eyes closed from the pain that was building behind them. Cairo waited patiently across the bar top. "Troy spoke at *gathering* tonight… well, last night. What time is it?"

"Three till change," Cairo replied with a chuckle. "Notice the empty bar?" He winked at Lowell and nodded for the boy to glance around the room.

Lowell hadn't noticed.

"Anyhow," Lowell continued, "she said the time to act is growing near and ended with a call for new military recruits."

“Good information indeed,” Cairo replied, eyebrows raised. “Anything else?”

“Yes,” Lowell hesitated. “A bit more information... with an ask.”

“Go on…”

“Do you know a girl named Tacita? She was a *Robin* with me…” his mind strayed, a robin, a bird… he brought it back. “She got picked up by Gemma about a year ago.”

“Yes. Mute. Big jagged scar across her neck…” Cairo appeared to shiver slightly at the recollection.

“That's her. She's in the Lower Half on Orville’s bidding. I'm trying to find out why.”

“At whose behest?” Cairo inquired.

Lowell hesitated, unsure if he should disclose his most recent employer.

“I need to know,” Cairo said. “Make sure I don't get my lines crossed, got it?”

“Yeah,” Lowell understood. Cairo juggled information from numerous sources and kept the lines clean with a finesse only he could manage. “Ruya.”

“Of course,” Cairo’s face brightened. “Well, what have you found so far?”

“Tacita was with the Uprisen. She was front and center at *gathering*, beating her fists on the ground with the most ardent.”

“Interesting…” Cairo observed, “and odd.” He stroked the sparse whiskers on his chin in concentration while Lowell took a few more bites. The kettle began to whistle and Cairo turned to pour the steaming water through the glass *drip*. “So, what's the ask?”

“Maps,” Lowell answered. “Nobody has seen her come or go from the Lower Half. I spent all day yesterday asking around at the inns and amongst the corner groups.”

“So you think she's gaining access from the Upper?”

"Maybe," Lowell paused for a moment, weighing his next words carefully. "Or maybe Orville's crew have their own passage?"

"That would make sense," Cairo said as he poured coffee from the *drip* into Lowell's cup. "Perhaps they've intersected one of the older tunnels in High Side?"

"That's what I'm thinking," Lowell replied, wrinkling his nose at the first sip of coffee. "Old trading passages."

"I believe…" Cairo's reply was cut short by the creek of the pub door. Lowell focused on his coffee as Cairo busied himself wiping dishes further down the bar.

"Troy, what a wonderful surprise!" Cairo exclaimed, smiling broadly.

Lowell's heart quickened as he stared into his coffee cup. He had never actually met Troy but had done her bidding through the request of her partner, Liam. Liam was a hard man, rigid in both physical appearance and in his social interactions. He neither smiled nor raised his voice, never appeared tired or overly energetic. Blunt, clear, and concise, one always knew what to expect with Liam. Troy, on the other hand, seemed cunning, more volatile by nature. Lowell's nerves felt raw at the thought of Troy discovering his current assignment. After all, Ruya's relationship with the Uprisen, or lack thereof, was slightly contentious. Thankfully, Troy took little notice of the shaggy youth perched at the end of Cairo's bar.

"Cairo, Brac, good evening… make that morning," Troy said. "Glad to see you're still open."

"Do I ever really close?" Cairo asked with a wink.

"I suppose not, old friend," Troy responded with a tired smile as she took a seat at the bar top. "Do you happen to have any goat's milk?"

"Goat's milk?" Cairo replied with mild amusement. "Well, I do, but seems a strange request. No wine?"

"Not this time," Troy replied, her tone a little less jovial. "This thing… it's all getting a bit crazy. I wonder…" she paused and Lowell barely made out her gesture in his direction.

"It's safe," Cairo assured her.

"I wonder if you might be able to bring me some clarity…" Troy continued.

"I'll do my best. But what is it that has you so frazzled at such an hour?"

"The crackdowns from the Tri and the Lex have been bad enough, but now we've been infiltrated. I didn't place the girl until after she left with a group of youth, but realized I'd seen her with Orville's servant, Isaac."

"Tacita," Cairo affirmed. "Yes, I've already heard she made her way into your meeting."

"You've heard?" Panic rose in Troy's voice. "How?"

"Well…" Cairo shrugged, "it appears you two should be the ones having this conversation."

Lowell's heart lurched into his chest. What was Cairo playing at? He of all people should know this was a dangerous game. Lowell took a deep breath, brushed his shaggy hair out of his face and looked up to meet Troy's puzzled gaze, though holding it proved to be more than his eyes could tolerate.

"You," Troy observed. "You've been helping Liam?"

"Yes, ma'am," Lowell responded, his voice raspy, wavering, as his eyes focused on the details of wood grain on the counter. He had been helping Liam navigate some of the older tunnels to create new outposts for the Uprisen for nearly a year.

"Why does Liam have you looking for this girl?"

"I had the boy on that errand," Cairo interjected.

Lowell breathed a sigh of relief as he realized Cairo's tactic. Of course the Gatekeeper would know how to navigate this exchange without giving away Ruya.

"We think Orville's men may have tunneled into one of the old trading passages in High Side," Cairo continued, "and I intend to find out where. This boy here knows our maps better than I could ever hope to. Keeps every detail stored in his head."

Lowell looked down at his hands, cheeks flushing with the unexpected praise. Not just anybody could read the maps. Their creators had hoped to prevent full knowledge of the underground from falling into the wrong hands. They were coded, each map detailing broken layers of the network without any points of context. To assemble the puzzle, one must already have familiarity with the overall underground and knowledge of at least a few access points on each map or they would become lost entirely. Cairo had learned the hard way, spending the majority of his young life getting lost in, and ultimately finding his way out of, the complex underground. But for Lowell, the layers came together in his mind. Dozens of cryptic maps meshed into one beautiful labyrinth that only he could see.

The Uprisen had recently begun restoring a number of the higher and more open tunnels, with the hope of creating a fluid underground transport. The Green Tunnels would allow the people to move about the city in full avoidance of the Lex and Orville's spying leaves.

"That's why Liam has him working with navigation," Cairo went on. "I was hoping if he followed Tacita, he might be able to discover her access point. It was not until a few moments ago that I learned she was with your people tonight, so your visit is timely, indeed."

Lowell felt Troy's gaze on him as he drained the last of his cup of coffee. He watched Cairo load a plate with pickled beets and wedged potatoes and set it on top of the bar in between Troy and Lowell.

"Ah, but how often are important conversations held over food?" Cairo asked the room, "Eat. I expect you two will have quite a lot to discuss this evening and food makes information stick."

CHAPTER 17
The Hermit

"Such silly children Sylvester has been brought to see," the crazed hermit cackled from the corner of the train car.

It was well into the morning. Dottie sat next to the fire with her forehead resting on her knees. She shivered, despite the warmth of the fire, as the combination of fear and fatigue settled into her back. She and Hudd had taken shifts through the night, while Ben and Penny slept – the one awake stoking the fire and keeping an eye on Sylvester along with Ari – yet when it was Dottie's turn, she had not been able to sleep, no matter how long she kept her eyes closed. The small fire gave off just enough warmth for comfort, but very little light. The morning brought with it a mingled sense of relief from the darkness and renewed dread at the thought of facing the day ahead.

“The leaves have brought Sylvester to see such noisy little children, indeed,” Sylvester continued.

Dottie looked up to find Hudd awake and glaring at the strange man.

“The dancing leaves do hear, you see,” Sylvester sang. “They follow.”

Dottie rested the side of her head on her knees and gazed out the windows of the train at the puffy flakes of snow drifting down from dark clouds. She wondered how much had fallen in the night, thinking how hard it would be to make their way to Aggie’s. Maybe they didn’t have to go at all. They could stay where they were and be like the Boxcar Kids from the book series she had loved when she was little.

“The leaves, they swirl,” Sylvester warbled. “They swirl. They follow. They listen.”

“What do you mean?” Hudd asked abruptly, making Dottie jump and snapping Sylvester from his sing-song trance. “What leaves?”

“The magnets,” Sylvester replied, rolling his head from side to side. “Sent to hear. They listen. They follow the noise wherever it may go.”

“Sent to hear?” Dottie echoed. “You or the leaves?”

“They. Sylvester. Both. We are *his*,” Sylvester answered, grinning wildly.

“Whose?” Dottie asked.

“The one who has sent Sylvester,” the hermit laughed. “Where is the other moon? The one must miss its friend, for one moon is such a lonely thing.”

“The guy’s a crackpot,” Hudd grumbled, placing a few small chunks of wood into the fire and prodding it with a length of stair railing. “Two moons….”

“Two moons… two worlds,” Sylvester continued, giggling.

“What’s going on?” Penny muttered, sitting up from her sleeping bag and rubbing the sleep from her eyes.

“The guy’s just talking nonsense,” Hudd said, waving dismissively at Sylvester.

Nonsense, indeed. And yet, there *had* been leaves, the swirling, humming, noisy leaves that seemed to be following them wherever they went. Dottie rose to her feet and went to the nearest window, looking for signs of them, but all she saw was falling snow.

“What are we gonna do with him?” Ben asked, sitting up and sleepily joining the conversation.

Dottie’s stomach grumbled.

“I say we just leave him here,” Hudd said bitterly.

“We can’t do that,” Penny replied indignantly. “That would be a terrible thing to do.”

“Well, he *did* attack us, so….” Hudd raised his eyebrows at Penny, who pursed her lips back at him.

“I’m sure he had a good reason,” Ben said with sarcasm, wincing as he tried to reposition his injured leg.

“Oh, you stop,” Penny said, frowning at them. “I’m serious, I don’t think he’s all there…”

“He’s definitely not all there,” Hudd cut in.

“So, we should take pity on him,” Penny said. “What do we *really* do now?”

“Well, we still need to get to Aggie’s,” Ben said, sweat gleaming on his forehead.

“We could stay here a few days,” Dottie suggested. “Maybe it’ll warm back up.”

“This wasn’t a normal snow storm, Dot. I wouldn’t count on that at this point,” Ben asked hoarsely.

“We still have some food and water,” Dottie said. “Lots of things we can turn into firewood.” Their small fire put off enough heat to keep them from freezing, but cracks in the windows and the biting cold of the early winter storm had Dottie longing to curl back up in her sleeping bag. They would need to improve the insulation of the car somehow if they wanted to stay here longer.

"Dottie, you've done a great job taking care of Ben's leg," Penny said without taking her eyes off Ben, "but I think he needs more help."

Ben's face was ashen. Dottie leaned forward and placed the back of her hand against his forehead. He was still feverish. Penny was right. They needed to get Ben to Aggie sooner rather than later.

"Let's see if we can catch a break in the storm this morning," Hudd suggested. "Dottie and I can take a short walk, get our bearings. We're maybe a couple miles from Breakneck. We climb to the top, see what we can see, then report back and go from there?"

"Why don't we all just go now?" Penny asked.

Dottie watched as Hudd looked up at Penny with a mouthful of pretzels, then around at the others while he finished chewing. His expression mirrored how drained Dottie felt, how exhausted she was.

"I think there were *more* people on this train than what we found earlier," Hudd began. "There are more bags in that luggage rack in the front than could have belonged to the bodies left behind."

"Where did they go," Ben asked, "and what would make them leave their stuff behind?"

"That's what I've been wondering. Look…" Hudd continued, sitting forward and extending an open palm as if he were about to shake hands with the fire, "evacuated neighborhoods, a derailed and abandoned train, leaves flying around like bugs, then Looney Tunes over there." He gestured to Sylvester, who was still in a trance and humming to himself. "Seems like maybe something else is going on here, and I don't want us wandering blindly with Ben in this condition. If something happens and we need to move fast…." He trailed off, leaving the thought to hang in the air.

"Well," Dottie searched for something to fill the silence, "if moving fast is what you're worried about, not sure I'm the right person to go with you." She received only frowns for her attempt to lighten the mood.

“Snow already seems to be falling a bit more slowly,” Hudd pointed out a few moments later. “Let’s just finish eating. Dottie and I will get geared up and head out, see what we’re working with, and then come back for you two. We won’t be gone long.” He nodded to Ben and Penny.

“Geared up?” Dottie asked.

“I have a few ideas,” Hudd replied, a slight smile breaking through his otherwise somber expression.

Dottie changed Ben’s bandage again after breakfast, applying more antibiotic ointment. She used alcohol wipes to clean away the oozing pus, revealing a spider web of bright red lines that spread radially around the gash.

“It's not hurting… as bad,” Ben said hoarsely as he lay back on the sleeping bag. “Arm itches like crazy though,” he went on, shivering and scratching furiously at his bicep.

“Let me see it,” Dottie instructed as she secured the clasps of the bandage around the newly treated wound.

Ben pulled his arm out from the inside of his hoodie. The tree shaped burn from the lightning strike was blistering. Dottie applied burn cream and instructed Ben not to scratch at it. Penny had said it was a relatively normal occurrence, this tree on Ben’s arm. But Dottie wasn't so sure. Something about it didn't feel right to her.

“The leaves do follow the tree,” Sylvester crooned from his corner, nodding toward Ben’s arm. “The energy in it. The energy in golden curls.”

Dottie shivered and turned back to Ben, who had appeared not to hear Sylvester’s comment. “You should try to get some sleep now,” she said, folding the flap of the sleeping bag over him and zipping him halfway in.

“Yeah, I should,” he mumbled as he closed his eyes.

Dottie turned to Penny, who sat picking at a loose thread on her jeans.

“I'll watch them,” Penny said, gesturing first to Ben and then to Sylvester.

“And keep the fire going…” Dottie added, lowering her voice in an attempt to be more instructive and less pushy. “You won't want to let it get any bigger, but don't let it die out either.”

“I can do that,” Penny replied with a sad smile.

Dottie bent down and dug through her pack for the utility belt, removing the switchblade and handing it to Penny.

“Just in case,” Dottie said. “You think you could use it… if you had to?”

Penny’s eyes widened as she reached out a shaky hand to take the knife.

“I don't know,” she muttered.

“We’ll leave Ari with you. He’s a good protector. But if you do need to use it… well, then you just *have* to. Don't overthink it, okay?”

“Okay,” Penny replied, taking the knife and returning her gaze to the little fire.

Dottie put the utility belt around her waist and grabbed her pack off the floor. She walked to the front of the car where Hudd had been tinkering with materials from one of the dining booths. She watched him work silently for a time until she understood what it was he was trying to make. The frame of the dining booths had curved pieces of wood, U-shaped. Hudd was carving notches into the wood every inch-and-a-half or so.

“I need laces, or strips, or something,” he told Dottie, gesturing to the polyester cushion cases.

Dottie grabbed a piece of the fabric and lay it flat on the floor, dropping to her hands and knees. She took out her pocket knife and sliced away long thin strips. It took most of the morning to cut and weave together the laces, but by midday, they had managed to fashion four clumsy snowshoes. With their makeshift gear in hand, Dottie and Hudd climbed down the stairs of the train car and out into the snow, leaving behind a delusional Sylvester under Ari’s guard, a sleeping Ben, and a fearful, but watchful, Penny.

The snow fell slowly. Fluffy flakes meandered their way down, joining in the waves of existing accumulation. The wind wasn’t too bad. Dottie had braced herself for worse given the volume of its howling on the *inside* of the train. She sat on the bottom step and strapped on the snowshoes as Hudd had just done. He was already making his way cautiously out in the snow.

"They're terrible," Hudd called, looking back at her over his shoulder, beaming, cheeks rosy from both the cold and the rush of pride and impending adventure, "but they work." He lifted his hands in the air as if he were flying on top of a cloud, rather than balancing precariously on the uneven drifts of snow.

Dottie allowed herself to relax a little, momentarily relieved from the crushing weight of sorrow. They owed sorrow nothing. They could smile, laugh, be free in this moment. It didn't mean they didn't miss the ones they had lost, the ones that had been taken. It meant they were refusing to allow death and darkness to cheat them of the beauty that still existed.

"Well," Hudd called from farther away, "you coming, or what?"

Dottie rose slowly to her feet on the makeshift snowshoes, laughing with nervous energy, invigorated by the crisp, cold air. The shoes were flimsy, but did the trick. She shuffled over to Hudd, becoming surer the further she went. They exchanged triumphant nods before heading silently off in the direction of Breakneck.

It was mid-afternoon when Dottie and Hudd padded up over the top of Breakneck Hill Road. Dottie slid a few yards down on the heels of her snowshoes before sinking completely to the ground, oblivious to the snow melting through her jeans.

"You seeing this?" Hudd said, his voice wavering uncharacteristically.

She followed his gaze out to the horizon. A shiver ran down her spine, though just a few moments ago she'd been sweating from their hike. Where she expected to see a sea of orange, red, and yellow treetops extending for miles, she saw the ocean. It was a mile away, maybe two. Instead of trees and buildings, homes and roads, the vast blue ocean rose and fell. Dottie glanced up and noticed that the clouds were different here, too–like a kaleidoscope reflection of the waves below, the dark clouds formed an ominous pattern.

"That's the ocean," she stated.

"Yes, it is."

"Well…" Dottie trailed off.

"What the hell is it doing here?" Hudd asked, to which Dottie had no reply.

And there, down at the base of the hill, along the newly defined coastline of an ocean that belonged some thirty or forty miles further away, she could just make out a swarm of swirling gold leaves.

"We need to move," she said hurriedly, pointing in the direction of the leaves, which crept towards them up the hillside. It was almost like they were trying to eavesdrop.

They listen.

Dottie and Hudd trudged back, following the tracks they had made earlier. They moved in silence, overwhelmed by confusion. The ocean was *here*, miles from where it was supposed to be, eerie and mirrored by those strange clouds. The snowfall picked up again as they started walking, gusts of wind that penetrated Dottie's soaked jeans. They weren't enough for this weather. She should have brought some snow pants from Penny's house. Despite feet that ached from the cold, days of walking and a mind that was increasingly unsettled, she willed herself forward. She had lost sight of the golden swarm by the time they made it back to the train, but her unease remained.

Hudd stopped at the corner of the derailed car that partially blocked the view of their own. As Dottie approached, she realized why he had stopped. Ben was standing in the middle of the snow a few yards from the train, his back to them, heaving as he fought to catch his breath. He reminded Dottie of a boxer waiting for the last round of a fight. Beaten, maybe even bloodied, but still coiled in that deeply ingrained and instinctive defensive posture. And across from Ben, just feet away, Sylvester rose to his feet, blood trickling from the corner of his mouth. He threw his hair out of his face and sneered at Ben defiantly. And then there was Penny. She was standing just behind Sylvester, legs pressed together like a baby deer, knock-kneed and vulnerable. She remained frozen, gripping the switchblade with both hands while tears rolled down her cheeks. Ari's bellowing bark echoed inside the train car.

Sylvester leaned forward and dove at Ben, tackling him back to the ground. Spurred into motion, Hudd barreled toward the pair. Dottie looked back up at Penny. It would take too long to shuffle around the brawl if she went one direction, and going the other way could end with her becoming jammed between them and the side of the train. The snow was higher there, drifted up against the car. Dottie was essentially trapped. Penny needed to use the knife, go for Sylvester's legs, do something to break things up. *Move.*

"Use it!" Dottie yelled to Penny.

The sound of Dottie's voice brought Penny out of her daze. She turned, eyes wide, shook her head, and dropped the knife into the snow, stumbling backward until she fell over the bottom step of the train car's stairway.

"Damn it," Dottie muttered. She sidestepped over a drift of snow until she could reach out and hold onto a ledge of the derailed car. As she shuffled forward, working her way around the inside toward Penny, the battling trio closed in on her. She was almost to Penny and could see the knife, gleaming in the snow. If she could just get a little further.

A shoulder crashed into her rib cage, driving her into the side of the train. Her legs became wedged under tumbling bodies, pressing down into the snow. She gripped at the window ledge with the tips of her fingers, trying to pull herself up. Her eyes locked with Ben's as his head slammed into her hand. She yelled out and released her grip on the ledge, fingers throbbing from the impact, pain radiating into her wrist and elbow.

"Get out, Dottie," Ben said through gritted teeth.

She reached her other hand down to her hip and pushed against the loose powder, snow blowing into her face. A foot kicked into her stomach, driving the air from her lungs and wedging her body deeper in the snow. She gasped, opening her mouth wider in an attempt to inhale. Her lungs failed to inflate for what seemed like minutes.

"I can't," she whispered as soon as her breath returned. A panicked whimper escaped her. The memory of being caught at the base of a tree with her skis still on her feet flashed through her mind. It had been like quicksand. She had gotten too close to the tree, sliding backward into the enormous trunk and sinking slowly into the deceptively deep drifts of snow piled there. Panic had overtaken her until Dad pulled her out. He had told her afterward that the worst thing she could do was panic. The more she flailed, the deeper she would sink as the layer of snow under her would be pushed to the sides.

Dottie leaned her head back against the side of the train and closed her eyes, allowing the stray blows from the fight to catch her as they came. She reminded herself that reacting to pain was an option, not a requirement. Calmly, she opened her eyes. Ben had managed to end up next to her, his feet braced against the train. He leaned his shoulder into the mass of limbs and drove them back enough for Dottie to slide up the side of the car and return to a standing position. Ben staggered forward into the struggle. Hudd was behind Sylvester, his arm around the snarling hermit's neck. Sylvester was driving his elbows repeatedly into Hudd's ribs. Dottie pulled her feet free from the snowshoes and struggled forward. She watched as Ben collapsed into a heap a few yards from Hudd and Sylvester. Sylvester slipped out of Hudd's headlock and turned on him, knocking him to the ground with one fierce blow.

Dottie's legs felt heavy as she pulled each out of the snow, continuing forward. Ben yelled in frustration and pain from where he was stuck in the snow. Penny's sobs echoed from higher up the stairs as Sylvester hovered over an unconscious Hudd, laughing. His laugh turned into a menacing growl, but then a second growl joined in. And down from the train barreled Ari. He headed straight for Sylvester. Plummeting through the drifts of snow, he lunged and clamped down hard on Sylvester's thigh. A high-pitched scream filled the air as Sylvester tried to pull away from Ari. The dog released his grip and charged forward, snarling and snapping as Sylvester stumbled backward, cursing. He turned away and crashed, limping, into the trees.

Dottie watched in awe as Ari came lumbering towards her with his beautiful, open-mouthed smile, tail wagging furiously. He lay next to her in the snow, nuzzling into her neck, grunting with happiness.

CHAPTER 18
The Warrior

The *magie's* scream sent a shiver up Haddi's spine and spurred him into motion. He retreated slowly until his back hit the wall. Turning and shoving the toe of his shoe into the only foothold he could find, he launched himself awkwardly up the side of the pocket. Haddi looked up in surprise as his hand caught hold of a ledge that had not been there seconds before. He pulled himself higher, flinging his other hand up and snagging yet another small ledge that appeared exactly where it was needed. He moved quickly, hand-over-hand, ascending with a determination fueled by the angry *magié* below him and confidence that grew with each inch upward.

Sweating and panting, Haddi dug his fingers into the cold ground at the top of the tunnel. He braced himself for one last thrust into the air, pressed the outside of his feet into the walls on either side of him, and drove up. His hips and arms extended in one fluid movement to bring his body out into the crisp mountain air.

He sat at the edge of the tunnel, letting his eyes adjust from darkness to the hazy light of a cloud covered day. A storm must have moved in while he was in the cavern. There were no trees around him, no shrubs, just ominous mountains of moss-covered *gelb* slate, dusted lightly with snow. He rose to his feet, backing away from the tunnel, finding it curious that the angered *magié* had not followed him. The sound of their hum and the ground vibrating beneath him made him feel ill at ease. The heel of his boot sank through a patch of crusty ice-covered mud. He stopped, turning slowly and realizing he was standing at the edge of a placid lake. The lip of the deep blue *clearwater* was only a few paces away, and he could barely make out the opposite bank. Far to his right, the water rippled as it appeared to fall off the edge of the horizon. Rivulets tumbled down from sheer cliffs of stacked slate and into the water from the other three sides.

Haddi squatted down on one heel and seized a clump of icy mud. The cut on his thumb, the one from the broken bottle of *magié* milk, had disappeared. Had he dreamt what happened in the cavern? Hallucinated? He took a closer look at where the glass had sliced but saw only a pale pink scar. Haddi was about to toss his handful of mud into the water when he heard a menacing growl.

For a moment, he contemplated not even turning around. He could just stay there, let his mind and soul get lost in the beauty that was before him and surrender to whatever was behind him – a bear, or maybe a mountain lion. Whether he made it to Mundabi or went to a different place entirely mattered little. He was worn down. He wished to be free of the demons that continued to torment his heart. Amar was sixteen and could probably take better care of himself than Haddi could at this point. He had taught the boy well, though it wasn't really a difficult task. Amar was brilliant, sure-handed. These days Haddi spent more time feeling like a burden to the boy, like he was the one who needed caring for, instead of the other way around. Perhaps Haddi could finally let go. And yet… a powerful emotion, curiosity. Haddi turned to face the rumbling at his back.

“What do ye think yer doin’ there?” A stout, bearded Irdish woman stood before him, arms crossed.

He offered no reply as he stared blankly. She was only the second of the trollian lineage that Haddi had encountered in his lifetime, and she caught him just as off guard as the first. This woman was built just like Trude, though perhaps a little older, more worn and rough around the edges, as if she’d fought a hundred battles. She barely passed his waist in height, but her girth doubled his circumference.

“Well?” she shook her fist at Haddi, demanding an answer.

“I, uh…” he trailed off, struggling to gather his thoughts. “I was just going to see if I could tell how deep the water was.”

“Deep enough,” the woman grumbled, “deep enough t’ swallow ye whole when I send ye into it. Cold, too.”

“I guessed as much,” Haddi replied, “about the water being cold that is, not you chucking me in.” An amusing thought, the idea of this woman hurling him into the inky water. She appeared fierce enough to make a light task of it.

“Ye don't seem t’ be too shaken by the idea,” she observed.

“I've faced darker things than death,” Haddi replied as he began wiping mud from the sides of his pants. He had always found the tunics worn by the Alterran people to be cumbersome and impractical, but it wasn’t until his dream about the golden-haired girl with her strange clothing that it occurred to him to fashion something different. He had time to spare in the early days after Shia’s death, once Nobi was secured, and focused a good part of his energy on making the pants. Haddi was grateful to have them, especially when scaling vertical tunnels to escape angry fairies. Yet, even after all this time, he had never really understood the point of the knee holes.

“Ay, I expect ye have,” the woman replied. “For the spirits t’ push ye all the way out the top like that. 'Tis a mixed soul they'll reject yet not devour.”

“A mixed soul?”

"Mixed," she repeated. "Darkened from the outside, yet not from within. Exposed t' the darkness, yet not consumed by it. Burnt, yet alive."

If it weren't for the dark things that he'd done with his hands, the death they had inflicted, Haddi might have believed that his soul was still somehow alive. Shriveled, struggling, yet still trying to exist. But he alone knew the carnage and desolation that he had both witnessed and perpetrated.

"Yer name," the Irdish woman demanded.

"Haddi," he replied.

"Ay…" she said.

Haddi thought he caught a glimpse of surprise in her expression.

"I'm Greta of the Mossgrown Irden," she added.

"Is that North or South?" Haddi remembered Trude discussing the coup that had taken place amongst the Old Irden, how she had been made to leave her home and settle further south in the Scalas.

"South," Greta replied, glaring at him now. "Old. And how do ye even know t' ask that question?"

"Years ago, I met an Old Irdish woman… 'of the ancient clans, not the rebels,'" Haddi recounted in Trude's brogue accent, though Greta didn't seem amused by the impression. "She saved my life."

"Well then that makes this a duplicate occurrence," Greta huffed.

"You're saving my life?" Haddi asked, unable to hide his smile.

"In ways you might never realize," she responded, a frown passing over her face. "Now, are ye goin' t' answer my question?"

"Question?"

"What do ye think yer doin' here?" The woman shifted impatiently, arms still wrapped around her broad chest.

"I guess I don't really know," Haddi replied, trying to buy some time. He knew exactly why he was here. He had let the darkness in his mind grow too strong while he was under the falls. He knew better, yet it had been almost out of his control. The emotionally driven *magié* had sensed his thoughts and could endure his presence no longer.

"Ye don't eh?" Greta raised her eyebrows at Haddi. "Ain't been a human up this way for thousands of years. The spirits have seen t' that. Excellent guardians, they are. But now it appears they've spit ye out right in front of me."

"Where am I, exactly?"

"Ye mean ye don't know?" Greta's eyebrows raised in surprise. "Yer in the higher realms, the realms of the spirit. Ye humans were banished from here long ago when a few of ye decided ye were better off without the Universe in yer lives. Plain foolishness, if ye ask me. Ain't nobody can escape the gift and discipline of the Universe. But up here, well, things are sacred, not t' be disturbed by the selfishness of men."

"I didn't intend to end up here," Haddi said defensively.

"Oh, I believe ye," Greta replied as she pulled a length of rope from her belt. "Ye know, our paths take us only t' the places we are meant t' be, Haddi. And yet, until I find out what exactly that meaning is this time, and how my fate is interwoven with it… I ain't gonna trust ye none."

Haddi braced himself as Greta strode toward him with the rope. She bound his wrists tightly behind his back with one end and held firmly to the other. He cringed as he recalled the leashes the Lex officers used for their dogs.

"Walk forward," Greta ordered. "Follow the lake and don't stop until I tell ye."

Haddi complied. He wasn't really in a position to argue, given the array of sharp and lethal objects attached to Greta's waist and possessing no such weaponry himself. He marched in silence with the Irdish woman close behind. She gave no further instruction, but huffed and grumbled as they went. His bare feet went from freezing to numb as the day waned. The ground was made of compressed clusters of darkened *gelb* stone. He was able to make out slight yellow trails of the mineral beneath his feet. The water itself was indeed *clearwater*, but a grainy indigo muck settled underneath, giving the lake an ominous appearance.

There was no sign of life. No fish in the water nor birds in the air, no goats on the cliff, not even the tracks of any wild creature. The water was still. The air was still. But Haddi's mind was not.

The sun began to dip down behind the drop off of the falls. Mesmerizing rays of sunlight bounced off the almost black surface of the water. The sunset graduated from orange to crimson, then purple as it stretched upward and outward into the infinite. Losing himself in the Universe's magical painting and suddenly overcome with weariness, Haddi stumbled. Greta yanked the rope that bound his wrists, dropping him backward so that he did not slide into the lake.

"We'll make camp here," she muttered.

Haddi sat in grateful silence as he watched Greta unload a sack of wood from her back.

"The journey around the lake is normally two days," Greta explained. "Might take three if ye don't keep yer head down and stay on course. Ye don't want t' go tumbling into that lake now. It's colder than ye might think."

Haddi's cheeks reddened slightly at the admonishment.

"We'll need to make this wood last," she went on. "Not going to find any more fuel for a fire out here." She stacked a few of the logs to one side.

"That won't burn more than a few hours," Haddi observed.

"Ye said ye met someone like me before, did ye?" Greta asked without acknowledging his concern. "Another of the old clans?"

"Yes," Haddi replied. "A long time ago. She called herself Trude, traveled with a Tor named Jeg."

Greta turned slowly to face Haddi, her prominent brow furrowed with a look that indicated either concern or disapproval, though Haddi was not sure which. She looked him up and down before returning to her work.

"I know the both," Greta muttered. She took a small metal pickaxe from her belt and began crawling around on all fours on top of a large slab of *gelb* stone, running her hand along its surface, tracing the yellow lines. Greta glanced up at Haddi before driving the pickaxe into one of the pale veins. She worked swiftly, picking away chunks of the yellow mineral, placing them into a small leather pouch at her waist.

"They showed me the *magié* clearing," Haddi added.

"Did they now?" Greta asked. "And did they tell ye what yer name means?"

"Yes," Haddi answered. "Where am I?" he asked for the second time that day, not satisfied with the first response.

"Where do ye think ye are?" Greta responded as she knelt down by the firewood.

"You said this was a spiritual realm."

"I did," Greta confirmed, removing a wooden pestle and mortar from her pack. She began crushing the *gelb* into a powder.

"This is not Mundabi… " Haddi knew that much.

"No," she replied with a soft smile. "Just one step closer, ye could say."

Haddi watched as Greta took a brush made from *hoch* needles from her belt, dipped it lightly into the water's edge, then used it to stir the *gelb* powder into a bright yellow paste.

"Do ye have ladders in Alterra?" Greta asked.

"Yes," Haddi replied, bristling at the apparent change in topic. "We did when I was young, though I haven't been within the city walls for many years."

"Really?" She raised her eyebrows in surprise. "A story for ye to tell me at another time perhaps. For now, I have one t' share." Greta brushed the yellow *gelb* paste onto the tops and sides of each piece of firewood.

"There is a story told amongst the Irden... in the time when the Universe was present amongst the creatures of Sum, and yer kind stood united with the Irden and the Tor. There was a ladder that one could climb either up or down. Down went the way to Incendi, up t' enlightenment." Greta paused to concentrate as she leaned the newly painted logs against one another.

Haddi waited eagerly, captivated both by her words and his curiosity over the purpose of the *gelb* painted wood.

"With each rung down," Greta continued, "the descended would become more anxious, saddened, disturbed. Physical pains would wrack the body. Yet, he or she would begin to crave more pain. Voices would urge them to go just a little bit further, promising the deepest desires o' their hearts. The further down one went, the more difficult it would be t' remember the way back up."

She began knocking stone against a piece of flint, throwing sparks into the center of the carefully stacked wood where she had placed the brush of *hoch* needles. "There was ne'er a one who made it back after crossing a certain point. So, we only guess how that part o' the way appears. Up from center was more complex. One had to work harder to scale the rungs against spitting rain and snow, fog, cold, enchantment. Atrofi might be considered one such rung. The *magié* you encountered, they are the spiritual gatekeepers for the highest steps, the spiritual realms."

A lone spark took to the brush, but no flame rose from it. A small blood red pool began to form in the place where the spark hit, the redness trailing outward slowly toward the logs on all sides. Greta continued her story.

"Now, the benefit o' the way up is this… the higher one can climb, the more significantly the strength of the Universe becomes a noticeable presence. The climb does not become easier, but the ascended become stronger from Her light. This place you have reached? This place is called Caerula and comes before Erit, which is believed t' be the highest point one could reach on the ladder before becoming entirely joined with the Universe. 'Tis the only path a *living* being can take to reach Mundabi."

A low blue flame grew like a halo around the logs as the crimson caught the wood. The unassuming fire put forth so much heat that Haddi had to back away to find comfort.

"No, the *magié* would not have let you pass," Greta went on, "if you were not indeed pure of spirit. Universe knows it took me nearly forty years of repeated attempts to humble myself enough to navigate past them. What it ultimately took was brokenness. In our brokenness, we lean on the only things that can save us–truth, faith, light–and in doing so we are washed clean of the hurt and pain we have either caused or experienced in a lifetime."

"Well, they must have made a mistake with me," Haddi replied, breaking his silence. "Broken I may indeed be, but that happened a long time ago, and I have been cleansed of nothing." This Irdish woman was wrong about him, just as the other had been. The *magié* were wrong about him. They must not know the things he had witnessed, thought, executed.

"The *magié* do not make mistakes," Greta replied calmly.

"I've done things," Haddi growled.

"We've all done things," Greta countered.

"I've killed men," Haddi shot back with more venom than he had intended. The look of surprise he anticipated from Greta never appeared. "I failed the first person I was ever given to love and protect," he went on. "I failed our child by not protecting her. I failed her because I was selfish and short-sighted, because I ignored the demons when I might have addressed them, because I thought I could depend on the Universe to protect us. But I was wrong. We are nothing, and to nothing we shall return when we die."

"Oh, but Haddi, ye were not wrong," Greta sighed, staring into the blue warmth. "We are all *sum*, Haddi. We simply *are*... I *am,* you *are*. We can pull and push as much as we like, strain against the momentum o' our existence, believing we have control over the direction we take, but 'tis a futile effort. All ye have control o'er in life is yer own perspective. The rest is up t' the Universe."

"Then the Universe is a selfish mistress," he said.

"Selfish only in Her love for us. She knows what she's doin' in our lives, Haddi. Ye may not see it now, nor even years from now, but in the end, it will all become clear. Humility is Her greatest gift, for it is where true freedom lies. Mundabi is indeed for the least among us."

Haddi glared into the blue halo of warmth.

"You know, Haddi," Greta continued, "there is energy in everything, in each one of us. We – the creatures, the plants, the water – we are all at once drawn t' and pressed away from one another in a delicate symbiosis. The problem is, if a force comes along that is strong enough to throw off that balance, the only way t' correct it is t' find an equally strong force t' push it back the other way, ye understand?"

"Not really," he replied, shaking his head.

"Look, there's a negative force at play in the Universe…"

"Orville."

"Yes," Greta agreed, "but there is another force who will come t' push things back into balance."

"The girl with the golden crown…" Haddi said, once again mimicking the accent of the other Irdish woman who had long ago discussed the salvation prophecy with him, though it was already well known by the people of Alterra.

"Ay." For the first time, a hint of something that could have been a smile crossed Greta's face. "Did Trude tell ye the rest, that there is one who would come before, clear the way?"

"She said that was me," Haddi replied, "but like I told you, she was wrong."

"She was not wrong. In the ancient tongue, yer name most closely translates into 'guide' or 'leader.' But in the context of the sacred Gelb, 'tis more accurately broken down as 'the one who lights the way.' 'Tis this light that the *magié* must have seen in you."

Haddi shook his head and chuckled. First Trude, now Greta. At some point, these people would be disappointed when they realized that their prophecy for salvation relied on a chronically flawed and bitter castoff.

“Ye need not be great t’ do great things, Haddi. Ye just need t’ be open to lettin’ the Universe work through ye. And the time for that is drawing near.”

He watched the Irdish woman gaze into the fire. She appeared suddenly tired, drained, as he now remembered Trude had been after talking of the prophecy.

“The circle will soon be complete. As we are all *sum*, Haddi, our fates are all on a continuum of *Pi*. No matter how hard we may fight, at some point, we will all end where we began.”

CHAPTER 19

The Leaves

Dottie dragged her numb feet forward, step after step. The snow had stopped falling and became more compact as the temperature rose, allowing them to walk without the snowshoes.

They had wasted little time packing up and moving on after Hudd came to. They didn't stop to assess or treat their injuries or to find out how exactly Sylvester got loose. There was no time to discuss what Hudd and Dottie found on their scouting trip. Dottie had grabbed her pack and sleeping bag, stuffed a few bottles of water into the pack, and ordered a hysterical Penny to do the same. But she had not taken the time to scour the train car for anything that might still be useful. She hadn't even checked the cash register. Was money even something that they needed anymore?

Driven by fear and fueled by the last dregs of adrenaline, the battered group made their way up and over Breakneck Hill Road. They paused only briefly as they came over the top for Hudd to lower Ben to the ground and rest. Ben and Penny saw the new coast for the first time, neither reacting to the realization that the ocean had migrated some thirty or forty miles inland. Was it that nothing surprised them anymore? Or could their brains simply not comprehend something so enormous? Somehow, they managed to forge ahead, and they found themselves walking up the path to Aggie's back door as the sun dipped below the horizon.

Aggie ushered the kids inside, scanning the woods and securing the door behind them. Dottie heard the deadbolt engage and watched as the woman turned to the children now huddled about her kitchen. Aggie was in her sixties, wiry in appearance, with long, salt-and-pepper hair. Her green eyes and colorful, high-waisted skirt reminded Dottie of a Romani.

"I've been expecting you all," she said, gesturing for them to sit. She looked from Ben to Penny to Hudd, then to Dottie, her gaze lingering on her mess of golden curls. "Where to begin?"

"You've been expecting us?" Dottie inquired.

"Oh, dear, yes. You're Dottie?"

"Uh, yes, but…"

"And how about you two?" She interrupted, gesturing at the others.

"That's Hudd Mead," Ben answered, "and Penny Tackett. They're from our neighborhood."

"Nice to meet you all, though I wish it were under more pleasant circumstances." Aggie turned her back to the table and stood on tiptoe to rifle through a cabinet of amber vials of varying sizes, mumbling to herself.

Dottie felt tension rise in her chest. How had Aggie known to expect them? Did she and Ben have some sort of pre-arranged plan for where to meet in a crisis? And she somehow knew her name, but not Hudd's or Penny's.

Dottie looked around the room as Aggie searched through the clanking vials. It was not a large kitchen, but it was well furnished with cherry cabinets and an old wood burning stove that filled the room with warmth. Houseplants were shoved into every possible space. Baskets and bundles of dried herbs hung from hooks over the one small window. A doorway at the back had been boarded off and draped with a floor runner. A set of four stairs to Dottie's left led down into a hallway with angled windows along the outside. Aggie appeared to have an entire greenhouse in there. Dottie inhaled the familiar fragrance of basil and saw the plant growing nearby. A single white and purple orchid bloomed on a shelf by her elbow.

"Okay, you first," Aggie directed as she approached Ben. She unscrewed the lid from one of the vials and poured a few tiny white pellets into the cap. "Now you all watch what I'm doing, 'cause I'm gonna have you do the same. Under the tongue."

Ben obediently opened his mouth, allowing Aggie to place the little beads under his tongue. She repeated the process with two more bottles before moving on to Hudd.

"Same for you now," she instructed. "Open and under the tongue."

Hudd complied, a subtle amusement playing in his eyes, as did Penny, though her expression remained devoid of any emotion.

"What are those?" Dottie asked once she swallowed the last of the beads.

"Remedies," Aggie responded, as if that somehow answered Dottie's question.

With the "remedies" administered, Aggie gave Penny, Hudd, and Dottie a quick once-over. Penny, having frozen up during the altercation with Sylvester, was no worse for the wear physically. Hudd had a mild concussion and a broken nose from the battle, but he made light of both. Stray kicks from the brawl had bruised Dottie's ribs, and two of her fingers were broken where Ben's head had smashed them into the side of the train car. She had hardly noticed the pain while they were walking. Whether from the cold or the adrenaline, it wasn't until she entered the warm kitchen that she became aware of her injuries.

"They don't need to be set at least," Aggie said, firmly pressing Dottie's wrist between the palms of her hands.

The pressure from Aggie's warm hands momentarily relieved the throbbing that pulsed up her arm. Dottie watched as Aggie broke a couple of popsicle sticks in half, using the pieces and some tape to splint the broken fingers.

"How are you feeling?" Aggie asked when she was done.

There was something about Aggie, her tone of voice, the warmth in it, that made Dottie want to tell her everything. Everything she felt, thought, and feared; every detail and memory that tormented her; the anxiety that plagued her, the headaches, the panic attacks. But she pushed all of that aside.

"I'm fine," she mumbled in response.

"Fine?" Aggie's eyebrows raised. "With what you all have been through the last few days, I'd wager you're just about anything but fine… anxious?"

"A little," Dottie replied.

"Skeptical?" Aggie asked, the corners of her mouth turning up into the slightest of smiles.

"Very," Dottie responded firmly.

Aggie continued the questioning, ignoring Dottie's reluctance to open up. "Anything hurt besides your side and hand?"

"My head," Dottie said. *My heart.*

"What have your dreams been like?"

"My dreams?"

"Yes. Clear? Foggy? Good? Bad?"

"Bad," Dottie admitted, "vivid… and weird. Morbid, with this strange door and snow that burns my hands." She looked down into her lap, embarrassed by what she had just said in front of the others. She needed to get more control over herself. This wasn't about her, this mess they found themselves in, and here she was complaining about bad dreams while people were dead and the ocean had relocated.

"Mmm, burning snow…" Aggie trailed off as she returned from the cabinet of remedies. "Open," she told Dottie, throwing a few more pellets under Dottie's tongue.

"Thank you," Dottie said quietly, not sure how to respond to the special attention. "Um, Aggie… Ben's probably the worst off of all of us. His leg's pretty torn up, and he has a burn on his arm."

"Benjamin Rutledge," Aggie scolded, turning on Ben, whose face flushed at her stern tone. "Why didn't you say something?"

"I figured I'd take the longest," he replied with a pained smile. "Wanted everybody else to get settled first."

"Up on the table," Aggie commanded. "Always trying to be a damn hero," she muttered as she moved quickly, unwrapping the bandage and gauze Dottie had applied the last time she cleaned the wound.

Dottie felt a growing warmth fill her stomach and a tingling buzz run along her scalp. Some of the panic that had been brewing in her chest began to subside. Perhaps it had something to do with those little white beads, or maybe some of the tension and fear from the last few days was beginning to ease here in the comfort of the cozy kitchen.

"This is going to take a little while," Aggie told them once she uncovered Ben's leg. "You all head on down past the garden, take a right. There are some snacks on the coffee table, afghans on the back of the couch if you're cold. Do me a favor and see if the fire needs some upkeep," she said to Hudd as he and Penny shuffled down the stairs.

"Can I stay and help?" Dottie asked.

"No, dear, go rest," Aggie replied. "This won't be the most pleasant thing, though at this point I gather you've seen worse. We'll join you in a few."

Dottie wandered the length of the hall-turned-greenhouse, stopping periodically to examine a vegetable or wonder about some unidentifiable bit of foliage. The last sliver of sunlight was escaping from the edge of the horizon, giving the indoor garden a hazy, dreamlike appearance. The end of the hall opened into a circular room, lined with shelves that looked ready to burst at the seams with books and reams of papers. A doorway to the right led to the living room, where Dottie could hear the fire crackling and Hudd humming to himself.

In the opposite window, a small desk sat buried under even more books and loose sheets of paper, pens, and something else that caught Dottie's eye. Here among the chaos on the desktop, barely noticeable in the dim light of the room, rested dozens of lifeless, metallic gold leaves. She took a few steps forward, squinting to be sure. But there they were, the magical leaves that had been haunting them throughout their journey, though they were much less intimidating in this sedentary state. She could see now that each one was engraved with two letters: O-Z. A lump rose in Dottie's throat.

Aggie had closed off the doorway at the end of the living room as she had done to the one in the kitchen. Penny sat curled into a Papasan chair, hugging herself and staring blankly into the fire as Hudd added another log. Dottie pulled an olive-green afghan from the back of the couch, wrapped it around her shoulders and sank into the cushions, one leg tucked underneath her. Ari jumped up and snuggled in next to her. She was warm, exhausted, and as safe as she could hope to be, at least for the moment. She made up her mind to ask Aggie about the leaves once Ben's leg was taken care of. For now, it was enough to be inside a home.

Hudd caught her gaze and smiled. It was far different from the confident grin she had always expected from him before last week. The creases at the corner of his eyes contained more sadness than mirth and his mouth softened while his chin tilted down. They had gotten here together, somehow, making it through the chaos, loss, and uncertainty. The four of them had somehow survived. Who knew what the future held for them? For now, it was enough to rest here in the warm room. She closed her eyes.

The painted door stands guard over trolls, giants, and fairies. She reaches out to trace the carvings in the wood. Her hand begins to burn. Something to her left catches her eye. It looks like a giant moth. Its body, antennae, and wings are iridescent, white with a tinge of blue and purple, like an opal, her birthstone. It hovers closer to her, fiery red eyes piercing her own.

"They listen," it whispers, before fluttering up the mountainside.

She takes a step back to watch it rise and hears a crunch. She looks down. Beneath her feet lie metallic gold leaves. They begin to hum and float together, raising her inches off the ground.

∝

Dottie's eyes opened and it took her a moment to recognize Aggie's living room. Morning light filtered in through the windows, waking her gradually from a sound sleep and bringing a sense of renewed warmth, casting out the fears that had haunted her through the night.

"Coffee?" Aggie walked into the room with a blue enamel percolator and a handful of mugs.

Dottie never really drank coffee, but the smell that filled the room was enticing.

"Yes, please," she replied, sitting up to stretch her back and rubbing the sleep from her eyes.

Ben was sitting next to her on the couch, sipping a glass of orange juice.

"Morning, Dot," he said.

"You don't look quite like hell anymore," she replied with a playful smile.

"Did I hear coffee?" Hudd picked his head up off the floor, eyes half open. The way his hair stood up flat on one side made Dottie snort.

"Yes, you did," Aggie replied.

"Penny, what about you, dear?" Aggie asked.

Penny was awake now but still cocooned in the chair. She shook her head without looking away from the fire. Dottie noticed that Penny looked more drained after sleeping than she did the night before. She was stone-faced, devoid of the happiness she had once radiated. As much as that charisma had once annoyed Dottie, she found that she missed it now.

Aggie poured the coffee and handed mugs to Dottie and Hudd. Dottie briefly considered asking for milk or cream, but getting used to drinking it black was probably best. It wasn't like she could go to the store for more milk.

"Alright, I think it's time for me to fill you all in then," Aggie said as she sat in her rocking chair. "So… where to begin?"

"There was an earthquake," Hudd suggested.

"Yes and no," Aggie replied. "The phenomenon that took place last Friday night did indeed seem to be an earthquake, a terrible one I might add, but it was not caused by the collision of layers of the Earth's crust, as quakes traditionally are. There was another force that generated the seismic activity." Aggie placed her crocheting in her lap. "When I was in grad school, I had a fellow student who was really into things like radios and magnets. He did some pretty interesting work, actually. The problem was that he never took adequate precautions, didn't follow the ethics or guidelines that other scientists did. No respect for boundaries. He disappeared suddenly forty years ago."

"What happened to him?" Ben asked.

"We had no idea… then," Aggie replied with raised eyebrows, still rocking. "Last we heard, he stole a good deal of equipment from the lab and took off into the Appalachians, chasing some random frequency readings he had picked up during his field research there."

"What was his name?" Dottie asked, suspicion dawning.

"Orville," Aggie answered. "And then, a few weeks ago, I received a package from an old colleague named Levi Hill. Levi, Orville and I had all been in school together. Well, Lee's team in D.C. stumbled on something that had Orville's signature literally stamped onto it and sent it my way for a second opinion. That man could turn anything into a machine, I swear."

“Even leaves,” Dottie interjected, no longer able to stop the web of connections weaving together in her mind.

“Precisely,” Aggie replied, her tone as grim as her expression.

“*They listen*,” Dottie mumbled to herself, recalling what the moth-like fairy had whispered in her dream, what Sylvester had repeated again and again in what they had all assumed were fits of insanity.

“They do,” Aggie affirmed, tilting her head to one side and considering Dottie. “They pick up and transport radio frequencies. How do you know that?”

“The humming,” Dottie said, sidestepping the question, “it’s like radio static or something, right?”

“In a way,” Aggie said, her brow furrowed. “They have had an awful lot to say about you.”

Dottie felt a sense of relief as she realized that her suspicions from the night before were more because of the leaves themselves than about Aggie. “That’s how you knew to expect us.”

“Yes,” Aggie replied with a slow nod, “and more…”

“Aggie,” Hudd interrupted from the floor before Dottie could ask another question. “Where did everybody go?”

“Well, Orville was behind the quake,” Aggie began to explain. “From some of the messaging I’ve been able to intercept… look, when we were in school, Orville thought those readings he picked up were from an alternate dimension.”

“An alternate… like another world?” Ben asked.

“Like another world,” Aggie answered. “These leaves, they don’t just transport what we *want* them to. They pick up and send everything within their range. So, I have been able to gather little snippets of information from this other side. Orville is indeed alive and well in this other world. He created some sort of pulse that caused the quake.”

“This *cannot* be real,” Hudd said skeptically.

“Look around you,” Aggie directed. “These are the only living faces you’ve seen for days, am I correct?”

“Except for the convicts and the crazy guy,” Hudd replied.

“Yes, except for them,” Aggie said. “You asked where everybody went? Well, this pulse actually changed the way the two worlds line up, though I haven’t quite figured out how. Nothing that runs off magnets or batteries works right now. No generators, no vehicles…”

“No trains,” Dottie added.

“Right,” Aggie said. “Now, this didn’t all happen immediately. Best I can tell, it took a matter of hours for full shutdown. In that time, the tools our first responders normally use to read chemical and nuclear activity went haywire. Law enforcement ordered a mass evacuation of residents toward the coast, where readings seemed to be lower. That’s when the tsunami hit.” She set her crocheting down in her lap and took her mug from the window sill next to her.

“All those people…” Ben breathed.

“All gone,” Aggie said, staring down at the now cooled coffee.

“Why… why didn’t the water recede after the tsunami?” Dottie asked, tears welling in her eyes. How many people were dead under that blue ocean they had passed by the day before? Their lost souls must have been reflected by those tormented clouds.

“Something has altered the atmospheric pull,” Aggie explained.

“Two moons,” Penny mumbled from her perch, breaking her silence. “Two moons,” she repeated, as if it made more sense the second time around. “Sylvester,” she said more forcefully, leaning forward in the chair.

“Sylvester?” Aggie repeated curiously.

“Crazy guy,” Dottie explained, “the one that attacked us. His name was Sylvester. He said somebody sent him, talked about two worlds, two moons. He must have been from there.”

“The ones Sylvester was sent to see,” Ben said, mimicking the hermit’s high-pitched voice.

“Damn it,” Aggie muttered, setting her crocheting down in the basket on the ground and rising to her feet.

"What?" the four asked in unison.

Aggie turned to face them. "There is something I'm going to ask of all of you," she said, eyes filled with an emotion Dottie could not quite pinpoint. Fear? Sadness? "Just know…" she paused, staring out the window, searching for something. "Just know I wouldn't ask if I thought there was any other way, okay?"

Dottie nodded, eyes locked on Aggie.

"We'll take a few days here, rest, refuel, heal, then we'll need to leave."

"Where will we go?" Ben asked.

"We need to get to D.C., to Levi," Aggie answered.

"What makes you think he's still alive?" Dottie asked.

"Same reason I knew Aggie was," Ben told Dottie.

"*Always have a plan*," Aggie clarified without turning from the window.

CHAPTER 20
The Maestro

The melody of Beethoven's *Sonata quasi una fantasia,* a sonata that Orville had so loved in his youth, filled his head. He closed his eyes and raised his hands to play the melody on an imaginary piano: the *Adagio sostenuto*, beginning quietly, slowly at first, *pianissimo,* the octave on the left with the melancholy triplet on the right. He had often wondered if he had missed his calling. Perhaps he should have left the highly-politicized science realm to become a conductor. Yet, had he changed course at any point, he would not be where he was today: executing what no other man had even attempted before, poised on the brink of scientific breakthrough, orchestrating his own epic symphony to the tune of freedom and prosperity for an entire bonded population.

Orville opened his eyes but continued to hum softly as he studied the chessboard in front of him. He had made the set himself, using polished squares of *gelb* alternating with marble to create the checkered pattern. A few lengths of wood for a frame and base and fine sand in between the stones had completed the work. The pieces themselves had been more complex, and had taken him months to whittle out of wood from the soft heart of the *hoch* tree. He had then painstakingly blackened one set of wood pieces and bleached the other.

The door to Orville's study creaked open, and he looked up to see Tacita standing in the entry.

"Come in," he instructed the young girl. "I expect you have something to report from the Lower Half?"

She nodded, her expression rigid.

While she still made him uneasy, Orville was starting to get used to the girl's grim appearance, the alarming scar no longer the *only* thing he saw when she was before him. The mute was of use to him. She was often privy to private conversations, people believing her incapable of repeating their words. Extracting the information Tacita gathered was the challenge. "My *leaves*, have they reported accurately? Has there been a rise in the street corner groups?"

Tacita nodded.

"And the resistance itself. It *is* increasing?"

Yes.

"What about the officers? Did you see any money exchange hands?"

No.

"Strange indeed." Orville twisted the wisps of beard that sprouted from his chin. How was such a large movement existing undetected by the Tri if they weren't paying off at least some of the officers? Perhaps Tacita simply didn't see the exchanges occurring. "How are these people staying out of sight?"

Tacita shrugged her shoulders.

"Are they congregating in homes?"

No.

"It's almost as if they were underground," Orville said sarcastically.

A small smile curled the edges of Tacita's mouth as she nodded *yes*.

"They're underground?" Orville asked, shocked.

Yes.

"You know where?"

Yes.

"Well, alright then, is there anything else? Shall I keep playing twenty questions?" The reference to the Earthen time-killing game was lost on the girl, who tilted her head to the side and raised her eyebrows for Orville to clarify.

"Shall I keep trying to guess what you learned?" Orville said more pointedly.

No.

"Go back to the Lower Half," Orville instructed, pulling the magnet from his coat pocket. "See what you can find out about who's leading this thing. Get close if you can, at least for a few days, then report back to me."

Tacita gave a curt nod, then turned to exit the room. After the door groaned closed behind her, Orville returned to his game, pensive. He moved a black bishop across the board just as Sylvester stumbled through the door, dragging a heavily bandaged leg behind him. Large strips of cloth were tied around his thigh, blood stains seeping through.

"What in the…" Orville began, but didn't know what to say to the filthy and injured old hermit who now stood before him.

"A dog," Sylvester explained as he entered the room, groaning.

"Go on…" Orville replied with a derisive smile.

"They had a dog. A snarling, biting dog."

"Who are *they*?"

"The youth, like goats, kids," Sylvester replied nonsensically. "The kids, yes, the boys… and girls. The golden girl in the center, leads."

"A golden girl," Orville echoed in a whisper, his mind reeling. "The girl with golden hair… you found her?"

"Not I, sir," Sylvester replied, panting as he tried to move his injured leg into a more comfortable position. "No, the *leaves* found the golden girl, the source of all the noise. So noisy is she."

"Where?"

"Through the back door. A little town, not far. Four days' hike. Six days *back* thanks to a snarling, biting dog." Sylvester looked longingly at the midnight colored armchair behind Orville's desk and pressed his hand to his leg.

"But she is not alone, you say?" Orville ignored Sylvester's unspoken plea to sit and attempted to picture the girl, but all he could muster was a less ghastly version of Tacita.

"Not alone. Two of each, boys and girls."

Orville felt his heartbeat quicken in his chest. "And what happened?"

"The children caught Sylvester, you see. But I tricked them. Such silly little children were they. Their world is a noisy mess." Sylvester rambled on about fire and flood, toppled buildings and openings in the earth as big as Alterra itself, painting for Orville a vivid picture of widespread devastation.

Orville listened to each word, his face grim as he began to understand that the effects of NEM on Earth were far worse than in Alterra. Perhaps it was the direction of the force. Or maybe she was too strong. Could he have miscalculated the amount of energy necessary to increase the size of the rupture? But no, his calculations were precise, exact. Something else must have come into play. It was a good thing he had decided to remain in Alterra and send Sylvester to follow the *leaves*. He had programmed them to stay within a twenty-mile radius of the back door, but it was not unusual for a wind current to blow them further on. It was entirely possible that the force radiating from NEM had pushed them several miles further away.

Whatever had happened didn't matter. They had found the girl with golden hair. He was sure this was the one from Ruya's prophecy. After all, people are magnetic creatures, and hostile energy would be particularly attractive to the *leaves.* And the carnage? Well, much could be justified in the name of progress.

"And they are coming here? How do these children know about Sum?" Orville asked.

"Oh, they did not know about Sum until Sylvester told them, sir. Such silly children." He shook his head from side to side with a high-pitched giggle.

"You told them…" Orville clenched his fists at his side. "You TOLD them? Probably led them straight through to Alterra, to *me."*

"No, I…" Sylvester stammered, looking up at Orville with pleading eyes.

"You should have neutralized the threat to me, you idiot, not facilitated it!" Orville's voice was rising, his face flushed with increasing rage.

"No, no… I warned them to stay away, you see. Such silly children. They only wanted to find their *aggie*." Sylvester's eyes met Orville's, silently begging for forgiveness.

"Their *aggie*?" Orville growled.

"They… they did not care for Alterra, sir," Sylvester said.

"What do you mean find an *aggie*?" Were the children playing marbles? The agate marbles, known as *aggies,* had been some of his favorite shooters when he was young.

"Not *an* aggie, sir, *their* Aggie, a she," Sylvester clarified.

"A woman?" Orville asked.

"Yes, yes, their Aggie is a noisy person, a very noisy person."

"Aggie." Orville began pacing the length of the room by the oversized fireplace, stopping only to stare into the flames. *Agatha*

Polson. It could be no other, for who else could be plotting his demise? Well, then, *let her come*.

Orville glanced over at Sylvester. The crazed man – who suddenly seemed so much older than him, though they were close in age – had done Orville's bidding for thirty-five years. While Sylvester was not somebody Orville considered to be intelligent, he possessed two characteristics that benefitted Orville. Like with Tacita, people often ignored Sylvester, speaking about all manner of things in front of him. And like Isaac, he was completely devoted to Orville. Sylvester had even turned aside his twin sister, the woman with whom he had shared a womb, as a show of his complete loyalty to Orville.

"Sylvester," Orville began without turning from the fire, "who do you serve?"

"You, sir, without end."

"Then I have a great service to ask of you."

"Anything."

"Go back. Find these children. Kill the golden girl. Kill their Aggie. Make sure they do not find their way to Alterra." Orville turned around to find Sylvester sitting on the floor, his legs sprawled in front of him like a child, a posture that echoed the naked fear on his face.

"Who do you serve?" Orville repeated.

"Sylvester… serves…" He hesitated.

"Who?" Orville demanded.

"You… Sylvester serves… Orville Zaide."

Orville smiled at the response from the broken creature as he returned to the chessboard, studying the pieces once more.

"Do not come back here again until you have done what I asked," Orville commanded. "Do you understand?"

"Sylvester… understands," the servant whispered.

Orville moved the white queen out from behind her pawns, then slid a black knight two squares up and one square over. The knight took out a white pawn and rested just one move away from the white queen.

"You may go," Orville said. He listened as Sylvester shuffled towards the door and pulled it closed behind him. The knight would fall to a rook on the next move before it could take the opposing queen.

The door to Orville's study creaked open once again. He took a measured breath, frustrated by yet another interruption, and looked up to find Rafi before him with Isaac close behind. The young Alterran reminded Orville of the wild horses he had once witnessed roaming the desert out in Arizona. Beautiful creatures, and powerful, but with an unbreakable spirit. Rafi became jumpy when he was cooped up inside stone walls for too long.

"Rafi, you've returned quickly," Orville observed as he walked over to his desk and settled into his chair. He pulled the dented pawn from his coat pocket and rolled it between his fingers. "This means you have something interesting to tell me."

"I do," Rafi replied, his tone wavering.

"Well, what has our Garrett been up to?"

Rafi remained silent. Isaac cleared his throat to urge the younger servant to speak.

"Was he simply enjoying a drink at the pub?" Orville asked.

Eyes cast downward, Rafi shifted his weight nervously from side to side.

"Meeting with somebody? A woman perhaps? Come on now, tell me and let's put this nonsense to rest." Orville leaned forward impatiently, placing his elbows on the desk in front of him. Why couldn't people just come out and say things?

"He was," Rafi replied slowly.

"Tell him who," Isaac ordered.

Orville straightened up slightly in his chair, becoming aware of the tension between Isaac and Rafi. This was not simply Rafi's nervousness. There was something else going on here that put both of his servants on edge.

“Yes, Rafi,” Orville ordered. “Tell me who.”

“I spoke with some of the tenants near Cairo’s pub,” Rafi began, taking a deep breath before he continued. “On the morning that Garrett was seen leaving the pub, all three confirmed seeing a woman exit shortly after.”

“And who was this woman?” What was Rafi playing at, taking so long to disclose what he had found?

“The seer,” Rafi stated in a hoarse whisper.

“Ruya,” Isaac added.

Ruya. Damn that woman.

“Did you question this… Cairo?” Orville asked, anxiety settling like a stone in the base of his stomach.

“I did not. I am not welcome inside the pub,” Rafi responded.

“Why?” Orville pressed.

“Cairo is my great uncle, sir,” Rafi explained. “His sister, my *avia*, she refuses to acknowledge me since I defected. Cairo would not speak to me out of respect for her if I...”

“It doesn't matter,” Orville snapped, cutting him off.

“Get to the rest,” Isaac commanded Rafi.

“Some day-workers who lived nearby. They confirmed that Ruya and Garrett sat at a table together from as early as two-past-change the night prior.” Rafi stumbled through his words, sweat trickling down his cheek. “It appears they spent the entire night in each other’s confidence.”

Orville gritted his teeth. First she teases, taunts, and then she deceives. He had been with Ruya before shift change the night this exchange took place. She must have known then that she would be going behind his back the moment he left her. And Garrett. The very next day he suggested increasing his guards. Part of their little scheme, no doubt, whatever it was. How long had the two of them been playing this game? Did they think he wouldn't find out?

“You've done well to bring this information to me,” Orville said after some time, trying to ignore the growing nausea and fire in his belly. *Damn her*.

“Thank you, sir,” Rafi replied, defeated.

“I know you have always seen Garrett as a… friend, a brother of sorts,” Orville waved his hand in the air as if to dispel such a sentiment, trying to keep his tone even. “You will be rewarded for your loyalty to me, make no mistake. But what I will ask of you now will be a difficult test. You must know, with a certainty, whose side you’re on. Do you understand?” He knew, as did the wild horse, Rafi, that there were no other options.

Orville pitied the men that allowed themselves to be backed into corners: Sylvester, Rafi. Orville would never let that happen to him. No, he always had options, even with Ruya. She thought she could play his game, and perhaps if she had kept to herself and remained respectful, he might have let her go on believing that. But now… now he had no choice but to show her who really held control over Alterra. Over *her*.

“What shall we do, sir?” Isaac asked as he stepped up next to Rafi, whose eyes remained on his feet.

“Eradicate the threat,” Orville said.

The two servants were silent. Isaac was steady, awaiting further instruction. Rafi was now shaking from the weight of betrayal.

“Ruya and Garrett knew the rules,” Orville stated flatly, “and now they must pay the price for breaking them.” He rose and walked back to his game of chess.

“Rafi, request that our most wise seer come to me immediately. Isaac, select a guard, somebody you trust, to watch Garrett. Do not allow him to leave Gemma. Speak of this to no one.”

Orville moved the black rook to castle the king on the other side.

“Oh, and Isaac,” he added, looking up from his game. “Follow Sylvester. He has found our golden girl. She is surrounded by other youth and an older woman, Aggie Polson. Help them find their way through to Alterra and bring them straight to Gemma.”

Would it not be all the sweeter to put an end to the coveted prophecy of the girl with golden crown in Alterra, on display for the people to see? *Let them all come to me.*

CHAPTER 21
The Quest

Time passed pleasantly at Aggie's, though a certain angst hung about them. The days were filled with warmth and a sense of safety that Dottie clung to furiously. She asked Aggie for some yarn and a crochet hook, determined to actually finish something she started now that she had the time. She was grateful that her broken fingers were on her left hand, the pinky and ring finger at that, so it hardly affected her ability to hold onto her project or perform any other basic tasks. Ari was in heaven, constantly cozied up either to Dottie or Ben, who he had developed an attachment to.

Ben was healing quickly, up and around for hours at a time. He and Dottie spent their evenings by the fire playing Rummy and listening to Hudd strum an old guitar he had found tucked in a corner. Things had certainly changed since the days of manhunt and childish name-calling, but something about being at Aggie's, maybe the routines that they quickly fell into, made Dottie feel almost normal. There were even times when she forgot why they were there to begin with, though such moments were fleeting. The faces of so many dead and gone, and orange, red and swirling leaves penetrated even the calmest moments.

Penny remained distant, keeping to herself most of the time and curling up with a book in the Papasan chair, no longer filled with warmth or optimism. Dottie wanted to make an effort to reach out to her but was battling her own feelings of frustration and disappointment. She wasn't quite sure what she had expected from Penny, but she couldn't understand how Penny had stood idly by while the rest of them almost got killed.

They worked, too, spending the warmer hours of the afternoon reinforcing the outside of the house, chopping firewood, or learning how to tend the indoor garden. The weather was returning to a more normal temperature for late October. You could even see patches of ground where the sun had worn through the snow.

Ever the devoted teacher, Aggie insisted they read for a time throughout the day. And each night as they sat down to dinner, she called on them to share something new that they learned with the rest of the group.

"We must never stop learning from each other," she said one night, "for we all have a different set of experiences and skills to bring to the table. Collaboration is one of our strongest mechanisms as thinking people."

The next day, Aggie took that sentiment one step further, having each of them think of unique skills they could teach or share with the others.

Hudd had been a Boy Scout when he was younger and taught the group how to tie a bowline knot.

"It's relatively simple," he said, holding up his example for the rest to see, "but extremely dependable. This thing isn't going anywhere." He gave either end a firm tug to demonstrate.

They spent an afternoon out in the trees with Ben, who had a particular interest and talent for making shelters from tree branches and foliage.

Dottie taught them all some basic sewing techniques, demonstrating how to thread the eye of a needle and make a knot. She then showed them how to do a straight stitch, a simple way to bind two things together, before demonstrating how to execute an overstitch to close off a hem. She ended her lesson by teaching them how to use a cross stitch for added strength and stability.

Penny silently sat through these group lessons, but claimed that she had no useful skills to offer the group "other than how to do makeup or hair."

Any time one of them pressed Aggie about D.C. and the quest on which they were all supposed to embark, she simply asked them to be patient and rest. They would need it, she told them. Whatever mission she had in mind could not bring their families back and would not fix the widespread devastation that had taken out a majority of their world. And Dottie didn't feel ready to move on from this little life they had established. As she watched the others settle into their new routine, she wondered if they felt the same way.

Dottie kept track of the days on a calendar that hung from a pushpin in Aggie's office. It was a Wednesday morning in early November, two full weeks after they had found their way, broken and stumbling, to Aggie's back door. Dottie looked up from her crocheting to see Aggie standing with the percolator and stash of mugs that were their start to each morning.

"It's time to go," Aggie stated abruptly.

Dottie felt blindsided by the words. She knew, in the back of her mind, that they would eventually come, but not *this* morning, not *so* soon. Not when she was so close to finishing her scarf.

"Why?" Dottie asked, trying not to betray the trepidation she felt. "How do you know it's time?"

"Follow me," Aggie replied somberly, setting the coffee and mugs down on the corner desk, "all of you."

Dottie rose uneasily. Ari leaped off the couch and led the way.

Aggie led them all down into the green hall, then gestured toward the windows. "Look," she said, "what do you see?"

Dottie followed Aggie's finger out to the line of the trees and covered her mouth with her hand. On the edge of Aggie's yard, a swarm of Orville's leaves had gathered, thousands of them, the largest grouping Dottie had ever seen. Ari growled next to her.

"Why are they following us?" Dottie asked.

"Hmm," Aggie glanced down at Dottie, the corners of her mouth turned down. "I'm still trying to figure that out," she replied, looking away from Dottie and turning toward the kitchen. "You all get your things collected from the living room. Bring everything into the kitchen. Hudd, can you grab Ben's things? Ben, I need your help with something."

Dottie went with Hudd and Penny back into the living room while Ben followed Aggie into the kitchen. Penny let out a frustrated sigh as she sunk back into her chair, ignoring Aggie's instructions.

"What's going on with you?" Dottie asked Penny in annoyance. The girl glared at her in response. Fear and frustration overrode Dottie's usual patience with Penny, and the words came tumbling forth. "You were so damn cheerful when all this started. Now that we've come through the worst of it and we have a plan, and we know more about what has happened in the world, you're miserable. I don't get it."

"Well, I was an idiot before," Penny shot back.

"You weren't," Dottie replied.

"I was. I was naive," Penny said. "I thought… well, I definitely didn't think all the things that have happened ever could. And I almost got Ben killed."

"What are you talking about?" Dottie asked, knowing what was haunting Penny but wanting to give her the chance to explain.

"Back at the train," Penny began, voice slightly lowered now, "you told me when you handed me the knife, you said if I had to use it you needed me to try, remember?"

“I do.”

“Well, I kind of thought you were crazy. I didn't think I would ever actually have to. And then when I *did*….” Penny trailed off, dropping her head into her hands.

“You didn’t fail, you know,” Dottie said quietly, trying to sound reassuring, “you just….” She grasped for some way to spin it. “…you just have a greater sense of compassion than the rest of us do. The idea of having to cause harm to somebody else, regardless of what they’re doing….”

“Look, Dottie,” Penny cut in, looking down at her hands. “I get it, okay.”

“You get what?”

“I get that you’ve been looking out for me, you all have. I don’t have things to offer like you guys do, the knots and shelters and sewing things.”

“Penny,” Dottie said, kneeling down directly into her line of sight. “You don’t need the *same* things because what you offer us is just as important: optimism and energy. If we don’t have that, we’re getting nowhere.” She reached out a hand and awkwardly patted Penny’s knee, then rose and finished gathering her belongings. As she neared the kitchen, pack slung onto her shoulder, she heard Ben and Aggie conversing in hushed tones.

“She should know,” Ben whispered to Aggie.

“Not yet,” Aggie replied. “If she knows the truth, she might not agree to go along with us.”

Ben caught sight of Dottie out of the corner of his eye and sat back in his chair, smiling at her sheepishly.

“What are you guys talking about?” Dottie asked.

“Oh, uh, we were just debating,” Ben began, “whether or not to tell Penny that there are likely no bathrooms along the way to D.C….”

Dottie smiled in reply, but something felt off. The uneasy feeling she had experienced when they first arrived crept back into her stomach. They wanted her to take off blindly on some quest that they had just admitted to themselves she would not attempt if she "knew the truth." The truth about what? Were they trying to protect her from something, or were they trying to deceive her?

She felt it then, just a small tickle at first. Panic. It rose, crawling like spiders up her back. She squirmed, moving her shoulders side to side to release the energy trapped there. *Damn it, not now.*

"Anxious again?" Aggie asked.

"Very," Dottie replied, eyes downcast. "Feels like I need to curl up in a ball, run away, punch something, and scream all at the same time."

"Anxiety can have that effect," Aggie replied. "How long have you had it?"

"As long as I can remember," Dottie said, "my whole life." She shuffled into the kitchen and took a seat across from Ben.

"Can I teach you a little trick?" Aggie asked.

Dottie nodded, her renewed suspicions about Aggie defeated by her need to gain control of herself.

"Close your eyes, sit back in the chair."

Dottie did as she was told.

"Where are you?" Aggie asked.

"In your kitchen," Dottie answered. She felt Ari lay his heavy head in her lap and placed a hand on it.

"What do you smell?"

"The cook stove," Dottie replied, "coffee, the basil in the garden. That reminds me of my mom."

"Your mom is gone?" Aggie asked.

"Yes, but I can't think about that now."

"No, don't push aside the thoughts that come to you. They'll begin to build up and come back with more strength when you are least able to navigate them. Negative thoughts become toxic and can sabotage our ability to self-regulate. You are here. Allow yourself to *be* here."

Dottie slipped into silence, then found herself talking. “My mom always grew basil in our garden with the tomatoes,” she said. “She’d chop the two up on a plate with fresh mozzarella, make a little balsamic reduction to drizzle on top, slice some nice fresh baked bread. The smell of it filled our house when I got home from school on those days. Fresh Caprese was our favorite meal to share.”

“Well, maybe when all this is done you could make it for me sometime,” Aggie said, her voice sounding distant to Dottie. “Sometimes the best way to honor the memory of somebody we’ve lost is to share the most special parts of them with others.”

Another surge of trapped energy ricocheted back and forth across Dottie’s back. She shivered in response.

“Don’t tense up,” Aggie instructed, “just let it flow. You’re here, in my kitchen, smelling basil and coffee and fire. What do you hear?”

“Hudd in the living room, moving the guitar.”

“Now, bring your mind to the very tips of your fingers,” Aggie continued. “What do you feel?”

“Ari’s head, the table…” Dottie replied, patting the dog, then gently brushing the fingers of her other hand over the surface of the wood. “The lines of the grain.”

“Good,” Aggie said. “Now, are you safe?”

“At this moment,” Dottie replied, “I hope I am.” Her breathing had slowed, and the anxiety started to ease.

“That is all you need to know,” Aggie assured, her voice calm. “Take a few more deep breaths, feel the table, hear the guitar, smell the basil, know you’re safe… and open your eyes.”

Dottie blinked, feeling almost as if she had just woken from a nap.

“How do you feel?” Aggie asked.

“Better,” Dottie said, looking around the room, conscious of Ben’s gaze on her. A flush crept into her cheeks as she realized that she had done it again, made the moment about her because of her weakness. There seemed to be no judgment in Ben's eyes, just compassion and maybe understanding.

"What you just worked through," Aggie said, rising from in front of Dottie and sitting back in the seat next to her, "it's called mindfulness. When your mind wants to take your body for a ride, the best way to keep it on the right track is to plant yourself firmly in the present. Stop what you're doing, and *be* where you are."

Dottie nodded.

Hudd and Penny joined them in the kitchen with the rest of their belongings. Aggie made them all sit and eat.

"Fuel," she stated. "We've got a long trek ahead of us."

"How exactly are we doing this?" Hudd asked.

"Slowly," Aggie replied. "D.C. is about 450 miles away. The distance will take us around twenty days to travel, and that's assuming we can tackle at least twenty-three miles per day, without any setbacks." She took a map out of her pack and set it on the table, tracing the path with her finger as she spoke. "The new coastline seems to push us in roughly thirty-six miles. Now, I don't know that that's the case the whole way down, but it's probably the best guess we can make."

"How do we even know the damage extends that far?" Ben asked.

"If it didn't," Aggie replied, "things would be back up and running by now. Now, we'll head up to Hartford first, make sure we stay just inland from the new coast."

"What about the leaves?" Dottie asked.

"They aren't able to pick up our conversations in here, but that changes once we go outside. I still don't know how Orville powers them, some form of magnetism, but one that doesn't play by the rules. What I do know is that Ari senses their presence before we can see them. We'll need him to help us lose them and then stay clear of them as we travel.

They finished their breakfast, bundled up, and shuffled out the back door in silence, moving away from the house in the opposite direction from the leaves. Dottie paused.

"Just put on blinders," Aggie whispered, stepping to Dottie's side. "Close your eyes to the things you recognize, the devastation. Close your mind to the things you once had or that you wish could be. Open your ears to the sounds around you." She turned to address the others. "Remember, if I was able to stay behind ad not evacuate, I'm sure others did as well. Though," she added, "the other types of people who might want to avoid law enforcement are likely to be less trustworthy than me, as you have already been unfortunate enough to experience."

They stayed off the main roads, pausing every few hours to check the map, following the smaller streets and trails that wove in and out along their route. They maintained the same routine round the clock, stopping for meals and snacks, breaking well before sunset to put up a campsite and shelter, taking shifts throughout the night. The only break to this pattern would come when Ari's growl and warning posture signaled the presence of Orville's leaves, forcing them to move on more quickly. They reached the outskirts of Hartford just before sunset on the third day but found themselves in an area with little cover for the night.

"I think we need to keep moving," Ben said.

"Yes," Aggie agreed, "but I don't know this area well. Without a solid view of the map…"

"We could follow the stars," Penny suggested.

"I hate to say it," Aggie replied, "but that's one skill I do not claim to possess."

"Well, I guess it's a good thing that I do," Penny said, smiling for the first time since the train. "My family likes to sail," she added to the collection of raised eyebrows.

They moved around the outskirts of the city well into the night, Penny making sure they were still heading in the right direction. She showed them how to find the North Star using the Big Dipper, how to estimate latitude with an outstretched fist, and how to find true east and true west with the rising and setting of Orion's belt.

"Not that estimating latitude would help us at this point," she added, "who needs to know that anyway?"

Dottie chuckled, happy to see a little bit of Penny's spirit coming back. Once they were a few miles past the city, they hunkered down for the rest of the night and rotated watch shifts, each getting a few hours of sleep until morning.

They stayed on course over the next few days, winding down through Waterbury, Southbury, Newton. They spotted a few solo vagrants here and there, usually hanging around deserted grocery or convenience stores, some sleeping in doorways. But the group never approached them and remained hidden. Mid-afternoon on the fifth day, as they moved through the neighborhoods surrounding Danbury, Aggie stopped them for an unplanned break.

They were about twenty feet into the tree line behind a cluster of homes that reminded Dottie of her own. The eeriness of passing through abandoned neighborhoods had waned a few days into their trek, but a child's playhouse in the nearby yard gave Dottie pause. It was not that long ago that she had been wandering through the woods playing manhunt, debating the ethics of whether or not to hide out in such a yard, fully expecting to make her way back to a warm house that night. Oh, what a difference a few weeks can make when the world comes crashing down around you.

"I told you all I had something important to ask you," Aggie began, once they had settled onto the ground in a circle, passing around a bag of trail mix and a bottle of water.

Dottie offered some of the water to Ari, who lay panting in the cold dirt. He was starting to lean out quite a bit with all this walking.

"When Orville first disappeared, Levi and I tried following up on some of his work, thinking it might help us find him. What we discovered was that the field of competing magnetic force was duplicated in other parts of New England. With what we know now, this would suggest multiple entrances into this other world."

Aggie's eyes met Dottie's briefly before she continued. "You will be going the rest of the way to D.C. without me."

"Why?!" Dottie's breath quickened. Here they were, days away from anything they knew. And now Aggie was going to leave them?

"Orville's EMP, or Electromagnetic Pulse, would have come through from one of the entrances. If I find the origination of the pulse, I find a door. You have everything you need," Aggie said hurriedly, trying to reassure them. "You have the map and the supplies, but most of all, you have each other. I must say the four of you make one hell of a team. You don't need me."

"I'm pretty sure we do," Penny said, eyes wide with disbelief.

"The leaves have followed us this far," Aggie said. "They're going to keep following you. This is my chance to slip away without them noticing."

"Where are you going to go?" Hudd asked, face somber.

"To the source," Aggie answered. "The energy that did all this has a specific frequency. I can't hear it." She paused, reaching down to pat Ari's head as he dozed by her feet, "but *he* can, just like with the leaves. Dottie… I need to take Ari with me."

"No," Dottie responded immediately. "He's *my* dog." She instinctively moved closer to the last connection she had to her family, placing an arm around his neck.

"I know," Aggie replied, keeping eye contact with Dottie, "but there is no other way. He alone can lead me to the source of all this, and maybe I can put a stop to it. In the meantime, the knowledge you carry with you is valuable. I need you to take it to Levi."

"Then I'll go with you and Ari," Dottie suggested. "The others will be fine without me."

"We need you with us, Dottie," Ben said, moving closer to Dottie and placing a hand on her knee. "This could save whatever world we have left."

Dottie searched Ben's face, silently pleading with him.

"This is bigger than us, Dot."

She nodded, tears pooling in her eyes.

"You all need to go the rest of the way down through Danbury," Aggie said, flattening the map out on the ground, though Dottie could hardly see a thing in front of her. "I would say to then head up to Carmel and Fishkill, but the Tappan Zee bridge is just barely over thirty-six miles inland and already sits below sea level. I doubt it's still above water. You'll have to move further north, over Schaefer Ridge to the bridge that runs from Beacon to Newbury." She traced the path with her finger. "If *that* is no longer standing, you are going to lose additional days finding a point and means of crossing. But if you can get past the Hudson, then you'll move a little further south to Allentown, then through Lancaster, York, and Hanover, then make a quick cut down into D.C. or as close as you're able to get with the water."

It was a quick goodbye. Dottie should have made it longer, should have hugged Ari one more time, scratched that spot behind his ear that made his face scrunch up all funny. But she felt too numb for all of that and the moment passed more quickly than her aching heart could process.

"You'll see him again, Dot," Ben told her as they stood watching Aggie and Ari sneak away into the trees.

"No," Dottie said sadly, straining to keep Ari in her sights for just a little bit longer. "No, I'm pretty sure I won't." She turned to face Ben, clenching her fists at her sides, resisting the urge to sock him. "And you knew."

"I did," he said.

"The day we left, when I walked into the kitchen…"

"Aggie had just told me."

"And what else did she tell you? Was this all she intended to take from me, or is there more?"

"There's a reason those leaves are gonna keep following us, Dottie," Ben said quietly.

"What reason is that?"

"You," Ben replied, before grabbing his pack off the ground and stomping off in the opposite direction.

CHAPTER 22
The Robins

Lowell slid back into his seat at the bar and placed his forehead in his hands. It was just after shift change. He had spent the early hours of that morning poring over the underground map system with Troy and Cairo, mostly just trying to help the other two make sense of the network. They were at least able to identify a few likely points of penetration, vulnerable areas of the tunnel where Orville and his crew may have been able to intercept from Gemma.

Cairo came around the bar in front of Lowell, face drawn from fatigue. "Drink this," he instructed, placing a cup of cold, black coffee in front of Lowell. "Then go home, wherever that is, and get some sleep."

"No time for sleep today," Lowell replied. "It's our turn for instruction."

“Ah, yes, time with the old Hawk is worth a hundred sleepless nights,” Cairo said with a wink.

“Worth a few at least,” Lowell replied as he swirled his coffee. He wasn’t sure he could get used to the stuff, hot or cold. Hawk had recommended Lowell start drinking coffee to help with the headaches. It had been nearly three weeks since the *Robins* last had an instruction day with the aged leader of the Uprisen and Lowell’s mind ached for a challenge even as his body screamed for rest and solitude.

“Just chug it,” Cairo suggested. “Probably won’t taste great, but it’ll give you a little kick.”

Lowell drained the cup in three large swigs and waited for the bitter aftertaste to subside before opening his eyes.

“Do you like cards, Cairo?”

“Never cared for them much myself,” Cairo replied. “Much prefer to play the particular game of strategy that *people* provide so readily. Though I expect you do quite well with the numbers?”

Lowell nodded. It was like the maps for him – a few steps into the game and all the counts and suits came together in his mind. Cards were how Hawk preferred to teach sums and logic to the streetcorner groups. It had gotten to the point where the other Robins wouldn’t play against Lowell anymore. Hawk had promised him a game soon.

“Well, anyway…” Cairo said, signaling it was time for Lowell to get going. “You enjoy your lessons, my young friend. Glean what you can from Hawk. Fit some rest in when you can. But then it’s back to searching for our silent little spy, yes?”

“Yes,” Lowell agreed. “There's another sit-in tonight. Strange that they're hosting them back-to-back…”

“From what Troy was saying, they're trying to beef up their ranks quickly.”

“Sounds right… but I'll try there, follow the girl best I can, then in the morning scout out those tunnels. Best not to go underground at night anyway.”

“Dark down there either way, isn’t it?” Cairo asked.

Lowell considered the old smuggler for a moment. Cairo had first begun to navigate the tunnels when he was not much older than Lowell. Still, he only understood the routes he had taken frequently enough to remember. It was a pity. The natural talent Lowell possessed should belong to men like Cairo, who had years enough to make use of it.

"When you were making runs," Lowell began, "did you ever feel like the tunnels pulled you down further than you ever planned to go?"

Cairo nodded.

"Or like your soul might become lost down there, even though your mind knew the way back out?"

"And yet there was always something so sweet in it…" Cairo recalled.

"That magic… it knows when the sun sleeps."

"Best not to be caught up in it when it is at its strongest then. You are wise for one so young," Cairo said, lifting his cup of coffee in salute. "Far wiser than I was at your age. That power did indeed almost swallow me whole once. But that, my friend, is a story for another day."

∝

The worn street youth stepped out into piercing daylight. He squatted against the wall outside the pub for a few minutes, letting his eyes adjust. He was tired, much too tired for somebody his age; he knew that. He had never really expected to make it this long. Lowell was born cursed with magic the old healers in the *Innova* did not understand. He was a frail infant, constantly covered in bumpy rashes and wailing incessantly. From his earliest days, he had suffered from terrible headaches and joint pain. Changes in light or bad weather were the worst triggers. After a long night spent squinting over the intricate puzzle of maps, the throbbing in his head was particularly severe.

Lowell tilted his head back, stretching the tense muscles in his neck as he rolled his head slowly from side to side, inhaling deeply as Ruya had once taught him to do in order to ease some of the tension. She had been with his mother in the *Innova* when he was born. The old woman, Basira, had not expected him to live long, so Ruya performed a reading to see if there was anything that she could foretell about his particular fate. She later told Lowell how his mother, Lin, had clung to his tiny body, clutched him to her breast, attempting to nourish him as best she could during the divination. But the prophecy was not comforting. Her baby would live, but his path would be short and rocky at best. *Sometimes the shortest flames give the greatest warmth*, Ruya had told Lowell after his mother died.

Well, if he was going to be a short flame, he better get going and make the most of what time he had. Lowell opened his eyes slowly, the sun warming his face, chest, and arms. The pain in his head began to subside. The gong signaled one past change as he rose, straightening the folds of his tattered purple tunic. He was running late. He would have to cut through the center of the Lower Half to get to Hawk's in time. That meant venturing closer to Triplica than he wanted to, but he couldn't avoid it.

The triangular set of buildings that formed Triplica was the home of the Tri-Commission's Division of Subjugation, the center for all things related to the licensing and bondage of the city's indentured class. Triplica was heavily guarded, and the Lex officers did not like seeing anything too brightly colored within their sight. It made them itchy, unpredictable.

The Lex would not want to see someone like Lowell hanging about, but there was another more compelling reason that he avoided Triplica. The tower at its center sang a song he wished not to hear, brought back memories better left behind him. But the gong did not lie–he was late and had no time to waste on another route. He braced himself as he bounded down a set of stairs that led into the open hub of the Lower Half, Triplica at its center. He measured his pace. It was best to navigate this intersection quickly, but not so quickly as to draw attention from the guard. There were more people in the junction than he had anticipated, most wandering about aimlessly, causing the flow of foot traffic to become stuck at different points. Lowell moved purposefully amongst the people, keeping his gaze a few steps ahead, planning his course.

As he neared the northeast corner of Triplica, a scuffle broke out between two pedestrians, driving a sea of bodies into him. He became wedged between the crowd and the stone wall as bystanders formed a circle around the grappling men. Some were friends of the men, while others were just fans of physical confrontation who yelled directions:

"Get him!"

"Hook his ribs!"

"Stick his chin!"

"Don't let him come around on you!"

The crowd buzzed with an aggressive frenzy. Lowell found himself pressed against the walls of Triplica with the mob at his back. He closed his eyes and reminded himself to breathe as the suffocating force of so many bodies pressed in on him. He raised his face to the sky and fixed his gaze on the stream of smoke spiraling out from the top of the central tower. A heavy heel crushed the toes of his left foot. Lowell clenched his jaw and groaned, resisting the urge to cry out.

Just when he felt he may be trampled, a chilling scream emerged from the top of the tower that formed the center of Triplica, followed by another, and still another. Dozens of wailing voices, the screams of children, filled the air. The angry men responsible for the chaos seemed to forget what they had been fighting about and the crowd at once became still. The people of the Lower Half exchanged looks of defeat, only a few brave enough to cast their eyes upon the tower before they moved on.

Lowell's heart beat painfully in his chest and he swallowed hard to quell the acid rising in his throat. His hands were shaking and his toes throbbed. The traffic around him moved smoothly once again as pedestrians returned their eyes to the ground and started walking to where they needed to go. Lowell knew he needed to keep moving. He was already too close to Triplica and its inhabitants and feared the attention his bright clothing and hobbling walk might bring.

He turned and leaned against the wall and looked down at his foot, finding his canvas shoes a bloody mess. He kicked them off, tore a strip of cloth from the bottom of his purple tunic, and wrapped it around his big toe which no longer had a nail. His stomach clenched at the sight of the brand on his calf. 3-1-3-8. It had been burned into his flesh up in that tower – his own terrified and pain-filled screams had once pierced the air just like those of the children he'd just heard.

∝

Despite his efforts to be on time, Lowell arrived late to Hawk's for instruction. As he entered, the old man glanced up, observed Lowell's haggard appearance, and waved him in with a look of concern. All the other boys were there, sitting cross-legged in a semi-circle around their teacher. Tacita had been the only girl in their streetcorner group before she left, though she had also been the fiercest among them. The *Robins* had remained the same group of six since: Lowell, Elys, Vin, the brothers Nail and Nadim, and the grocer's bastard son, Pam.

"Today, we are talking about the power of words," Hawk began, his raspy voice filling the little dirt room. "And not just in telling stories." He nodded at Lowell to come take his seat on the floor amongst his peers. "Though storytelling is, as we have so often discussed, the strongest link that holds us to one another and, of course, to previous generations."

Hawk was as old a man as Lowell had ever known, and often joked that once he hit eighty, he stopped counting the years. The concept of counting one's age from birth was strange enough to Lowell, but he also knew that, had he been able to do so, he would not need to count long enough to lose track.

"Any moment in time is an intersection of numerous stories: stories of how we arrived there, stories yet to be told that hinge on that moment, stories that belong to another, but run parallel to our own… in every instance of our lives, there are stories to tell, stories to hear, and still others that are transferred through action and emotion, rather than words." Hawk paused to clear his throat before continuing his instruction.

"This is the very framework of our existence as social beings," he went on. "We learn from stories, develop our perspective of the *self* and the *other* based on our interaction and experience with them. Stories are the way we connect with the people for whom we develop an affinity, and they are the way we experience disconnect with those we ultimately choose to keep at a distance." He paused once more to take a sip of water and give the boys time for his message to settle. "Stories are our filter for how we experience our world, the foundation for our sense of self. And *words*, words are the bricks that make up that foundation."

Lowell, interested though he was, felt his eyelids becoming heavy from the lull of Hawk's gravelly voice.

"Anyway, an ironic thing it is," Hawk continued, "to exercise the *use* of words to discuss the very act itself. We sometimes say that words can tear a man down more cruelly than swords. It could also be said that words are themselves the swords that free us from oppression. And why are we oppressed?" He waited patiently for an answer.

"Because of the Tri," Nail offered.

"The Tri wasn't even around when all this started, you idiot," Nadim hissed at his younger brother, who rolled his eyes in response.

"True, true," Hawk added with a chuckle. "But what *was* around when it started, Nadim?"

"The Council of Elders," the older brother answered.

"Well, that's what I meant, same thing…" Nail mumbled.

"Not quite the same thing, Nail," Hawk said, pointing a bony finger at the boy, "though, in a way you are both correct since the Tri is simply a reinforcement of the Agency of Universal Truth. But, my young friends, how is it that we find ourselves oppressed? By what means did the Agency manage to institute such oppression?"

Lowell dug the tips of his fingers into the dirt floor, remaining silent along with the other boys.

"I'll give you the first reason," Hawk offered. "Movement… the first measures taken by the Agency aimed to restrict movement, or *mobility*. Shift change mandates, curfews, closures of the Upper

Half to residents of the Lower. Now, why does restricting movement contribute to oppression?"

"It's isolating," Vin said. "They cut people off from each other. Those who had the most got even more, and those who had less became the least."

"Yes, yes, very good," Hawk affirmed. "So, movement. What else?"

"*Commeri,*" Pam volunteered.

"Currency," Hawk replied. "Good, Pam. If the people of the Lower Half can hardly obtain enough *commeri* to survive, it takes away their ability to alter their station in society."

"No chance for upward mobility," Lowell recalled aloud from Troy's speech the previous night.

"Exactly!" Hawk's voice filled with excitement as he leaned forward, resting his hands on his knees. "There was a time, hundreds of years ago, when the exchange of currency for work happened freely between the Upper and Lower Halves, but this was all before the *Bondage Commission* mandated licensing and took over the distribution of compensation. Alright, we have movement and currency. What is one more component of the weapon of oppression that has been used against us?"

"Mind." Lowell looked up from where he dug at the sand with his fingers to the room of his peers and teacher. "Uh, our minds are oppressed," he attempted to clarify, before quickly returning his gaze to the ground.

"Go on," Hawk urged.

"They use fear," Lowell explained. "They restrict information, keep us in the dark. They tell us that this is the only way."

"Yes!" Hawk's eyes sparkled at Lowell's understanding. "Now, earlier we likened words to swords, but it is through context that you learn what you ought to think about them. One can persuade another to think either positively or negatively about words as swords depending on the words used and how they are put together. This is something known as *rhetoric*."

Lowell watched Hawk take a deep breath, face brightening as he straightened his back and dove into the part of his lesson where he brought everything back full circle.

"Now, the majority of us use rhetoric without even realizing it," Hawk continued. "You choose your words carefully and use them differently depending on the situation. Sometimes you use them to escape a confrontation with somebody on the street and other times you need to navigate the social hierarchy of your community groups or deal amongst yourselves. That is just a normal part of our daily interactions. However, *some* use rhetoric more nefariously."

Lowell thought of the way Troy had addressed the crowd at sit-in the night before and the change in her tone and word use when she was expressing her concern to Cairo.

"As an example," Hawk went on, his bushy white eyebrows furrowed, "the Agency maintains that the written Universal Faith supports the state of indenture, right?"

The boys nodded, some shifting their weight or tucking a stray limb underneath themselves. Pam's head jerked periodically as he fought to remain awake next to Lowell. Hawk continued.

"The Universal Truth that the oppressors use to justify our servitude states: 'the Universe made slaves to use their hands and masters to use their minds.' When this passage was discussed in the council, they determined that the Universe had destined certain men to be slaves and certain others to be masters. This was both how they formed and how they continue to defend the oppressive mission of the Agency."

Lowell squinted as the old man spoke, hungrily trying to understand this new information.

"However... and this is a *big* however... another translation of the earliest text is read 'The Universe made slaves of men who use their hands *alone* and masters of men who use their minds *alone*.' And, perhaps more importantly, the passage that follows this states, 'for those who do not think become slaves to the will of others, and those who do not work become masters only to their own self-indulgence.' This," Hawk continued, raising a hand emphatically into the air, "this is *rhetoric*, my young friends. A set of words that appear to be so innocently altered creates an entirely different, and in this case, dangerous meaning!"

The room was still. Lowell's mind was reeling, trying to keep up with all he had just heard. Was it true that a simple passage, translated incorrectly, was to blame for thousands of years of abuse and indenture?

"Hawk," Elys broke the silence with caution, "may I ask… how do you know these things?"

"That's a very good question, Elys," Hawk replied, the rows of wrinkles surrounding his eyes and mouth softening. He gazed at the faces around the room, his topknot of stark white hair resting lopsided on his head.

"But first, I believe I owe you all an apology," Hawk said. "If there is one thing I would like for you to learn from me, it is always to question the source of information you are given. Question all… origin, intent, impact. And what evidence have I offered you to support my own credibility?"

"You help us," Vin replied. "You lift us up, teach us how to think and act as enlightened people. That's credibility enough for me."

Lowell and the other boys nodded in agreement with Vin.

"Ah, for that, I thank you. Nevertheless…" Hawk continued with a gentle smile. "I spent a number of years in the Upper Half amongst the elite, the literate. I read some of the most incredible scrolls, telling of this city's history, some of which have since been lost to this world, burned for the dangerous truths they told. But those truths have a place here…" He pressed an index finger to his temple.

"You read," Lowell observed aloud.

"I do."

"Can you teach us?" Elys asked excitedly.

"Yes," Hawk stated. "Up until now, I had not seen the point in spending what limited time we have for lessons on reading when you have no access to scrolls and logic and numbers better serve your day-to-day purposes. But that may indeed be changing moving forward."

Yes. Lowell felt excited by the promise of more learning. Perhaps his short flame would last long enough to shed some light on the written word.

"Hawk," Nail's voice shook a little as he struggled to form the words. "Why… why would somebody want to use words to, you know, make one thing seem like another?"

Hawk considered the youngest of the group, staring down at him.

"Not everybody goes through life with good intentions, Nail," Hawk replied. "You know, I don't believe I've ever told you boys this, but I am not actually from Alterra. But *that* is a story for another time, perhaps." He waved away the flood of surprised questions that came from the boys. "But where I am from, there once was a tyrant, one who used persuasive rhetoric to convince otherwise good and decent people to do the most insidious things. At his orders, an entire group of people was all but wiped out. Mass genocide…"

"What's genocide?" Lowell cut in, his voice wavering.

"The worst kind of evil," Hawk intoned, voice barely more than a whisper.

Before Lowell had a chance to question Hawk further, the door to the little dirt room opened suddenly, and Tacita entered.

CHAPTER 23
The Giant

The gong from Triplica signaled four past shift change when Ruya followed the dark alleyways back to Cairo's. The nights were getting cold quickly, and she shivered as she left the biting chill behind her for the warmth of the pub. A clay fire pit sat in in the middle of the room, the chairs and tables pushed off to the sides to accommodate it. Ruya offered a nod to Cairo behind the bar. He smiled in reply without breaking his one-sided conversation with Brac. She settled into her usual seat at the corner table with a weary sigh. Much had changed in the two weeks since she had last been here: the ground was not the only thing that had been shaken up in Alterra.

The Tri-Commission had rocked the Lower Half with a series of crackdowns, doubling the Lex guard at each post and around

Triplica. They shortened the amount of time that shift workers had access to the Belt during change, resulting in chaos as day and night workers pushed against each other in a frenzy to get through to the other side. Those stranded north of the Belt were left hungry and unable to get to their families overnight, while the unexpected closures resulted in fines and imprisonment for those who were unable to make it north to their shift.

Days later, officers raided the south market, making a series of unwarranted arrests and shutting down what little commerce remained for the Lower Alterrans. Just that morning, the Tri had issued a new decree forbidding any travel on foot through the Lower Half in between shift change – hence, the empty pub. Ruya had been worried, though she did not see a single officer on her way. Fear was as powerful an enforcer as any officer and sufficient to keep most people in their homes.

Cairo came around from behind the bar with a cup of water. "Will Garrett be able to join us tonight, Ruya?"

"I'm not sure," she said without looking up, concentrating on the wood tabletop in front of her, tracing the grain with the tips of her fingers. "The alleyways were completely clear, none except the street youth huddled in their doorways. No Lex. I just don't know how Garrett would be able to get into the city from Gemma."

"I guess we'll just wait and see," Cairo said. He placed the cup on the table and patted her hand. "Can I get you anything else?"

"Not right now," Ruya replied, managing a grateful smile. "You are always so generous, Cairo, both with sustenance *and* information. But no gossip for me today?" She teased the old barkeep, more to ease her anxiety about Garrett than anything else.

"I wasn't sure you were in the mood for trivialities," Cairo said with a sympathetic smile as he took a seat next to her.

"Something to pass the time," Ruya replied and leaned against the back of her chair. Closing her eyes and sipping the water, she listening to the latest news of the Lower Half, though it was far less light-hearted than Cairo's usual buzz.

There had been a riot outside Triplica that morning, just after they issued the new movement restrictions. More than two hundred bonded night-workers crowded the intersection surrounding the three-building structure, chanting, "We will move!" and demanding the release of their licensing contracts.

"It was magnificent, really, from what I hear," Cairo said. "They all pooled their *commeri*, accruing enough to buy out the contracts of two of their members. Apparently, the strategy is for the two freed individuals – one man, one woman – to obtain work out of bond and make enough *commeri* to buy out more contracts."

"A noble plan," Ruya observed, "yet, no law-abiding citizen of the Upper Half would risk hiring them. Has there been a response?"

"Not yet," Cairo replied. "From what I understand, the group is still holed up outside the Licensing office."

"Where do these free-people seek to gain employment, should Licensing comply with their purchase and release?"

"Orville." Cairo's eyes gleamed as he delivered this juicy detail.

"But Orville would have little use for skill-labor," Ruya replied.

"Oh, perhaps in the past. But things have changed at Gemma," Cairo said. "There has been a small… shift in plans, which you may hear from Garrett this evening, should he arrive."

"In which direction?" Ruya asked.

"Disruption."

"With whom?" She could barely get the question out. What was Orville about to do?

"The Tri," Cairo answered. He rose from the table and headed back behind the bar just as Lowell materialized in the low doorway of the pub, leaving Ruya little time to process this new information.

Lowell looked like he had aged years over the last few weeks, growing taller and leaner, but something about his manner of walking and the dark circles under his eyes gave him an almost ancient appearance. Then again, the boy had always looked an odd combination of young and worn. Ruya recalled the sickly infant that Lowell had been, his jaundiced complexion and long, knobby fingers. He had outlived her interpretation of his prophecy, though she had purposefully not disclosed that detail to anyone. Length of time was difficult to determine accurately from the cryptic tarnish trails.

"Cairo," Lowell nodded to the barkeep as he approached Ruya and took a seat, keeping his eyes on the tabletop the whole way.

"Lowell," Cairo returned the nod. "Coffee?"

"Please," Lowell replied, rubbing his eyes and forehead with the palms of his hands.

"You're drinking coffee now?" Ruya asked.

"It seems to help… the headaches," Lowell answered, "and staying awake, of course."

"I'd take some as well, Cairo," Ruya said before turning back to her young friend. "You look tired. Have your long days yielded anything of interest?"

"Not much." Lowell shifted in his seat, leaning forward on his elbows with the backs of his hands pressed into the sides of his face. His speech was even more fragmented than normal. "It only…took a few days to find Tacita. Well… she sort of found me. She's back with… our group. Difficult to understand why… exactly, since I can't just come out and ask her, but… so far she's just been hanging around."

Ruya lowered her voice as she observed the boy's overwhelmed state. "How long has she been with the group?"

"Eight days, though she disappeared for the better part of yesterday," Lowell replied.

"Yet, in all this time, you have not been able to ascertain her motives? Have a conversation with her?"

"She can't speak," Lowell reminded Ruya, eyebrows raised as he made momentary eye contact with her.

"Right," Ruya replied, shaking her head. "I knew that." Sleep, coffee, she needed more of both. "Well, perhaps she is simply homesick. That or Orville has her keeping an eye on the Lower Half. She would certainly be able to access parts of the city where

Isaac would be unwelcome." Ruya paused as Cairo placed two cups of hot coffee and a small bowl of grapes on the table.

"But why did Tacita ever go to Orville in the first place?" Cairo raised a valid question. "Perhaps she is playing both sides."

"Perhaps… but which is she really on?" Ruya added that question to her figurative plate of worry. "Thank you for the information you've gathered, Lowell. Look, I…"

Lowell waited in silence across the table as Ruya struggled to find the right words. She needed to express to him both the seriousness of the task at hand and the fact that he was not obligated to take it on, to convey the severity of the risk as well as the magnitude of the payoff should they be successful. How could she let him know that she wished she did not have to ask him but that she also had no choice?

She had predicted that Lowell's life would be a short one. She was about to ask him to sacrifice what little remained of it for a greater good, a good from which neither he nor she would live to benefit from.

"You helped my mother," Lowell said suddenly, interrupting Ruya's thoughts.

"I did little," she managed to reply, watching as a tear trailed down through a layer of dirt on Lowell's cheek. "I wish I could have done more."

"You did more than anyone else," he said. "You did all you could, for her… and for me. So… whatever it is you need to ask me, ask me. And know that I will do all *I* can to return a favor I can never fully repay."

Ruya blinked repeatedly, tasting the salt from her tears as she struggled to speak. She had tried, for Lowell, for Lin. The Universe knew how hard she had tried.

"What I will ask of you is dangerous," she began. "Much of what you will face is unknown. You may never reach what I will send you to find."

"Ask me."

“Cairo,” Ruya said without looking up. “You and Brac might want to hear this too. I have a request for you next.”

Brac and Cairo made their way around the bar and took the two remaining seats at the table before she continued.

“Orville did not simply come here from another city or land, nor was he divinely sent, which I know is not a surprise to anyone at this table. You have all borne witness in one way or another to his… flaws.” Ruya paused, taking a deep breath. “He is from another *world*, and what he has been doing, as best I understand, is trying to widen the opening from which he first entered Sum, and others he has discovered since, so that resources can be rerouted from his world into ours. This other world runs alongside us somehow, like two roads that lead in the same direction. Our worlds were never meant to overlap, yet something happened years ago to fuse them together, and now there are doorways at the places where they’re connected.”

“And people can just walk right through?” Cairo asked.

“Yes,” Ruya replied, “as long as you know where to look.” Ruya glanced around the table: Cairo wide-eyed, combing his fingers through his hair; Lowell sitting motionless, mouth parted in disbelief; and Brac, his calm and smiling expression unchanged as he focused his blank eyes on Ruya.

“Orville’s *leaves*,” she pressed on, “they’re sort of like spies, though I have no idea how they work. But by using them, he learns things he would not otherwise be able to know. Two weeks ago, before I last met here with Garrett, Orville came to me. There was a new reading that foretold his inevitable downfall at the hands of a *girl with golden hair*.”

“New reading...” Cairo interjected, “that means there is an old one.”

Ruya hesitated. “There is,” she admitted. She had held onto this information for too long, thinking she could carry the weight of her secrets alone. It was time to tell. “The first reading, forty years ago, foretold that Orville’s work would destroy us all if he did not set it aside. It has remained the same, year after year.”

“But now,” Lowell muttered, “something new.”

“This girl,” Ruya nodded. “Orville will try to find her using his leaves so he can kill her and thwart fate. But there is one thing he does not understand. The ancient salvation prophecy, as you all know, tells a story of a girl with a golden crown who will unite us all.”

“You believe this girl and the one from your foretelling are one and the same?” Cairo asked.

“I do,” Ruya said, pausing to take a sip of her coffee. “There is a specific patterning to the salvation prophecy. Its strength lies in its consistency. The question of salvation can be posed a hundred different ways by a hundred different seers and the divination will be identical. This is not the case with any other foretelling. Orville’s prophecy shares strong patterns with the salvation prophecy. This is a rare, if not singularly occurring, phenomenon.

“I recently followed my brother from Gemma up through the Scalas…”

“That’s very odd,” Cairo interjected, "what was Sylvester doing that far out?”

Sylvester and Ruya were not only siblings, but they had shared a womb and come into this world just minutes apart, both gifted with an immense power to foresee the future. Ruya’s abilities were more useful than Sylvester’s, who was plagued by voices and hallucinations. Her brother had been easily swayed by Orville in those early years, turning against her and remaining with Orville after she left.

“Odd indeed,” Ruya replied. “Basira said some of the women had seen him outside the walls of the *Innova* on multiple occasions. So, I spent a few days with them and waited till he passed again. I followed him up over the ridge. He kept muttering about a ‘back door.’ Then I saw him go through one of these... openings between the worlds. I cannot describe it.” Ruya shivered at the memory of her brother crashing through the brush, mumbling to himself about a “dog” and “noisy children,” about not failing his master again, before disappearing entirely between two *hoch* trunks.

“I could follow him,” Lowell whispered.

Ruya nodded.

“Find the girl?” Lowell asked.

“Before Sylvester does,” Ruya said. “He left this morning. He appeared to be injured and was moving slowly. It might take you a day or so to catch up to and pass him, but he would be easy to track the way his leg was dragging. Find him. Then find the leaves.”

“Then once I find the leaves,” Lowell said, his voice steady, “they’ll lead me to *her*?”

“Hopefully, and if you find her and the others she is with, you can warn them about Sylvester and give them enough time to prepare to defend themselves. Orville is sending my brother to take out the threat.”

“Or at least cause a delay…” Cairo added.

“... at my brother’s expense.” Ruya’s voice cracked.

“And after I warn them,” Lowell continued, “what then?”

“Then you must be their guide, lead them back here, to us, to…” Ruya hesitated. She hadn’t thought that far ahead. She had been so focused on how to protect the girl that she had no plan for what happened next.

“... to the underground,” Cairo said firmly, a sly smile curling one corner of his mouth upward.

“The under…” Ruya looked back and forth between the faces of the man, the boy, and the giant before her.

“Ruya,” Cairo began, “I do think, my dear friend, that it is time to bring you into the light.”

“The light of what?”

“Of whom, more accurately,” Cairo corrected. “That of the Uprisen, the enlightened movement of the underground.”

“It still exists?” Ruya breathed the question. She could almost hear a click in her head as Cairo and Lowell told her about the people of the Uprisen. It all started to make sense: the colorful garments she had noticed throughout the Lower Half; the way Lowell and the other street youth congregated in organized groups and were far more quick-witted and well-spoken than children growing up on the street should be.

The movement, Cairo explained with a knowing smile, was led by an elderly intellectual they called Hawk.

"Theo," she whispered, then laughed like she hadn't in years.

He had done it. He had built his movement, and she had been completely oblivious. Her relationship with Theo had been sixteen sweet, tormented years where she tried to recover from the damage that Orville had caused. But in the end, neither her efforts nor Theo's patience could free her. When Shia died, she severed ties with him. But he had kept his promise. He had left her out of the Uprisen movement while they were together, and she had remained in the dark to this very day. But how could she not have seen it building and rising into the spirit of the city? For surely such energy should have been as obvious to her as a giant walking through the market.

As it had been planned so many years ago, the Uprisen identified themselves as a resistance movement, Cairo continued, counter to both the governing elite and Orville's radical anti-enlightenment rhetoric. He explained that they had long occupied an intricate system of underground tunnels known only to them and that they called him the gatekeeper, the one who held close all information about the movement.

Ruya thought about the conversations she had had with Cairo over the years. There were so many times when this information could have helped her, might have changed her course, yet he had never disclosed it.

"Why?" Ruya asked. "Why did you not tell me this before? Did you think I would betray my own people? Take the information to Orville?"

"Ruya," Cairo said, palms up in defense. "Please know that you were not kept in the dark because we felt you untrustworthy–quite the opposite, in fact. Theo and I spent many a late night debating the issue. We did not want to endanger you. Who knows what Orville would have done… but now, we no longer have the luxury of precaution. I believe it is time to bring you into the fold."

Enlightened movements, secret tunnels, the luxury of precaution, Theo, and Orville… this would bring Orville down. At the very least this meant she would not have to do it alone. She held tight to that realization, knowing she had no choice but to keep moving forward. And Theo…

"Ruya, can these kids find sanctuary in the *Innova* for a time once they are through?" Cairo asked.

"I believe so," she answered, shaking loose the cobwebbed memories of Theo. "I can go see Basira and arrange it."

"There's an old passage," Lowell added, "a tunnel that runs from Triplica out to the *Innova*. It will be difficult to navigate past that entry point to the city, and I have no idea what kind of shape it's in, but it's the only way I can get there undetected."

"Then that's the way you must go," Ruya said gravely.

The four of them sat in silence while the city bells chimed midnight. Only six more hours to morning shift change.

"Lowell, you shouldn't wait too much longer to get going," Cairo said when the ringing stopped. "You'll need to navigate Triplica at change when it is most busy. The more people around, the better your cover, and I expect you'll want to get a few hours rest first."

Ruya watched Cairo as he filled a small canvas bag with apples, a few potatoes, a jar of pickled beets, and two full loaves of *pan*. He stepped down into the cellar and returned with a small bladder of water and a bland, oatmeal colored tunic.

"Go put this on," Cairo instructed Lowell. "You need to be even more discreet than usual. With the riots around Licensing, purple makes you a target."

Lowell reached out a shaky hand and took the tunic.

"Rub some more dirt on your face," Cairo ordered, placing his hands on Lowell's shoulders and holding him at arm's length, "and into your hair. Keep your head down. Play dumb, deaf, and blind should anyone question you. Watch your back… but don't ever turn around." Cairo's voice cracked as he held firmly to the boy. "You hear me?"

"I hear you," Lowell replied with a nod before turning to Ruya. "I *will* find this girl, Ruya. I will bring her here."

"I know you will," Ruya choked, a lump in her throat. She rose to her feet and embraced Lowell; the sickly baby now turned into a frail but fearless boy, a boy for whom she felt so much devotion. "When you get to the *Innova*, have Basira send a messenger to Cairo."

"Not to you?" Cairo asked.

"Not to me," Ruya said. "*May your path be calm.*"

"*May your path be calm*," Lowell replied, eyes downcast but tinged with fear despite the confidence in his voice.

Ruya's stomach lurched as she watched him leave. She listened to his footfalls echoing as he headed on his way.

"And now, my dear Ruya..." Cairo said behind her, voice heavy. "What role do you have for me in this?"

"You will not like it," she replied without turning to face him.

"We are not living life fully if we like every part we play in it," Cairo said.

Ruya turned toward him with a sad smile, considering him for a moment. She had thought she knew him well: his habits, mannerisms, his history. But he was also someone else entirely, the Gatekeeper. It would take some time to reconcile these two versions of him, but he stood before her now, the same charismatic and genuine person she had grown to trust.

"I will not be here when Lowell returns," Ruya told him finally. "Yet now, more than before, I feel it is your destiny and not mine to play this role. If Lowell can guide the children through to this world, to the *Innova*, I will need you to lead them through the underground, to Theo."

"I have spent the better part of a lifetime as a gatekeeper of information," Cairo said. "I shall act in such a capacity for these children as well."

"There is one more thing, Cairo."

"What more can be asked?" he replied with wide eyes and a nervous chuckle.

"There is more at play here than a corrupt government and the ego of a crazed man," Ruya began. "Orville's actions, the actions of the Tri, they are affecting the Scalas, nature, the Klar. The Universe herself is out of sorts."

"How do you know this?" Cairo asked.

"Haddi."

"Of course," Cairo nodded in understanding.

"I know somebody who might be able to help, who might have some answers for us. But she is a long way from here, and I am not welcome there… and yet, there is somebody else who would be." Ruya nodded toward the man that still sat at the table, uncomfortably large for the chair that held him. She had long suspected Brac was descended from the giant Tor, though most no longer believed in such magical creatures of folklore. Ruya knew they were real, yet also understood that this knowledge was dangerous to the safety of their existence and was best kept secret.

Cairo looked slowly from Ruya to Brac, his expression darkening with sorrow as he realized what she was asking of him. He walked over to Brac and placed a hand on his elbow. Tears filled Ruya's eyes once again as she witnessed Cairo's grief at the thought of parting with his lifelong friend. She suspected that Cairo knew Brac was unlikely to return. If they succeeded, it would mean Brac would be reunited with the Tor. Ruya hoped they might even take him back into the scion. *If* they made it that far….

"Brac," Cairo began, voice hoarse with grief. "You, uh… you need to go with Ruya for a bit, okay?"

Brac nodded at his friend and caretaker with a placid smile.

"I wish there were another way, Cairo," Ruya said. If they pulled this off, whole generations of people would live out their days happily, unaware of the sacrifices that had been made to allow this to be so. Lowell, Cairo, Brac, Ruya–they each had a thankless role to play.

Cairo busied himself putting together travel packs for both Ruya and Brac as he had done for Lowell. Ruya sat sipping a cup of water, mulling over Garrett's concerning absence. He had not shown, and likely would not so late into the morning. She tried to convince herself that he was simply unable to enter the city and remained safely inside Gemma's walls.

The city gong signaled one hour to change when Ruya and Brac left a sniffling Cairo, who was polishing the glass coffee drip for the third time. The slightest hint of peach streaked the horizon as their breath rose like clouds into the cold morning air. The south gates were closed indefinitely thanks to the new movement restrictions. They would have to navigate north and try to exit the city via the Belt during shift change.

They had not gone far when a shuffling in an adjacent alley caused Ruya to halt, placing a hand on Brac's arm to stop him as well. She jumped, inhaling sharply as Rafi appeared from around a corner a few feet in front of her. A veteran of Orville's guard and Garrett's right hand, Rafi made her feel uneasy. He was too quick, too smooth, too pleasant.

"Sorry to startle you, *Avia*," Rafi said, teeth flashing.

"What are you doing here, Rafi?" Ruya asked, more harshly than she intended.

"I have a message for you," Rafi replied.

"Who from?" Ruya asked.

"From Orville…"

"What does Orville say?" Ruya asked, her mind racing.

"He requests that you come to him immediately," Rafi stated.

"Why?" In the forty years Ruya had known Orville, he had never once sent a messenger to her.

"I would do as he says, *Avia*," Rafi replied, his voice lowered.

Ruya's voice shook. "You call me Grandmother, yet I am of no relation to you…"

"Bring the giant along, too," Rafi whispered with a wink before disappearing down the dark alley.

CHAPTER 24

The Rupture

"Me?" Dottie snagged her pack and hurried after him. Why was *she* the reason for the leaves following them?

"Look, it's hard to explain, okay," Ben said, walking fast, keeping his eyes on the path in front of him. Hudd and Penny scrambled to grab their things and catch up.

"Bull," Dottie shot back. "Slow down!" She reached out and pulled at one of his shoulder straps.

Ben whirled around to face her, wide-eyed and breathing heavily.

"What is going on with you two?" Penny called after them.

Dottie stared at Ben, waiting for him to explain.

"Look," he said at last, shoulders slumping in defeat, "this will all make sense soon, okay? I promise. But right now we need to keep moving and I need you to trust me?"

Trust him. She would trust him, for the most part, if it weren't for the suspicious conversation between him and Aggie that she had witnessed. But maybe she was just paranoid. Suddenly, as if in response to Ben's plea to keep going, the roving cluster of leaves made their way out of the trees behind them.

"We need to move," Hudd said. "You two can argue later."

The group traveled together at a run until they put some distance between themselves and their metallic shadows, but Dottie's mind continued to race faster than her feet. They spent the rest of that day and all through the next mostly in silence, reaching Schaefer Ridge in the late afternoon. After some debate, they decided to hike up a few hundred feet to the base of the ridge, rest there until the next morning, then tackle the full journey up and down in a single shot the next day.

As they came over the top of the ridge the following morning, Dottie stopped to examine a massive rupture running along the surface of the ground a couple hundred yards or so from the base. According to their map, it was exactly where the Hudson River should have been. It made her think of the pictures she had seen of the Grand Canyon, except this was narrower and lined with black boulders and displaced earth. If the ocean itself hadn't moved inland some thirty-six miles, the canyon might have shocked her, but she just shook her head sadly and moved on.

Dottie's legs burned and her hands were shaking as she neared the end of the descent. She sat on the lip above the last steep section, catching her breath and scanning the ground below, wondering how much of the terrain had always looked this way and what portion of the jutting rock was the result of the quake. That's when she saw him. A boy a few years younger than herself, scrawny, dirty, with a mess of thick brown hair sitting like a mop on his head. He had on a tattered tunic, not unlike the one Sylvester had worn, and stood up straight on a piece of displaced land, staring right at her, motionless.

Dottie hit Ben's arm repeatedly after he slid down the rock next to her, trying to get his attention without taking her eyes off the silent observer.

"What? Hey! Stop hitting me!" Ben yelled, scooting away from Dottie.

She stopped looking at the strange boy long enough to roll her eyes at Ben as Hudd scooted down between them.

"What's going on?" Hudd asked as he stood, reaching up to offer a hand to Penny, who then accidentally slid straight into his legs, taking him out, the two of them tumbling into Ben.

The scene reminded Dottie of something out of *The Three Stooges* episodes she had watched with her dad growing up. "Hey, Larry, Curly and Moe? We have company." She tilted her head in the direction of the boy, who now wore an amused smirk.

"So, there's that," Hudd said, rising to his feet and straightening one of his pant legs that had gotten twisted in the tumble. "What's up buddy?" He called down to the boy, who calmly sat down on the rock, crossing his legs in front of him in response.

They slowly approached the boy, who stood to greet them.

"You're from *there*," Dottie said.

"I'm from Sum," he confirmed, tilting his head slightly to one side, not meeting her eyes.

"Sum," Dottie echoed. "What's your name?"

"Lowell," he replied, patting his hands on his legs.

"And Lowell," Hudd began, "are you a friend or… not so much?"

"Friend," he said with a smile, though he did not look directly at any of them.

"How do we know that's true?" Ben asked.

"You don't," Lowell responded.

"Fair enough," Hudd said. "Well, what are you doing here?"

"I'm here to show the girl with golden hair the way through," Lowell said.

"Through a door?" Dottie asked. *The girl with golden hair*. That's exactly what Sylvester had called her.

"Come on," Lowell replied, gesturing for the others to follow him as he turned and hopped down from the ledge, moving quickly in the opposite direction. "I'll show you."

"I'll bite," Hudd said, looking around at the others before turning to follow Lowell.

They walked closely behind the boy for the better part of an hour, winding in and out of a section of conservation land and passing through a golf course and a street filled with quaint houses. Dottie knew they were heading in the direction of the rupture she had seen before. Was it possible that Aggie and Ari had already made it through to this other world, to Sum, as the boy had called it?

"Did Aggie send you?" Dottie called to Lowell.

"Don't know any Aggie," he replied, without looking back or stopping.

"Then who did?" Dottie asked as they came out from between two buildings into an open field.

"Somebody who wants to see you live," the boy said bluntly, trudging forward into the mess of frostbitten weeds and grass that covered the field.

They drew closer to the edge of the rift and Lowell gestured for them to continue moving northeast alongside it.

"Wait," Ben called. "We need to cross this thing."

"I need to take you that way," Lowell replied.

"No," Ben said, his voice firm. "We have a job to do. We need to get across and stay on track to D.C."

"Don't know any D.C." Lowell countered. "But I do…" he paused awkwardly, mid-sentence. "I know who wants you all dead and who can keep you safe."

"Wait," Dottie cut in, shaking her head, "*who* wants us dead?"

“Him,” Lowell said, gesturing to the ever-present shadow of golden leaves that peeked out from between the warehouses on the other side of the field.

“Orville,” Penny muttered.

“Yep,” Lowell said.

“He wants us dead so we can't get the information where it needs to go,” Ben said accusingly, glaring at Lowell. “All the more reason we *have* to succeed in doing just that.”

Lowell shrugged his shoulders in response.

“Look, we need to make camp either way,” Hudd said, lowering his pack onto the ground. “It’s getting late, and to be honest, I'm not liking the look of those clouds out over the water.”

Hudd was right. Dottie didn't know much about clouds, but the dense, grey fog moving in from the ocean seemed ominous. They were too far from any kind of cover to build a shelter and would have to wait out the night exposed to the elements. Dottie sighed. At least it had been warmer the last few days. Ben got a good fire going, and Penny went through what little food and water stores they had left, rationing out a meal for each them. She offered some to Lowell, who perched on the ground with his legs crossed in front of him. He hesitated, looked at the piece of jerky in Penny’s hand up to the girl’s face and out to the water.

“It’s okay,” Penny said. “I promise.”

Lowell nodded his thanks as he took the jerky and devoured the savory meat in two bites.

“When was the last time you ate, Lowell?” Penny asked.

Lowell shrugged his shoulders in response. “Couple o’ days, I guess.”

Penny dug through the snacks for a granola bar to hand him next, which he accepted and devoured like the jerky.

“Why haven’t you eaten in days?” Penny asked. “Where is your family? Your home?”

“No family…” Lowell muttered with a mouthful of food. “I’m in a corner group. We sleep where we can find shelter from the wind.”

“You’re homeless…” Penny breathed.

“Why you?” Hudd cut in. “Why would somebody send a boy who hasn’t eaten in days through to another world, on rough terrain, to fetch a couple of other kids?”

Lowell made brief eye contact with Dottie. The momentary connection caught her off guard, so powerful was the light in his eyes.

“I see things… differently,” Lowell explained. “When we go back, we have to go underground, through tunnels… I can… navigate those tunnels.”

“And others can’t?” Ben asked.

“Few… and even then, not as well as I can.” Lowell began scooping up handfuls of rocks and weeds and arranging them in a circle on the ground. “What do you see?”

“Rocks… weeds,” Hudd replied.

“A circle,” Penny observed.

“It is between us, yes?” Lowell asked.

The group nodded.

“I look at this and I see seven and six hundred and thirty-nine one-hundredths,” Lowell said. He began to rock back and forth on his heels. “The circle is divided into quadrants with rocks and weeds alternating at six pieces per quadrant. Six, four times is twenty-four. Twenty-four divided by pi is seven and six hundred and thirty-nine one-hundredths. The diameter, *or* the space from me to you. Or forty-five, as the whole of the mass that lies between us.” Lowell wiped away his mathematic example. “You might see a shape between us, or an element or set of elements, or perhaps even a visually estimated physical distance. I see numbers.”

“And how does this help us get into Sum?” Dottie asked. This boy could do more math in his head than she could do on a calculator.

“The tunnels… there are millions of them. They have only ever been recorded once and on a series of maps that few can read. One must not only possess the maps, or mentally retain them as I can, but one must also be able to piece them together using a concept of thirty-six overlapping, abstract matrices, each possessing an infinite dimension.”

“So… you have a photographic memory?” Hudd asked.

Lowell nodded.

“And because of the way you see life as numbers…” Penny began.

“I can navigate the underground,” Lowell finished.

∝

Dottie nibbled on a couple of almonds as the sun dropped low in the sky. The storm clouds over the water became more menacing, and the sun’s rays streamed through sheets of rain that fell on the horizon. She stood and scanned the length of the rupture path. At its base, a massive wall of interwoven roots held the water from the ocean at bay. The way down and back up the rupture was steeper closer to the cusp and widest at the bottom – though it wasn’t the bottom, just the place where the visible walls stopped and dropped off into a dark abyss. The walls became slightly less inclined, and the chasm narrowed as she looked up the path. At the northernmost point of what she could see of the rupture, for it continued past her line of sight, a red glow became visible through the darkness.

“What’s that light over there?” she asked the others.

“I’m not sure what it’s called,” Lowell said, “but I passed by it earlier. It looks like mud that’s on fire. Black and red, and puts off a lot of heat.”

“Lava,” Ben muttered, jumping to his feet and coming to stand by Dottie.

“Sure is what it seems like,” Hudd replied, joining them.

“What next, tornados?” Penny scoffed.

Dottie shook her head. At this point, nothing would surprise her.

"Look at the water," Ben said, pointing in the opposite direction, "down by all those roots."

"What about it?" Hudd asked.

"It's risen since we got here, a couple of feet at least."

Ben was right.

"Doesn't the water go up and down with the tide or something?" Dottie asked.

"Not like that," Ben replied.

With each rush of waves the water rose. They stood there for a time, watching the height of the water closely.

"Keeps going up like this," Hudd said after a time, "it's gonna fill this chasm before we wake up tomorrow."

"We need to cross tonight," Dottie said. "Guys… we need to cross now."

CHAPTER 25
The Guard

Ruya stood at the entrance to Orville's compound, the afternoon sun glistening off the freshly lacquered wood and oiled iron. Orville demanded the gate be kept pristine along with all the other doors inside Gemma's walls. She had once heard him assert that "a worn front door is a sign of weakness to one's enemies." But she believed Orville's true intent was to intimidate his own people, rather than those who meant him harm. Even *she* fell victim to the atmosphere of this place. There was something about it that drove her mad.

"You've arrived," a voice crooned down to Ruya from the tower window above. She looked up to see Rafi's smile flashing at her.

“Well,” she called up to the man, shielding her eyes from the glare of the sun, “are you going to make me stand out here all morning?” Gemma’s stone walls towered high over Ruya, and she had to lean back to see him.

“Let her in,” Rafi called to the guards inside the gate below, then disappeared as he jumped down from the ledge.

Ruya heard the sound of iron latches sliding open. She waited as the gate creaked inward, uncomfortably aware of the remnants of the dirt road wedged inside her canvas shoes. She forced a smile when Rafi bounded down the last few stairs at the tower base and strode towards her. She knew he had meant to intimidate her back in the alley outside Cairo’s and she had no intention of letting him know he had succeeded.

He embraced her gently and placed a kiss on her cheek, as Garrett would have done. Ruya was not sure what unsettled her more, the way Rafi treated her as if she were some fragile thing, or that he took the liberty to embrace her at all. Though Rafi was younger than Garrett, the two men had grown to be friends in the six years since Rafi joined Orville’s guard. The old seer relied heavily on her intuition – which usually manifested in the rumblings and churnings of her stomach – to navigate the world. Rafi’s affections felt like a punch in the gut, and because of that and his newfound arrogance, she hoped to keep him at a distance.

“Orville is expecting you,” Rafi said as he led Ruya through the military section of the encampment. “I believe he is looking forward to your… visit.” He was friendly as they passed through the Plaza, remarking on the improvements their masonry division had made to the inner walls. Orville’s camp had started as a small two-bedroom lean-to located to the west of the northern orb of the city. He had lived there alone for the first few years, coming and going from Alterra under close scrutiny of the Lex by order of the Council. Ruya had visited him regularly until he disappeared for the better part of two years and returned to her changed in so many ways.

She walked alongside Rafi through the back half of the compound and up three flights of narrow stairs. Bodyguards dressed in charcoal grey tunics and armed with scimitars were stationed at each level of the winding stairwell. The long, curved blades of the illegal weapons rested sheathed at the guards' sides. That was intentional too. Orville could have armed his men with any kind of legal weaponry but chose one banned by the Tri as an insult to the elders. Ruya's heart beat harder as she followed Rafi through yet another glistening door. She placed a sweaty palm on the perfectly lacquered wood and passed through into Orville's parlor.

A large oval table and chairs filled the space, scrolls and maps strewn about its surface. A fireplace warmed the room from one end. Orville's entourage stood in clusters around its edges, discussing and debating amongst themselves as Orville lounged arrogantly with his feet propped up on the table in front of him. Ruya briefly caught the menacing glare of the servant, Zaila, wrenching her stomach anew. She scolded herself for not preparing for this encounter. Had Orville placed Zaila there intentionally to intimidate Ruya? Surely Zaila would be by Orville's side regardless, as she always was… Amaya's daughter. Ruya was quick to redirect her gaze from the girl. She must not appear to be searching for Garrett.

Ruya caught a glimpse of Garrett from the corner of her eye. She let her eyes wander the room, noting the numerous respected leaders of both the Lower and Upper Half that Orville had attracted and corrupted over the years. His council was nothing but a farce. He made deals with the members under the table, bribing them to make sure their expert opinions supported his already solidified plans, promising each some coveted power or resource. These men both feared Ruya and looked down on her. She was a bonded woman of the Lower Half, the least of the least. At the same time, she held the power of prophecy and had earned the good favor and trust of the people. She was at once lowly, yet powerful; base, yet influential; insignificant, yet dangerous. Men such as these did not know what to make of Ruya, and they often chose to ignore her entirely. This had bothered her in the past, but now she was grateful that she didn't need to acknowledge them.

"Ah, Rafi, I see you've found our long-lost prophetess!" Orville mocked from his chair. His cheeks were flushed, and a mostly-empty cup of wine sat next to him on the table. "I believe I requested Ruya come immediately, didn't I Zaila?" The girl nodded, the corners of her mouth turned up in a sneer. "Why was I made to wait for so many days?"

"I came as quickly as I was able," Ruya said. "Might I know why I'm so urgently needed?"

"You may ask," Orville replied gruffly, "though I may choose not to answer you." He drew his feet off the table and lurched forward, refilling his cup and taking a long drink. "You have not asked about NEM."

"I've only just arrived," Ruya deflected. Orville was far more drunk and unsettled than he had been when she had last seen him.

"Well, I'll tell you about her anyway," Orville said. "Her first performance was a success, you know. That was no simple quake. More powerful than I could have ever dreamed," he boasted. "She's recovering marvelously. I do believe I was too cautious with her before."

"She succeeded?" Ruya whispered, her heart dropping. Orville had been working on NEM for thirty-five years. A giant "magnet," he called it, though she didn't understand most of the specifics.

"We have yet to verify that, Sir," Garrett interjected. "But we have field teams out now looking to confirm…"

"Yes, yes, get your confirmation," Orville snapped. "You might need it, but I don't. You *felt* her power. She succeeded. You all felt it."

"Yes, but Orville," said Linos, one of Orville's advisors, "was it powerful enough to cause destabilization?" The elderly man had led the city's Small Council on Science and Agriculture for years before it was abandoned as a result of the decline in agricultural trade. He leaned against the table, stroking his chin.

"That's what we're working to find out," Garrett answered for Orville as the inebriated man took another swig of wine and turned his chair away from the rest of the room, glaring into the fire.

"If it did," Ioram, a former temple host, began shakily, "would it hold? For how long, Garrett?"

“There's no way to know,” Garrett replied, eyebrows raised, as he stepped forward into the center of the room and into Ruya’s direct line of sight.

She breathed a sigh of relief to see him standing as sure as ever. His absence from their meeting at Cairo’s, followed so closely by Rafi’s surprise request had made her worry that something terrible had happened. In the time needed to deliver Brac to the *Innova* for safe keeping and to speak with Basira about sanctuary for the girl with golden hair, she had imagined Garrett suffering a hundred different deaths.

“There’s been no way to test for these things.” Garrett faced the advisers and spoke with confidence. “The electromagnetic pulse from NEM would have had to be strong enough to both destabilize the magnetic field that holds the worlds apart *and* generate enough power to cause an impact between the two surfaces that could widen the rupture.”

“Pin-point accuracy!” Orville blurted without turning from the fire.

“Yes,” Garrett continued. “This is all assuming that the pulse was placed accurately.”

“Do you doubt my formulas, Garrett?” Orville demanded as he swung his chair around and rose to his feet, swaying.

“I do not doubt the formulas, sir,” Garrett responded coolly, undeterred by the fire in Orville’s eyes. “As I’ve stated before, I simply acknowledge that we may have missed something, or that there may be an element of which we are not yet aware.”

“I’ve accounted for shifts in time, lunar activity, and gravitational pull,” Orville boomed. “I’ve adjusted for molecular stability and mineral influence!” He moved towards Garrett, waving his now empty wine cup in the air. “My algorithms are flawless. I will not allow you to call them into question…you or anyone else!”

Ruya watched as Garrett drew his shoulders back and took a deep breath.

"Yes sir," he responded slowly. "My apologies. I was not trying to question your expertise. Rather, I was attempting to explain the unknown variables to the others in the room who may not be capable of fully understanding the complex algorithms you've generated."

Orville looked up into Garrett's face, wavering under the influence of too much wine. Ruya felt increasingly nervous as an uncomfortable silence filled the room. Orville was the first to look away, glancing down at his cup.

"Zaila, my dear," Orville stated, voice lower and steadier now, "more wine."

"Yes, sir," the girl replied, quickly retrieving the jug and refilling Orville's cup.

"This is an exceptional vintage," Orville said to no one in particular. "A fifty-year-old bottle. Came over on one of the last trade ships from *Procul* shortly after I found this broken world." He paused to swirl the blood-red liquid, lifting the cup to his nose, lips parted slightly, taking in its fragrance through flared nostrils before he continued. "Oh, so broken were you all. Trade practically non-existent, agriculture faltering, civil unrest growing. And it has gotten worse. If only you had listened to me sooner, the last forty years might not have been filled with such hardship."

Rafi, who had thus far remained silent at Ruya's side said, "*We* heed your words, sir," as he stepped forward into the room.

Ruya saw Garrett cast a warning look in Rafi's direction. After all this debate and confrontation, she still had no idea why she was here. Given Orville's present state, she was growing increasingly fearful.

"*You…*" Orville's gaze turned to Rafi. "You who served the elite, our opposition? Who only came to join us as a last resort?"

Rafi's confident smile evaporated.

"You heed my words now, perhaps," Orville ranted. "Though it was not always so, and you have yet to conduct yourself in a manner that will make me forget it. You came here, Rafi, at the direct request of Garrett, yet how will you repay him?"

Rafi's cheeks reddened from Orville's rebuke, and he silently returned to Ruya's side. What did Orville mean about repayment?

"*Out*," Orville whispered and then yelled the command, his voice filling the room as he ordered all but Ruya, Garrett, and Zaila from the room. His servant, Isaac, entered just as the last of Orville's advisors filed out the door.

"Have I not always taken care of my children?" Orville asked the wall next to him, then returned his gaze to the swirling wine that seemed to mesmerize him. "Well?" he asked the wall again, almost comically. "Have you no response?"

Ruya shifted uncomfortably from one aching foot to the other. The movement attracted Orville's attention.

"Have I not always taken care of my children?" This time he directed the question at Ruya.

"You… you have," she conceded nervously.

"Have I not loved them?" Orville pressed.

"You have loved them," Ruya replied, her voice cracking.

"And yet…" He paused. "You despise me for it."

"I do not," Ruya said. This was a dangerous game she was being asked to play. Orville was rarely reckless with his words. And she was normally better able to guess at his intentions and to identify the ever-changing rules of his game, navigating safely to the outcome that would benefit them all. But this… this was a new situation entirely.

"You do not show me the gratitude I deserve for carrying such a heavy burden all these years," Orville continued. He returned to his seat by the fire, affectionately patting the hand Zaila placed on his shoulder.

Ruya forced herself to regain control of her emotions as she felt tears well in her eyes. She clasped her shaking hands to steady them.

"Does our son not look well, Ruya?" Orville asked pointedly. Ruya focused on Garrett, whose posture and expression had not changed at all.

Good boy, she thought, *I may be weak, but you must be strong.*

"Have I not done all I promised for him? For all my children?" Orville pressed, though he did not wait for a response. "In fact, my dear, I'd argue that removing him from you was the best thing I could have done for him. Perhaps Shia would still be with us if I'd taken her as well."

And there it was. His words were a dagger that stabbed into her core.

"At least I've kept one daughter," he said as he patted Zaila's hand again. "No thanks to you, of course."

"*My* mother kept *me* close," Zaila added.

Ruya noticed Garrett's hands tense slightly and silently begged the Universe to steady them both. Her head spun as she focused all her energy into remaining on her feet. Had Orville simply brought her here to torture her? Them? Did anything other than spite drive him? Or did he know… had he somehow found out about her meetings with Garrett?

Ruya thought briefly of Shia, her fair-skinned and free-spirited little girl who had turned so dark. She had had too much of Orville in her. Ruya had never found a way to tame the demons that eventually consumed her daughter. She had felt hopeful when Haddi came along. The boy had a way of bringing out the good in her girl. Oh, how she could light up a room with her laughter when she was with Haddi. But in the end, the darkness was too much for her to bear, destroying her soul completely.

"Yes..." Orville's voice broke through Ruya's thoughts. "Yes, Zaila, your mother knew better than to let you wander off. Ruya… you could have learned a thing or two from Amaya. Particularly about proper child-rearing… and loyalty."

"Loyal till death," Zaila said.

Ruya's head spun with the memory of saying goodbye to Garrett at Gemma's gates when he was just a young boy, a barely walking Shia clinging to her brother's waist, screaming for him as if her heart was being torn from her chest. Ruya's own heart ached with the memory of Shia's years of torment, these painful memories resurfacing because of Orville's petty cruelty.

"All that I have done," Orville went on, "all that I continue to do… and you two conspire."

"No," Ruya whispered.

"No?" Orville replied. "Have you not been meeting in secret? Consorting at all hours of the night and day to plot my demise?"

"No," Ruya's voice was hoarse, warped by the sob that rested in her throat.

"Don't lie to me!" Orville yelled. "I *know* you were."

"We were," Garrett said.

"... but not to see to your end, Orville," Ruya stammered. How could things be spinning out of control so quickly? "You must believe me. It was my fault. I have been pressuring Garrett for years to meet me. I missed my son so…"

"Lies," Orville growled. "And now what choice does that leave me?" He went on, more to himself and his glass of wine than to the others in the room. "If you had just been honest, perhaps… but no. It must be done."

"What?" Ruya sobbed, knowing all too well the cruelty he could inflict. "*What* must be done? Whatever you're thinking, I assure you this was *my* fault, Orville. I convinced Garrett that he must meet with me to help you. He only ever wanted to see you succeed!"

"Let us say for a moment," Orville said, "that you're telling the truth, that Garrett had no ill intent, and that *you* are solely to blame. Well then, Ruya, you deserve a punishment that is much more severe."

Yes, yes… she would face whatever came, as long as it meant keeping Garrett safe. What she said, after all, was not entirely untrue. Garrett would never have initiated contact with her out of loyalty to his father. He had only agreed to it on her suggestion.

"Yet…" Orville paused, taking the chipped pawn from his pocket, rolling it between his thumb and forefinger. "Yet, the way to make an impression on you, make the punishment fit the crime, so to speak, would be not to harm *you* at all."

No.

"Isaac," Orville called.

The servant stepped out from behind Rafi.

"Take Garrett to the courtyard."

No.

"Have all the men assemble."

Universe, no!

"Blind him. He shall never *see* his beloved mother again… and she shall live with that pain for the rest of her life."

CHAPTER 26
The Pass

A clinging dampness filled the space around Dottie. She sat perched on the edge of the rupture path, using the last bit of sunlight to try and see down to the bottom. She tried to memorize as much of the path as she could since they would likely end up navigating a good amount of it in darkness. The way up the other side appeared steeper than the way down. That might pose a problem. But it was truly now or never as the ocean waves crashed against the base of the rupture, the water rising quickly against the wall of ancient roots that formed the makeshift dam.

They had to get far enough up the other side before the water broke over the top of the roots. She watched Lowell go first. He dropped down into the chasm and scampered over the black boulders. He was a bit like Mowgli from the *Jungle Book*, using his hands and bare feet to cling to the slippery surfaces.

Penny went next, lowering herself cautiously down into the rocks and moving slowly from one to the other.

Dottie tried to focus. She imagined that this was how it felt when facing tough ski moguls on a double black diamond. Always trying to think a few steps ahead, choosing your course wisely, but keeping up some momentum. She had always hummed during times like that. It kept her calm and steady. She began to hum quietly then, no particular song, just whatever came to mind.

"That's a pretty epic tune," Hudd said as he plopped down next to her, making her jump.

"Look, I… I hum when I'm nervous," Dottie replied, embarrassed.

"Seriously?" Hudd flung his legs over the edge on which Dottie sat, grinning, amused with himself for catching Dottie off guard. "Like you give yourself a theme song?"

"Yeah, it's a thing, okay," Dottie said, grinning and shaking her head.

Hudd chuckled, but his smile softened as he paused, looking back up at Dottie with a hint of sadness in his eyes.

"See you on the other end of this thing, okay Dot?" Hudd said. "Take your time, hum a damn tune, whatever gets you there."

Tears filled Dottie's eyes as the weight of Hudd's words and the challenge they now faced hit her. She let Hudd navigate down a couple of yards before taking a deep breath and launching her own body over the side and into the mess of boulders. She stood, holding onto the lip where she had been sitting, foot wedged awkwardly between two sloping faces of rock.

"You good?" Ben asked from a few feet away.

"Yeah," Dottie replied, voice shaking. She was far from good.

"Take your time," Ben said. "Move with purpose."

Dottie nodded. She made her way down into the rupture, carefully, methodically, pausing only a few times to adjust her course. Some of the flatter surfaces were slippery from ocean mist, but the shallower places, where two rocks met or chunks of gritty earth sprouted from the wall, made for easier maneuvering. Dottie wasn't sure how long it took, an hour, maybe two, but she eventually joined Lowell, Hudd, and Penny at the bottom of the visible portion. Ben joined them shortly after.

They sat together and peered down into the chasm, the rupture path at its center. The crevice was about six feet wide at that point, which seemed to be as narrow as it got. Lowell tilted his head at the others before springing effortlessly across the rupture to the other side. Dottie held her breath, panic stirring once again in her chest.

The best way to keep your mind from going off the tracks is to plant yourself firmly in the present. Dottie remembered Aggie's words. *Be where you are*. She closed her eyes, feeling the mist settle on her cheeks, digging her fingernails into the layer of gritty dirt.

She opened her eyes to find that she was able to see very little as the storm clouds moved across the sky and covered the moon. A few weak stars and the faint red glow of the lava trail were all that lit their way, and that only enough to see a few feet ahead.

She felt a hand rest on her upper arm.

"Your turn," Ben said behind her. "Penny and Hudd both made it across."

Dottie reached up and squeezed his hand before crawling forward to where the ground dropped off. She stood slowly, perching precariously with one foot against the edge and the other behind her. Dottie stepped back, mentally measuring the distance between her and the infinite darkness. Deep breath in, forward, step, leap. Her arms swung in circles as her body flew, suspended in the darkness. She closed her eyes, and for one brief moment she thought she must have missed the other side before her knees slammed hard into a brutal, but very real and very stable, rock face. She climbed up a few yards, moving quickly as she searched through the darkness for any sign of Ben.

"I made it!" she yelled over the increasing volume of howling wind and crashing waves. The mist had now turned to full droplets of water as the rain began to fall. "Damn it," she muttered, sliding back down toward her landing point, straining to see back across the chasm.

A second wave of relief hit her as Ben came hurtling through the darkness and landed at her feet. He pushed himself away from the edge and towards her quickly, looking up at her through nervous laughter.

They were over halfway there now. The rain was falling, the water was rising, and gusts of wind were picking up, but Dottie knew that it would be over soon. They pressed on. She came close enough to Hudd at one point to shout up to him through the noise of the storm and got a thumbs-up in return. Flashes of lightning began to alternate with crashing thunder as they worked their way up. During the next burst of lightning, Dottie caught a glimpse of Lowell wriggling up over the very top ledge.

One safe, Dottie thought, *four to go.* She took a deep breath, shifting a foot to one side, stretching to reach the next handhold. The rock underneath her foot gave way, the tips of her fingers slipping from the notch above. She skidded down hard onto a narrow, flat ledge. Pressing her back against the wall of the cliff, a single sob escaped her. She had almost made it to the end, and God she was just so tired. She tilted her head back, letting the falling rain beat on her face. She let out a yell of frustration, releasing some of the anger, fear, and sorrow that continued to build inside her. She sat forward, searching the darkness for any clues about where she was.

As another strike of lightning lit up the rupture, Dottie covered her mouth to stifle a scream, not that anybody would hear her. Ben was within view, but it was the hulking figure of a man not far below him that caused her alarm. Had she seen him? Was her mind just playing tricks on her? Another strike. The shadowy figure was gaining on Ben. Dottie shifted as far to her left as she could go on the ledge, reaching a hand out into the darkness in search of anything to grab hold of so she could get down to Ben. Nothing. She scrambled to the other side, again stretching as far as she could reach, clawing at the empty air.

Another bolt of lightning struck a cluster of trees on one side of the root dam. One of the trees erupted into flame, creating enough light for Dottie to see Ben's pursuer more clearly. She could make out the wild hair and crazy eyes that unmistakably belonged to Sylvester. Ben was working his way up to Dottie's right, about twenty yards down. She called his name as loudly as she could, but the wind stole her words before they could reach him. She yelled to him again, but he still did not hear. Just above her to her side Penny perched on the edge of a boulder, Hudd having helped her up at some point. Dottie made eye contact with Penny, whose look of desperation said that she had seen him too.

I'm stuck, Dottie mouthed, looking from Penny up to Hudd. He lifted a hand in the air and shrugged questioningly. He didn't see him. Dottie watched as Penny began making her way down to Ben with an uncharacteristic determination. Waving to Hudd, Dottie pointed at Ben and the pursuing menace of Sylvester just feet below him on the rocks. She continued to observe helplessly as Penny descended. Hudd scrambled, trying to find his way to Ben as well, but he was too far away.

Dottie continued to search for a way off the ledge. Standing on her tiptoes and pressing her chest flat across the wall behind her, she reached up, blindly groping for a reasonable handhold. Her fingertips caught hold of a ridge of rock and she pulled with all her might. The rock broke loose and slammed into her forehead, knocking her down. The world spun as she pulled herself on her stomach over to the edge, trying to stay focused on what was happening.

"Go!" she screamed down at Ben, "behind you!" But it was no use. The wind was too strong, and the waves that now crashed up and over the wall of woven tree roots drowned out any other sound. The dam whined as the rising ocean began to trickle over the top and spill into the rupture. Dottie saw it all but was powerless to influence the outcome, trapped on the ledge.

Ben paused briefly to rest his forehead against the surface of a boulder in front of him. Just as he looked up and caught Dottie's terrified gaze, Sylvester's hand came up out of the darkness and clamped down on his leg. Dottie briefly glimpsed the terror that filled Ben's face before he whirled around to face Sylvester. Ben tried to swing an arm down at his attacker but was unable to land a blow. He kicked back with his free leg, driving hard into Sylvester's shoulder, knocking the hermit loose from the rocks. Sylvester slid backward toward the chasm at the center of the rupture, dragging Ben with him. The root dam groaned again as the ocean waves continued to break through. Once that buckled, water and mud would come rushing straight at all of them.

"No, please God," Dottie begged. Penny was closing in on Ben and Sylvester, moving deftly down from one boulder to the next. She paused just above Ben as he clawed at the rocks, trying to stop his downward momentum. Sylvester's feet slipped over the edge of the chasm. Penny lunged forward, propelling her body toward Sylvester. The force of her momentum caused them both to fall as one, plummeting over the edge of the chasm and down into the black abyss.

The scream that left Dottie was neither of this world nor the other. But in the moment that followed, despite the wind and crashing waves, a devastating silence fell over her like a wet blanket, stifling, suffocating. Ben lay on his stomach below, peering down into the chasm. Was he screaming for Penny the way Dottie had? She wouldn't be able to hear him if he was.

The dam moaned louder still, and chilling pops filled the air as roots began to snap under the weight of the rising water, stirring Ben into motion. Dottie watched as he moved with determination up the side of the rupture toward her. Something brushed her arm, and she looked up to see a rope dangling from where Hudd perched above them. Ben grabbed hold of the rope and climbed the rest of the way to Dottie.

"Climb," he ordered, grabbing her by both shoulders.

"Penny!" Dottie screamed in response, pushing against him to look down into the chasm where Penny had disappeared.

"She's gone," Ben yelled over the din.

Dottie remained frozen, looking from Ben to the black below.

"She's gone… climb!" Ben commanded her more forcefully, tears streaking the mud on his face.

A crash from the root dam set her in motion. Dottie had just wrapped the rope around her ankle, pressing it between the top of one foot and the bottom of the other – as she had once learned in gym class, a lifetime ago – when the last of the roots tore apart. A cascading wall of water and mud rushed into the deep cavern at the center of the rupture.

"Go!" Ben yelled.

And Dottie climbed. Shoulder pressing against the wall of rocks, she worked her way up the rope like an inchworm, hand-over-hand to extend her body, then pulling her legs to her chest and rearranging the rope between her feet. Once she reached a point where she could get a decent hold on the rocks, she released the rope and climbed the rest of the way on her own, Ben close behind. Clinging to the ledge at the top, she turned back to watch the rushing waves fill the entire length of the rupture, covering all the way up to the trails of lava and extinguishing any last hope for Penny. Hudd grabbed Dottie by the shoulders and heaved her up and over the ledge, then offered a hand to Ben. The three of them fell to the ground, drenched through and with hearts demolished from the weight of so much loss.

They stayed there, a huddled mass of grief and exhaustion while Lowell crouched nearby. The sun came up, revealing a perfectly calm ocean. Brilliant red filled the clear morning sky. Dottie felt numb. Ben built a small fire from some brush and leaves – not the kind of leaves that had been pursuing them, just some regular dead ones – and handed around the last bottle of water and a few MREs. Dottie took a few bites of "beef stew" before setting it aside.

"We need to keep moving," Ben said after a time.

Dottie knew he was right, but anger filled her all the same. "We can't leave without..." she began.

"Damn it, Dottie," Ben shot back with tears in his eyes. "Don't you think I'm hurting just the same as you? I watched it all too, you know! I watched her fall into that rift. I watched her take Sylvester with her. She... she died... saving *me*. She died... to keep *you* alive. She died so that we could accomplish something that's bigger than you or me, bigger than any of us. We *need* to keep going."

Dottie shook some of the cobwebs from her head and rose to her feet.

"I'm sorry," she told Ben, putting a hand on his arm and searching his eyes for forgiveness. "You're right. Let's go."

Ben wrapped his arms around her and drew her against his chest, firmly, briefly, before taking her by the shoulders and holding her at arm's length.

"When we get there," he said, "when this is over, we can mourn, we can hurt, we can try to make sense of it all, but there's no place for it now. Okay?"

Dottie nodded.

Ben had not let her go. His eyes searched hers as he reached a hand up, brushed a frizzy curl off of her forehead and then turned away.

They walked through dried out farmland for the better part of the morning, stopping only once to take a sip of water. As Dottie rested briefly, leaning up against the wall of a still-standing barn, a loud hum filled her ears. She peered around the corner of the barn, but the leafy metallic swarm that she expected was not there. It had remained stranded on the other side of the rupture-turned-river. The hum grew louder.

A helicopter.

It was like something out of a dream. A grey helicopter zoomed through the sky and landed in the open field. The group shuffled out from behind the barn, wind from the propeller making Dottie's frizzy golden curls dance wildly. A man jumped down, dressed in camo fatigues and wearing a helmet. He raced toward them, ducking under the propeller blades and jogging across the field.

"I'm Echo," he shouted. "Come with me. Stay low, move quickly."

Dottie recognized the pattern of his fatigues as belonging to the Marine Corps. And who could be trusted if not a Marine? Dottie's feet carried her across the field, under the thumping blades of the propeller, and she took one step up into the helicopter before Echo lifted her the rest of the way. They all piled in, and Dottie instinctively grabbed Ben's hand as they rose shaking into the air.

CHAPTER 27
The Prophecy

"How is this thing even working?!" Ben yelled to Echo as the helicopter lifted into the air.

"It was underground!" Echo shouted back.

"Like a bunker?" Dottie's voice was no more than a hoarse whisper. Echo shook his head and pointed to the side of his helmet to let her know he couldn't hear her.

They rose up high over the field. Dottie leaned close enough to the open edge to peer down at the world below them, this strange terrain of vacant homes, jutting ridges of displaced land and road, mudslides, and sunken buildings. They lifted higher still, and the flooded rupture path came into view. It was even larger than she had thought. The section that they had navigated the night before was only part of the base. It extended up and out in the shape of a tree, not unlike the mark left by the lightning strike on Ben's arm -- now healed into a pink scar -- or the one the snowflake left on her hand in her dream.

Dottie looked down at Lowell next to her. He was curled up into a ball, hands over his ears and repeating something aloud. She tried to put an arm around him, but he cowered at the touch. She wondered if there were helicopters in Sum, but considered it doubtful given what she had learned about the other world so far. The experience must be incredibly overwhelming to the young boy, who already seemed to process the world around him differently.

Dottie sat back against the thinly cushioned seat and closed her eyes, remaining that way until she felt the helicopter begin to descend. They landed in another open field. She followed Echo's instructions to duck down and run until she no longer felt the force of the blades at her back. A woman stood in the middle of the field waiting for them. Where had she come from? There were no vehicles or buildings nearby.

"This is Miss Morrow," Echo said, loudly making the introduction. He wasn't used to speaking normally after the noise of the helicopter.

"Please, call me Rebecca," she corrected gently. "Follow me." She offered a pained smile and a curt nod before turning to walk, heading into the middle of nowhere. They walked about a hundred yards before Dottie saw what looked like a woodshed, draped with huge camouflage blankets and textured netting. Lowell, Dottie, Ben, and Hudd followed Rebecca into the shed, through two heavy metal doors, and into a dimly lit stairwell.

"How are the lights working?" Ben asked Echo, who secured each door behind them with heavy hinge locks.

"Protected power grid," he replied. "Everything that was inside the bunker when the initial electromagnetic pulse struck is still functional."

Of course the military would have protection against this sort of thing.

They trudged down four flights of stairs and through another heavy metal door, which opened into a parking garage with only a few scattered vehicles present. They passed quickly through to the other side. Dottie's feet ached, and the pounding in her head made it hard to focus. After passing another metal door and a set of hallways flanked by darkened rooms, Dottie found herself in a triage room where a team of nurses was waiting. She climbed up onto the gurney as instructed, aware of how plush the mattress felt beneath her after so many nights sleeping on the hard ground. She was safe. But Penny was still gone, had tumbled into the darkness with Sylvester after giving *her* life for theirs.

"I don't think she even knows she's bleeding," a woman's voice said from somewhere far away. "Dorothy, do you remember how you hit your head?"

Dorothy.

"We need to get that stitched up," a man's voice added.

It sounded like they were all under water. Dottie couldn't muster a reply and only vaguely noticed the pressure applied over her right eye. Through the haze that built up like a tunnel around her line of vision, she made out the figure of Audrey, Penny's sister. She hadn't seen Audrey since before manhunt the night everything happened, hadn't thought much about her since Hudd asked about her in the middle of that first night. Dottie watched as Hudd stood from the chair where he had been sitting, eyes wide as Audrey crossed the room to him. She fell into his arms and he embraced her, kissing the top of her head and holding on as if he would never let go. It was like watching a silent movie. Dottie guessed at their conversation based on their expressions. Hudd was telling Audrey the truth, but perhaps she had expected it all along.

Dottie struggled with the guilt she felt, mixed with another emotion she didn't recognize. Were these feelings all because of Penny? She had played a role in her death – she should certainly have been able to find a way down to Ben. It should have been *her* who toppled over that ledge with Sylvester, not innocent Penny. If she had never given Penny that knife back at the train, she might still be with them now.

Suddenly Dottie knew what that other emotion was. Jealousy. She was jealous over the ease with which Audrey and Hudd interacted, how genuinely they comforted one another, embraced each other, how they spoke so freely. She didn't need to know the exact words being exchanged to read the full story. And Hudd hadn't brought Audrey up once during all their weeks together. Dottie hadn't had a clue.

Audrey suddenly turned to study Dottie. What was Hudd saying about her? He was probably telling her how Dottie had dragged Penny kicking and screaming away from her home, had pushed her too far, had shown little compassion for her when she was scared.

"You're all done dear," the nurse's muffled voice said. "Stay here and rest for a few minutes though, okay?" Dottie nodded, then shoved her hands under her legs as Audrey approached her.

"Thank you," Audrey said simply, placing a hand on Dottie's arm.

"I don't deserve your thanks," Dottie muttered.

"Hudson said you took care of my sister from day one," Audrey replied, tilting her head to one side in the same cocker-spaniel way as Penny always had. "You protected her, cared for her, and shared everything you had left with her."

"Well, I… I owed her," Dottie replied.

"For what?" Audrey asked.

"She stuck up for me in school," Dottie said, "more than once. She always treated me like an equal." She looked up at Audrey, who was smiling with a warmth that reminded her of Penny. She sensed sadness behind the smile.

"What makes you think you weren't her equal?" Ben asked, coming to sit next to her on the bed.

Dottie shrugged. They wouldn't understand. She wasn't kind like Penny, not good with people, and definitely not selfless. She was awkward and self-centered.

"No, you didn't do those things because you owed her," Audrey said firmly. "You buy somebody lunch for stuff like that."

"You helped her because you cared about her," Ben said.

“Same reason you helped all of us,” Hudd added from behind Audrey. “Even me, even though I was always kind of a jerk to you… before.”

Audrey frowned at Hudd, who shrugged his shoulders in apology. The exchange made Dottie smile. They were actually kind of cute together.

“My sister always knew how to be kind,” Audrey said, turning back to Dottie, “but from what little I can gather, you showed her she was just as capable of being brave.”

“I had to,” Dottie said, some of the buzz in her head beginning to fade as tears welled in her eyes. “She wasn’t going to survive on optimism, but then… her being so damn brave is what got her killed.”

“You’re wrong,” Ben said firmly.

“Her love for you,” Audrey said, “for her friends, is why she did what she did.”

“There is always a place in this world for kindness, Dottie,” Ben said. “Penny would have wanted us to remember that.”

∝

The fairies had red eyes. The snow burned. The leaves rose, lifting her high into the air above the falls. A snowy cliff.

A knock on the metal door startled Dottie out of a fitful sleep. Memories from the night before came flooding back, unbidden. Her whole body ached in tandem with her heart. She sat up, wiggled her toes, rotated her ankles and extended her fingers, and then pressed her palms down into the mattress. Dottie traced her fingers gently over the stitches above her right eye. She was wearing somebody else’s clothes, but they were clean and dry.

Another knock. She rose shakily, almost toppling a tray of cold breakfast food off the table at her elbow. She moved across the floor on wobbly legs.

“Grab your shoes,” Ben said, smiling down at her when she opened the door.

Dottie resisted the urge to reach out and wrap her arms around his waist, lay her head on his chest, and hold on for dear life. The impulse surprised her. She was desperate to hold on to the people that mattered to her. She had never told Penny how much she meant to her, how many times Penny's positivity and kindness had been the only bright spot in her day. She never even thanked her for that day in the cafeteria. Did that even happen? Or was the life that existed before some kind of dream?

Dottie stared blankly at Ben, her mind struggling to focus on the present.

"You in there?" Ben asked, his voice reassuring as he placed a hand on her shoulder. His smile faded slightly when he saw her face and his eyes searched hers for understanding.

Dottie reached up and held his hand in her own, briefly pressing her cheek against it, before ducking quickly back into her room. She looked for the hiking boots she had been wearing since leaving her basement, but only found a pair of combat boots a size too big.

"Where are we going?" Dottie asked as she rejoined Ben outside her room.

Ben took her hand in his and started walking without a word. They walked down more dim hallways past metal doorways before entering a conference room. Ben opened the door for her and ushered her inside. Hudd and Audrey rested together on a bench along the back wall, Lowell nearby. Rebecca, the woman from the field the night before, stood in the corner next to them. A handful of men and women Dottie did not recognize sat around the conference table in various exhausted postures.

"I don't know, Mar," one man said, "earthquakes, heavy rains, volcanic activity, a tsunami, wildfires, landslides all over New England, and an electromagnetic pulse radiating across the ocean all the way to Europe… who knows how many have perished? We cannot stand idly by and do nothing to help those still alive."

"I do not suggest we do nothing, Caleb," the woman replied. "I suggest we solve the problem before more innocent lives are lost. Our resources are limited and cannot easily be replenished. We must stop the bleeding by finding and clamping the vein, rather than trying to mop it up as it overflows."

"Seismic readings remain… unusual," another man added, "which suggests the possibility of another quake. I agree with Marilyn – we cannot afford to expend our resources on anything but a solution to the root cause of the problem."

"We *need* to consider the human element of all this, Owen," Caleb argued.

An older man in a white lab coat stepped away from the wall near Ben.

"I must point out..." he began, "that this other dimension contains two moons, which is likely the cause of the change in tide and sea level. If we go to the center…."

"Levi, this business about another dimension is not helpful," Rebecca scolded from the corner. "It's an earthquake, an unusual one to be sure, but there is nothing to suggest a parallel Universe or that this was an attack by aliens."

Levi Hill, Aggie's old colleague, only smiled patiently. He wasn't as well-polished as Dottie had imagined, and his tousled grey hair suggested that he often ran his fingers through it nervously. His glasses sat crookedly on his nose, and he adjusted them a dozen times over the course of a few minutes.

"Ah, quite to the contrary Miss Morrow," he said. "There's evidence to suggest this is far more than a simple earthquake. Though, I do agree that we are not talking about aliens," he added with a wink.

"You suspect something sinister, Levi?" Caleb asked.

"I did suspect it, yes, but these young people," Levi said, "the ones rescued from the base of the rupture yesterday, have brought information with them that confirms my suspicions."

"And what information is that?" Owen asked.

"That this was no earthquake," Levi said, taking a few steps closer to the table. "The seismic activity was manufactured using a massive neodymium earth magnet, and it was created and carried out by a man who was acting with ill intent…."

“Who is this information coming from, Lee?” Marilyn interrupted.

“From an old colleague of mine, someone I trust completely,” Levi replied. “Agatha Polson.”

Dottie watched as a few of the others in the room shifted uncomfortably in their seats at the mention of Aggie.

“There's one more thing,” Levi continued. “This man… he believes in and is motivated by, at least to some extent, a foretelling put forth in this other world.”

“Prophecy can be a strong driver,” Marilyn observed.

“Indeed, it can,” Levi replied, glancing briefly over at Dottie. “He has been informed that a girl with golden hair will be his downfall.”

Dottie fought the urge to wrap one of her frizzy golden curls around her finger.

“He has been using magnetized radio receptors, disguised as autumn leaves, as spies in this world and his own. Something in their programming has drawn them to this young lady here.”

Dottie’s cheeks flushed. She clasped her hands together, gripping them as hard as she could to brace herself against the shock of Levi’s words. She looked down, uncomfortably aware of their stares, having briefly glimpsed some of their expressions: Rebecca wore a sly smile that made Dottie’s skin crawl; Lowell looked determined, stone-faced; Hudd and Audrey, his arm around her shoulders, wore matching expressions closely resembling pity. She looked at Ben. Was it regret she saw in his eyes? No one seemed surprised by Levi’s words. They had all known.

“What is this man’s name?” Caleb asked.

“Orville,” Levi replied as he held up a single stamped golden leaf for all to see. “Orville Zaide.”

Dorothy and Orville Zaide, O.Z. Now she’d never escape the damn Wizard of Oz references.

∝

Dottie stood at the top of a white, tarp-covered ramp, watching Echo and a couple of other military guys load supplies into an ATV. They were to leave that morning. No time to rest and recuperate. No time to come to terms with this prophecy, which everyone except for her had known about. She thought there had been something strange about the way the others treated her after Aggie's, but she had always harbored so many insecurities that she wrote it all off as misperception.

Ben came up alongside her.

"You should have told me," she muttered.

"I made a promise," he replied.

"I wouldn't have changed my mind, you know," she said, turning to face him. "You could have told me."

"I'm sorry, Dot," Ben took her hands in his. "We weren't sure you'd be able to wrap your head around it with everything we had just gone through."

"Well… you were wrong."

"Yes, we were… *I* was. I should have told you." His voice was husky with regret. He released her hands and wrapped his arms around her, pulling her close. The affectionate gesture caught her off guard. He was taller than she had realized before and she rested her head comfortably against his chest. "I should have trusted in your resilience," he whispered, gently pressing his lips to the top of her head. "I promise I won't be making that mistake again."

"*Good*," was the only reply she could produce.

"You know Dot…" he began, cupping her chin in his hand to raise her eyes to his. "You're stubborn as all hell.

Dottie suppressed a giggle at that. Laughter. What a funny response at such a time. She felt oddly comfortable so close to him. Nobody had ever held her like that. She lay her head back on his chest and wrapped her arms around his back, returning the embrace. She closed her eyes, stealing this momentary experience of comfort and safety, until Echo made the call for them to leave.

∝

They were a group of sixteen, or “four squared” as Lowell observed. But there was only room enough in the tunnel for them to walk three across. Lowell, Levi and Echo led the way… navigation, knowledge, safety. Dottie, Ben and Marilyn followed closely behind. Dottie liked Mar. Her voice was calm, confident. She spoke to Dottie without hesitation when some of the others seemed intimidated by her, or perhaps, thought her insignificant. She wondered how much they knew. If they had *all* been filled in on Greg and Mo, Sylvester, Penny, Aggie, Ari….

Dottie was supposed to bring down the man who caused all this. She wondered if the others doubted her ability to do so as much as she did.

“Walk quickly,” Echo instructed. “Keep your voice at a whisper, if you must speak at all.”

They had walked in silence for what Dottie guessed was around an hour when the cement walls of the first tunnel ended and nothing but dirt and wooden beams surround them. There was something both terrifying and comforting about the tunnels. Dottie felt as though she could stay down there forever, though a strange sadness simultaneously weighed heavy on her chest. The group wove in and out of tunnels for hours, breaking here and there to sit and rest, eat, drink some water. They turned and twisted through the last leg of their journey until they abruptly found themselves at the base of a set of wood slats embedded into the wall. A ladder. They climbed – a hundred rungs, maybe more – Dottie had lost count when she finally emerged out of the top.

She rose to her feet in a small wood paneled room. Lowell was waiting at a doorway ahead of them.

“Are you ready?” he asked Dottie – not the group – just her.

She nodded.

Dottie passed through the door and stepped out into a cavernous room. She wondered if a football stadium could fit in there. Tile and stone covered every inch of the floor and domed ceiling. Torches lined the walls. At the center of the room stood a group of women. They reminded Dottie of nuns, but their heads were not covered. They all wore the same charcoal grey, floor-length tunic. Lowell and Levi approached the woman at the center of the group. She was older than Dottie had realized at first, in her eighties perhaps, her face framed by wispy white curls. They had a brief, whispered exchange, and the woman stepped forward. She approached Dottie, lifting a hand to feel one of the golden ringlets that fell against her cheek. A smile spread across the woman's face and Dottie realized she was using her hands to see, as her eyes were unable to do.

"My name is Basira." The woman's grave voice echoed throughout the hall. "Welcome to the Sisterhood."

CHAPTER 28

The Setup

Orville paced back and forth in front of a marble fountain, now dry. Just like the other intricate water features found in the entryways of Alterran elite, it could no longer function after years of drought. His footsteps echoed down the stone hallway. He paused, considering the engravings along the side of the structure. *Aím nekroôsei borei zisonai pôi aím ôdigísei, aím frourísei, aím agapísei na aím enôsei ôlai*. He had seen such engravings before, scattered throughout the upper half, though he had no clue what the old language meant. He pressed the palms of his hands against his head, attempting to quell the incessant ringing that had plagued him since the unpleasantness with Ruya and Garrett. Rafi stood motionless against the wall behind him.

The sound of shuffling canvas shoes caught Orville's attention. Kain, the Council's Elder of Vocations – and a member of Orville's covert advisory board – made his way to Orville's side.

"What does this mean?" Orville asked Kain, skipping any greeting and gesturing toward the words on the fountain.

Kain folded his hands behind his back and considered the words for a moment. "Have you never seen Pnévema, Orville?"

"I have," Orville replied. "Though I confess I have not thought much of it before. A dead language, is it not?"

"It is," Kain replied, "as far as the spoken word is concerned. It does, however, remain a language of scholars."

"So you understand it?" Orville asked.

"Would you like a translation?" Kain offered.

Orville nodded, trying to hide how much the practice of answering a question with a question peeved him.

"*Aím nekroôsei borei zisonai*, the dead will live," Kain began, "*pôi aím haddísei*, with one to guide; *aím frourísei*, one to guard; *aím agapísei*, one to love; *na aím enôsei ôlai*, and one to unite all."

"It's all nonsense," Orville grumbled, agitated. It was just another worthless prophecy, such meaningless words.

"Yes," Kain agreed, bowing slightly. "Is this why you asked to meet?"

"Of course not," Orville replied. "Isaac says he heard something most concerning from a Gallery servant. It was said that the Council is preparing to execute an attack."

"They are," Kain replied. "In fact, if you hadn't asked to meet, I would have sought you out myself. The Council is planning to go after you, though they must take more care if such whispers have found their way down to the Gulley already."

"Where?" Orville demanded. "How?" Did they not understand the type of power he possessed, the level of loyalty he inspired among both his own men and the people of the Lower Half?

“They plan to start with a simultaneous attack on your northernmost outpost and your south field team at the Holt,” Kain said.

“That team is unarmed…” Orville reminded him.

“They are aware of this,” Kain replied, “but they plan to show no mercy.”

“You must stop them,” Orville demanded. “Convince them otherwise. I cannot take time from my current work to play at war with a bunch of bitter old men.”

“You know I cannot convince them of anything… and you are as old as we are, Orville.” Kain’s light-hearted demeanor made Orville’s skin crawl with the prickly beginnings of rage.

Orville turned to Rafi, hesitating only briefly before deciding to give his next instructions in front of Kain. The man was, after all, a close advisor.

“Rafi,” Orville continued, “I want you to go to the underground…”

“Not to our camps or outpost, sir?” Rafi interrupted, surprised by his master’s instructions.

“We will not be able to save them now,” Orville replied.

“You’ll sacrifice them?” Rafi questioned, eyes wide.

“It’s a strategic necessity,” Orville shot back. “Now, do as I say. Go find this Hawk character. Rally him to our cause. And see how many men he can spare to stand with us.”

“Sir, I do not believe we will find allies amongst the Uprisen,” Rafi said, his voice wavering.

“Rafi…” Orville paused, gathering his thoughts and trying to find the right words. “You say this Hawk runs an entire underground movement, and has done so with an expert finesse?”

“Yes,” Rafi replied, “but what he stands for…”

“There are rarely any differences between great men of power,” Orville interrupted. “This man… at the end of the day, I believe we will find he wants the same things that all-powerful men do… respect, influence. He and I… we both have a way of bringing people around." Orville had indeed become an expert at gathering up the disenfranchised of Alterra, recruiting them to his cause with promises of power, wealth, and freedom. Few of them needed further incentive than the opportunity to spit in the face of the Alterran Council. Yet, most of these recruits ended up at work camps and outposts. Should those areas be attacked by the elite of the Upper Half, they would be destroying their own sons.

Rafi gave a quick nod and salute, before backing his way out of the hall.

"There is one more thing," Kain said in a low tone behind Orville's back.

"Yes?" Orville said impatiently.

"Do not reach out to me again," Kain said, his voice shifting from jovial to menacing. "Do not come back into the city. And do not expect any additional aid or mercy from me or my fellow councilmen. You, Orville Zaide, may see yourself out. This will be the last time you walk freely in Alterra."

∝

Orville sat in his lab with a pile of the shiny metal leaves strewn on the table in front of him, a writing quill in hand as he prepared to take down the information the leaves had to share. He needed to find a way to program more units per recorder. Coding such small sets of leaves each time he needed to extract their information had grown particularly cumbersome after the increased intensity of recent weeks. Perhaps he could train someone else to do this tedious work, but who could he ever trust with the information? He couldn't afford to compromise what he had worked so hard to attain. No, this task must be completed by Orville alone.

As he flipped the switch on the recorder, the cluster of leaves became animated, rising from the surface of the table. Orville waited as the fragments of intercepted dialogue recorded onto an old cassette tape, one that had made its way into Sum with him a lifetime ago. He rewound the tape and pressed play.

"You're from there," a boy's voice shouted suddenly.

"… Alterra," a second voice spoke, though so far he recognized neither.

"Into the rift… she took Sylvester with her." The fragmented messages were broken up by intense static.

"Penny," a girl's voice came next.

"She died… to keep you alive," the boy's voice replied. "We need to keep going."

The recording was static from that point on. What had caused the leaves to stop transmitting? Sylvester was dead. This girl, Penny, was dead… but she was not the one that he had intended to kill. Not if they were still determined to get wherever they felt they needed to go…not if Penny had acted to keep her alive.

The girl with golden hair was still alive and had at least some allies with her. Who was "from there… Alterra?" Did they question Sylvester again before they killed him? Or was there someone else from Sum colluding with the others? He had not heard Aggie's voice after listening to multiple recordings from the last few days. Had she left the group? Was she coming for him even now as he sat in solitude, eavesdropping on a bunch of angst-filled adolescents?

Few things in life made Orville as irate as too many questions with too few answers. He flipped off the receiver and walked, brooding, to his game table. He moved the black knight up and over to take out a white pawn, then shifted a white rook two spots left, knocking the black knight off the board. He glared down at the board. The two moves had placed the black king in check, a defensive and reactive position. Sometimes, in games as well as in life, one must take a step back to get ahead. *Let them come.*

www.ingramcontent.com/pod-product-compliance
Lightning Source LLC
Chambersburg PA
CBHW030818310726
48980CB00006B/535/J

* 9 7 8 1 7 3 2 1 8 0 0 3 1 *